The Thistledown Connection

Spiderwize
Remus House
Coltsfoot Drive
Woodston
Peterborough
PE2 9BF

www.spiderwize.com

THE THISTLEDOWN CONNECTION

CHAPTER ONE

Sylvia Trent, the head housekeeper at one of London's five star hotels had been pushing a linen cart along the sixth floor, she had learnt long ago that there were no "OK" days. Things either went smoothly or were a complete disaster. Today was fast becoming one of the latter as two of the housekeepers had reported sick and fifty delegates were expected to arrive for a conference. So as well as organising the other housekeepers, ensuring there were enough sheets, towels, toilet rolls, shampoo and other bathroom items she found herself helping to make up rooms. Room 637 should have been vacated, but she knocked anyway and there being no answer, inserted the passkey and entered. Immediately reacting with shock on seeing a young woman sat crossed legged on the bed her arms hanging limply by her sides. "I'm sorry", she started, "I was expecting …." Her voice trailed off as she caught sight of the lifeless eyes staring at the floor and the syringe lying on the bed. "Oh shit!" she muttered reaching for her handset, and transmitting; "security urgent."

John Greenhall had been the hotel security manager for just over two years. A six foot ex-guards Captain he was a well-educated and articulate man who walked with the merest hint of a limp from the artificial left leg he wore having lost the lower half in the second Iraq conflict. He had just entered the control room when Sylvia's call came through and sensing the urgency in her voice he replied, "Go ahead." Sylvia's came back, "F1 in room 637." He noted the crack in her voice as if she was close to tears. "OK", he replied, "I'm on my way, don't touch anything or allow anyone else in." Turning to the duty controller he said, "Contact the Police and Ambulance services, and when you've done that, find out who was in the room and get every bit of CCTV footage from the time they booked in until now."

"Already on it" came the reply. F1 was code for fatality, it wasn't the first and he knew wouldn't be the last. Often guests passed quietly away in their sleep although there had been one or two suicides. Sylvia was a very experienced member of staff and had dealt with a few fatalities before, so the fact she sounded distressed worried him.

When John reached the sixth floor, Sylvia was stood outside the room, her arms folded in front of her in a vain attempt to stop herself from shaking. She was clearly in shock. "That poor girl, that poor girl", she muttered.

"OK" Sylvia he replied, "I'll get Danny up to look after you."

"No! No! I'll be ok if you want me I'll be in my office." Before he could object she was gone hurrying towards the lift. He shrugged then pushed the door open and entered the room. He was met with a sight that made him feel strangely cold. It was not the staring lifeless eyes, but the expression on her face, as if there was someone trapped alive and at any moment would let out a scream and burst from the lifeless body. He understood why Sylvia was so shocked, that and the fact that like him, she had obviously recognised the person before him, a fact that filled him with dread. His radio crackled. "I have a name for the room", the controller stated. "Mercedes Johnson," said Greenhall.

"Yeah", the controller cut in, "It's not."

"I'm afraid so", said Greenhall, "the press will be all over this like a rash, inform the duty manager and tell him to say as little as possible, but we need the sixth floor cleared, tell the guys on the door that no-one and I mean no-one comes in unless they have a reservation. Then advise the Police who it is we have here, this will need more than a beat bobby, oh! And get someone to check on Sylvia I expect the Police will need to speak to her."

Mercedes Johnson had rarely been out of the press recently, the daughter of wealthy businessman Albert Johnson she was rapidly gaining a reputation as a party girl, being seen in all the top nightspots and photographed with numerous celebrities. Heiress to a billion pound business empire with dark hair dark eyes and stunning figure she had graced the cover of all the top magazines and been romantically linked with film star Craig Radcliffe, although recent reports were of a breakdown in the relationship after he was photographed with the leading lady of his latest film. Her father Albert Johnson was born in Glasgow the son of a dockworker; he became a brilliant chemist, eventually setting up his own pharmaceutical company, which became a worldwide success. From there he branched out into shipping and ship building even buying the dockyard where his father once worked. Trading as AJ Associates he controlled subsidiaries and numerous front companies around the world. Although currently in London for a speaking engagement, after the death of his wife, his public appearances were few and far between. Most of his time was spent at his mansion set in one thousand acres of land on the west coast of Scotland. It boasted a runway and hangar facilities for his private jet and two helicopters, it also had a private bay and deep water jetty where his luxury yacht was often moored. In the grounds was a laboratory and accommodation for the army of technicians and security staff based there. This was discreetly hidden from view, being set in a forested valley half a mile to the right of the main house. The whole thousand acres was ringed with an eighteen-foot high security fence, which was constantly monitored from a control room, set on the top floor of the mansion. A large security post protected the one entrance by road, this had a double gate system, whether entering or leaving one gate would only open when the other was closed. Even those arriving by sea would need to pass through a security gate on the jetty prior to being driven up to the main house or laboratory by one of the security team. With most of the laboratory staff arriving or leaving by helicopter there was inevitable speculation amongst the locals as to what was being developed there.

John Greenhall had been stood outside room 637 for some twenty minutes, in that time it had been confirmed the sixth floor was clear. Luckily most of the rooms had been allocated to the delegates due in later that day, of the others all the guests appeared to have gone out, the one couple still in the room had agreed to leave as they were planning to go sightseeing and shopping anyway. Rather than tell them of the death, Sylvia had asked them if they minded their rooms being cleaned early as they were expecting several delegates to arrive for a conference. The sound of the lift doors caught Greenhall's attention and he turned to see Danny Herbert and two others step from the lift. Danny was deputy security manager and unlike John had started in hotels from school working in most areas and becoming a trainee manager. However he became fascinated with security after solving a series of thefts at a previous establishment. Danny was shorter than John being just five feet eight, but was always immaculately dressed currently he was wearing a neatly pressed white shirt, company tie, grey slacks with sharply pressed creases and highly polished shoes. He had short cut dark hair and bright blue eyes that couldn't fail to be noticed. His attention to his appearance was matched by his attention to detail. This along with his hotel experience made him a great asset within John's team. The two men with him were clearly police, the older one of the two John had met before,

Chief Inspector Penney, a person renowned for having a sharp mind who was well respected amongst his peers. John felt the inspector always looked as if he had just got out of bed, in contrast to Danny and his companion it looked as though his brown suit and cream shirt had never seen an iron nor his shoes any polish.

"OK what have we got John?" he asked negating any formalities or introduction of his companion. "Just as you see it", said John opening the door. "With the exception of the outer door handle nothing has been touched." The inspector walked to the foot of the bed, taking a long look at the body, noting the mark on her left arm where the syringe had entered and the syringe itself lying on the bed beside her it had not been fully depressed and had around two mils of substance still visible. There was a handbag and shoes on the floor and to the left and behind the body was a mobile phone. He then walked to the bathroom door nudging it open with his elbow, after a cursory look he turned to his companion. "OK Charlie I want this body out of here ASAP, before the press circus gets itself into gear. Being a Hotel there will be bloody fingerprints everywhere so tell the forensics to concentrate on the bathroom and inner door handles and I definitely want to know whose prints are on that syringe." There was a knock at the door and a young woman entered carrying a small pilot style case. John judged her to be in her late thirties, she wore a grey business suit of skirt and jacket over a white blouse that failed to hide her ample figure. With her soft features and long blonde hair she did not fit the preconceived ideas of how a pathologist should look. "Ah Doctor Stuart", Inspector Penney announced. "Have you been briefed who this is?"

"Yes", came the reply.

"Well in that case I want to know what's in that syringe and what other shit is in that girl's blood stream and I want to know today."

"I'll do my best", Doctor Stuart replied. "No" said the inspector, "with all the shit the press will throw at this, you won't do your best you'll bloody well do it." Turning to John he missed the pulled face and 'V' sign the doctor gave him as he continued, "As soon as the doctor here is ok with it can we get the body out via the back entrance, we'll arrange an unmarked vehicle I don't want the press ghouls photographing everything."

"That'll be fine", replied John. "Danny can you arrange that."

"No problem," came the reply.

John turned to the inspector, "I got Henry to pull out the CCTV tapes from last night, do you want to take a look?"

"Yeah, Charlie look after things here, let's see if we can find out who else was in the room." As they walked towards the lift John said, "You think someone else was with her then."

"Pretty certain", came the reply, "there are a couple of things not quite right, whatever killed her acted bloody quickly and then there's the position of the syringe, it's too far from her body to have fallen out of her arm."

"Bloody hell, I heard you were sharp but that's impressive."

7

"All in the detail John, all in the detail."

They entered the control room, "Meet our resident hippy", said John, "Henry this is Chief Inspector Penney have you got anything for him?"

"Sure have", came the reply. Henry Daws had been one of the controllers for the last five years, he wore his hair long and held back in a Ponytail with his short beard, jeans, flowery shirts and sandals, he fitted the hippy title well, yet under the façade was a clever electrical engineer and computer programmer it was he who installed and maintained the hotels CCTV and computerised booking systems. "I've been through last night's recordings, she came in at seven minutes past two this morning." He tapped on a keyboard and a monitor lit up showing Mercedes walking across the foyer to the reception desk where she collected her key card, as it was handed over: the inspector shouted "Stop there, can you rewind that bit ." A couple more taps on the keyboard and the scene was repeated. "Interesting," mouthed Penney. Restarting the recording, Henry said. "The next bit shows her arriving on the sixth floor where there's a man waiting for her." They watched as she walked, or staggered arm in arm with her companion and entered the room. "I guess you'll find a little alcohol in her blood stream", remarked John. "Have you got a better picture of the guy?"

"Not then, but forty minutes later he comes out of the room in a bit of a hurry, this time he's facing the camera." Henry stopped the recording and the monitor showed a clear picture of a face. "Can we print that?" asked the Inspector, "I'd like to see if we can identify him."

"That's easy", said Henry, "It's a DJ calls himself the Master of Sound, but I think his real name is Ralph Osborne or something similar."

"Are you sure about that?"

"Positive I did some work on his sound equipment, bit of a twat really likes to think he's up there with the A-listers." A voice cut in. "Control we have a problem here."

"In what way" Henry replied. "Mr Johnson has arrived insisting on seeing his daughter."

"Oh shit!" muttered John. "Let him in the Inspector and I will meet him in the foyer."

As John and the Inspector entered the foyer they could see Albert Johnson standing impatiently in the centre. He was around John's height and build and had the poise of a man that kept himself fit. His hair was unfashionably long and almost pure white as was his neatly trimmed moustache. John walked up to him and offered a hand which was not reciprocated. "I'm John Greenhall the security manager, this is Chief Inspector Penney from the Met." Johnson nodded.

"I'm afraid there has been an incident involving your daughter." Said the Inspector. "I'm aware she's dead," replied Johnson. "I would appreciate it if you would take me to see her." Both John and the Inspector were taken back by the cold manner in which the statement had been made. "I'm not sure you would want to see her as she is" John started. Johnson turned to the Inspector. "I take it you will want a formal identification."

"Well yes."

"Then I suggest you take me to see her, I will not be down to London again for several weeks." John called up Danny, "Have the team arrived to move the body yet?"

"Just here now", came the reply. "Tell them to hold off for a moment I'm bringing her father up, I take it you have no objections Inspector?" Penney gave a resigned shrug. "Let's get this done I don't want to delay the autopsy."

By the time they arrived at room 637, Danny had ushered the recovery and scene of crime teams next door and Doctor Stuart had left taking the syringe with her. When the three men entered the room, John was thankful the body was now lying face up on the bed having been prepared for the body bag in which she would be transported to the mortuary. Johnson walked over to the bed and stood motionless and expressionless looking at his daughter. He never reached out to touch her or showed any change of expression. He turned to the Inspector. "I can confirm that is my daughter Mercedes, let me know when her body can be released for burial." He then made for the door. "One thing sir", said the Inspector, "I think I know the answer but was your daughter right or left handed."

"Like her mother left handed", he replied then stopped and looked at his daughter once more. "I see", he said, and then abruptly left. "You know, when he mentioned his wife there was the smallest hint of emotion."

"I thought I'd seen it all", agreed Penney, "but that was hard totally emotionless I wouldn't like to cross him."

"So we have a murder then", said John. Danny had entered with the recovery team and overheard, "How do you come to that conclusion", he asked.

"Left handed people don't inject themselves in the left arm, is that right Inspector?"

"Pretty much", came the reply. "I had doubts when I saw where the syringe was, then I noticed she took her key card with her left hand. Well thanks for your help John but I think Charlie and I need to talk to a certain DJ."

The recovery team worked quickly placing the body in a body bag and loading it on to a folding trolley. The scene of crime unit had previously photographed everything and placed Mercedes belongings in evidence bags. Then while they continued taking samples and prints, the recovery team made their way down the service lift and out into the rear yard where an especially adapted unmarked van was waiting. Within minutes the body was loaded and the van driven from the yard, heading for the mortuary and Doctor Stuart's autopsy. Earlier, as Albert Johnson had left, a group of journalists and photographers tried to get a statement but were totally blanked. Saying nothing and remaining expressionless, he just got into his car and was rapidly driven away.

When Chief Inspector Penney left the hotel, he did make a short statement, advising there had been an incident involving a twenty four year old woman and that a body had been removed for autopsy. He added that there would be no statements from anyone at the hotel but if they contacted Scotland Yard a full statement would be made later that evening. That seemed to satisfy most but inevitably a few hung around the front of the hotel for some time. John put extra security on the front door and asked the manager to make sure no member of staff spoke to the press.

After watching the Inspector leave, John turned to make his way to his office but a voice called "Captain Greenhall." John turned to see a six foot heavily built man walking towards him; from the accent he could tell he was Scottish and there was a vague recognition but he could not put a name to the face. "It's a while since I was Captain anything", said John.

"Aye but I thought it was you, the last time I saw you we were on an 'evac-copter' and I was trying to hold your leg together." The memory flooded back, "Well you didn't do very well I lost this half" said John tapping his left leg. "Well you're looking well on it sir."

"I'm sorry" replied John "I'm trying but can't remember your name."

"Mac McCrae, ex SAS and army intelligence."

"Now I've got you Mac, what brings you here, it's not been a good day so far don't tell me I'm wanted back on active service."

"Hell no" Mac laughed. "I work for Albert Johnson now, I'm head of security for AJ Associates but spend most of my time at his laboratory compound in Scotland."

"Why does he need your skills to protect some test tubes?" Mac laughed again, "it's one hell of a place Capt. a thousand acres and over two hundred employees, lot of high tech stuff there, then there are the shipping companies docks etc. more than enough to keep me busy."

"I see so what can I do for you here?"

"Just wondered if you could shed any light on what happened, it would be nice to have some info if the boss asks." John shrugged "Can't tell you much Mac, she came in last night with some DJ according to Henry he calls himself the Master of Sound. He left about forty minutes later and this morning our housekeeper found her dead with a syringe by her side."

"Shit" replied Mac, "she was a great kid really just desperate for affection but I was sure she wasn't into drugs."

"I can tell you she didn't inject herself Mac."

"Thanks Capt. that gives me a heads up at least, nice to have met you again." He shook John's hand and turned to leave. "Just one thing Mac, how did Johnson find out she was dead?"

"He got a phone call some guy crying who told him she was here, guess it must have been that DJ."

After Sylvia had make a statement to the Inspector's companion and all the police had left. Her cleaners moved into room 637 and quickly had it stripped and cleaned. It would not be used that night but by late evening, the hotel was beginning to get back to some semblance of normality.

CHAPTER TWO

Michael 'Sticky' Wood wiped the sweat from his forehead with the back of his hand, even for Camp Bastion today was particularly hot. "Look on the bright side Capt." said his companion as he climbed into the front of the tandem seated Apache Helicopter. "This is the last sortie this tour, we start for home tomorrow."

"Ok Pony, let's get this one over before we celebrate." Fred 'Pony' Moore laughed, he had been co-pilot and armament operator with Sticky Wood ever since he first set foot in an Apache and he knew there was not a better pilot in the fleet. While he settled into his checks, Sticky continued his walk around inspection of the Apache, which was fully armed with hellfire missiles attached to its exterior pods. He looked up as the motor on the front mounted chain gun came to life and the gun began to rotate left and right as Pony checked his helmet controls, the gun being designed to follow his eyes, wherever he looked, the gun followed.

Satisfied with his inspection, Sticky climbed into the pilot's seat set behind but higher than Pony. He pulled on, then adjusted his helmet, checked communication and proceeded with his pre-start checks. Then, with a thumbs up from a ground mechanic, he started the engines the four six metre long rotors started to turn, picking up speed and throwing up a cloud of dust and sand causing the ground mechanic to retreat protecting his face as he did so. Sticky requested permission to take off from ground control and receiving a positive response, increased the engine power, and slowly lifted the Apache from the ground. Once in the air he swung the nose to the right and whilst continuing to gain height he increased forward momentum and sped out towards the desert. Some distance ahead two Chinook troop carriers were plodding through the air heading for the same destination. Members of the Taliban had caught the daughter of a local farmer reading, it being against their teachings to allow a woman to be educated, they beat her mercilessly and although disfigured she survived. Her father vowed vengeance and while keeping up a front of working with the Taliban, he was secretly passing intelligence to the allied troops. The week before he had led them to a major bomb making facility. If his information were correct, this time it would be an arms depot and a meeting between several of the Taliban leaders. If true they were expecting heavy resistance and were going in well prepared.

As they sped away from Camp Bastion, the scenery quickly turned to cultivated areas and large cornfields interspersed with barren patches. The three helicopters flew over a troop convoy and a truck recently hit with a roadside bomb an instant reminder that death or injury was never far away. As they neared the target they each changed course, the two

Chinooks planning to approach from either side while the Apache would come in from behind, along with the Chinook's door gunners they would be able to give the troops cover as they disembarked.

The target was a large single storey farmhouse set in its own grounds, there were cornfields on either side with the corn standing around two metres high. It gave cover to both sides but was notorious for concealing IED's (improvised explosive devices). The area to the front of the building was ploughed, providing no cover and a clear field of fire for anyone in the building. To the left of the farmhouse was an old long abandoned lorry quietly rusting its rear springs had already given away leaving it sitting at an angle to the ground. To the rear of the building, the ground rose steeply reaching a height level with the roof and providing a week spot in the buildings defences. Sticky swung the Apache to the right about three kilometres from the target taking a wide angle his intention was to come in low from behind the raised ground.

The timing was to the second, both Chinooks arriving either side of the front of the building at the same time, while the Apache swooped up from behind the high ground Pony sweeping the area for targets, almost too late he spotted the insurgent under the lorry aiming a self-propelled grenade directly at them. He engaged with the chain gun there was a short "buurrrrrp" of fire as the gun unleashed its shells at over six hundred rounds a minute, parts of metal, rust and human flesh disintegrated into a cloud surrounding the target area. Almost simultaneously the insurgent had pulled the trigger and the grenade exploded into the bank below them. The blast threw them upwards but Sticky quickly had it under control. Insurgents began to appear on the roof aiming fire at the advancing troops. Another blast from the chain gun quickly silenced that threat, then it promptly jammed, "Shit" muttered Pony. Then with heavy fire coming from both the front and rear he unleashed two hellfire missiles that slammed into the back of the building, one went straight through a door and the explosion that followed took everyone by surprise. Some troops were thrown off their feet while others hit the ground as the blast showered stone, brick and cement fragments around them. Luckily as soon as the hellfire's were released Sticky had swung the Apache over to the right intending to sweep back in towards the left side of the farmhouse. They still took some hits and were buffeted around Sticky countering each movement with a deftness that kept the helicopter as stable as possible. The Apache was not known as a flying tank for nothing, his main concern was for the rotors but all the aircrafts instruments remained registering normal.

As the dust settled it was clear that most of the building and its occupants was completely destroyed, troops started to get to their feet dusting themselves off and checking others for injuries. Against all protocol one of the Chinook pilots radioed. "What the hell did you hit Pony?' Keeping in the spirit of the conversation, "God knows" came the reply, "but I guess the info about an arms dump might have been correct." The ground troops rapidly moved in, two of the bodies found inside the house were identified as wanted Taliban leaders while others were beyond identification. The blast had also exposed an underground bunker stuffed with arms and bomb making material, as well as maps and plans for future attacks. Two of the insurgents were found injured but alive in the underground bunker and were ferried out where they would later provide vital information.

With the all clear, the troops were left to secure the area while Sticky and Pony headed back to Camp Bastion. After a survey of the external damage to the Apache, They later attended a debrief, where they were informed that a document had been found giving the names of officials in the Governments of both Afghanistan and Pakistan who were providing support and intelligence to the Taliban. "A great way to end the trip" said Pony, Sticky nodded but could never celebrate seeing people being blown to pieces, whatever side they were on. They both had a shower and then started to pack their kit. At last they were heading home.

Sally Wood was a slim brunette with brown eyes and a permanent smile, she had met Michael when they were both eighteen and had been together ever since, they married when they were twenty three and had a son Peter a couple of years later. He was now four years old and had been excited all day on hearing his father was coming home. Sally put the phone down after ringing her brother and then Michael's parents. Tomorrow was forecast as being a hot day. So she had invited them all to a barbeque as a welcome home. They had all agreed to come so after a quick check of the fridge and freezer, she decided to go to the local supermarket rather than leave it until the next morning.

"Come on Peter" she said "Let's go and get some food for daddy and if you're good I'll buy you a treat", He didn't need asking twice and was quickly running for the door. Sally picked up her keys and bag, then after securing Peter safely in the car seat she started the engine and headed off. Leaving her driveway, she turned left onto the road that led from their housing estate and within minutes had joined a dual carriageway, heading to the supermarket which was a little under two miles away. As she came up behind a lorry she checked the mirror indicated and pulled out, another quick glance in the mirror brought a smile as she saw little Peter quietly singing to himself, looking forward again she was horrified to see a car heading directly at her, instinctively she braked and swung left but as she was already partly overtaking, her car struck the lorries rear wheels throwing it sideways where it was impacted by the other vehicle. To Sally everything seemed to go into slow motion as her car flipped into the air and rolled over smashing into the central reservation. In reality there was a thunderous series of noises as metal and glass smashed and crumpled around her, this was quickly followed by total silence. "Peter! Peter!" she screamed but there was no reply then her body went into convulsion and she lost consciousness.

The flight back from Afghanistan had seemed longer than normal, there had been a stop off in Cyprus followed by another four and a half hours of flying, but now the Airbus A320 was on final approach and there was a tangible feeling of relief on board. Fred and Michael were sat together and other than commenting that the flight on a civil aircraft beat the hell out of flying in the Hercules, they had spoken little either watching the on board film or catching up with sleep. It was the same for many others on the aircraft, the constant need to be on alert and the twenty four seven tension while on deployment means exhaustion becomes a way of life so when able to fully relax that need for sleep takes over.

With a sudden jolt, the airbus touched down the passengers momentarily thrown forward as the combination of reverse thrust and braking began to take effect a spontaneous cheer spread through the cabin as the aircraft slowed and turned onto the taxiway. As it slowly moved towards the parking apron someone called out "Hey guys there's a load of scrambled egg waiting for us."

"Must have heard how good we are" someone responded. Fred looked out the window and could see two vehicles parked on the apron with their commanding officer and some unknown General stood next to them. Their senior officer stood up and took over the PA system from the Senior Cabin crewmember. "OK guys" he started "I don't know why they are here, but for the first time we have come home with everyone we left with, we have a good squad and it's been my pleasure to work with every single one of you. So let's show them, be properly dressed when you leave this aircraft, do so smartly and with pride and don't forget to salute."

By the time everyone had done up buttons fitted their headgear and collected items from the overhead lockers, the doors were open and steps in place. Led by their senior officer one by one they departed, as Fred and Michael got to the doorway they could see their senior officer talking to the General and Commander while everyone else walked smartly by saluting as they did so. As Michael stepped off the aircraft steps onto the tarmac, the Commander called "Captain Wood, a moment please." Michael walked over came to attention and saluted. A loud call of "No! No" rang out causing Fred to look around in time to see Michael drop to his knees on the tarmac. Immediately he dropped his bag and ran over towards him, only for his senior officer to step forward and grab his shoulder. "Give him a minute Pony" he said, "they have just told him his wife and son were killed in a car accident last night."

CHAPTER THREE

Ralph Osborne was sitting in his room in a little hotel just off the Quai de Montebello in central Paris. After ringing Albert Johnson, he had gone home, grabbed his passport and packed some clothes in an overnight bag then caught a taxi to St Pancreas station. There he bought a ticket for the Eurostar and after a nervous fifteen-minute wait he boarded the train to Paris. Although he had had a lot to drink and would normally consider himself drunk, he suddenly felt very sober. The speed with which Mercedes reacted and died had totally freaked him out. As he sat on the train he was uncontrollably shaking reliving the moment over and over. I killed her I killed her he kept repeating to himself. He just felt the need to run, to get away and clear his head.

The train sped through the Kent countryside then entered the tunnel for the trip below the channel before emerging again in France. Less than three hours after leaving St Pancreas, it was still early morning when he stepped off the train at Gare du Nord. After withdrawing Euros from an ATM, he took a taxi, requesting a hotel he knew having stayed there before. It was an apart-hotel each room having a small lounge, kitchen and on-suite bathroom. He could stay here a few days and once he had bought some supplies, there would be no need to go out, giving him time to think. What he didn't know was that he had been identified back in London, belatedly the border agency had flagged up that his passport was used on Eurostar and by lunchtime his face would be adorning all the British television news channels and by tomorrow it would also be in the national papers and continental press.

Now exhausted, he finally fell asleep. Waking just a few hours later he decided to freshen up then order room service. As he got up to go to the bathroom there was a knock on the door. Without thinking he went to answer it and as he turned the latch the door was flung forcibly open throwing him across the room where he landed heavily on his back. Immediately he was grabbed from either side, lifted and thrown into a chair. "Mr Osborne I presume," said one of the men. Dazed he looked up to see one man close the door while the other stood immediately in front of him. He was around six foot tall of heavy build, although smartly dressed it was obvious it was all muscle and he was not someone you would want to pick a fight with. It was this man who had spoken and Osborne noted a thick Scottish accent. "How did you find me?" Osborne replied with a noticeable tremor in his voice. "When you run away you shouldn't hide in places you've been before laddie, now I think you have some talking to do." Osborne sat forward and placed his head in his hands and started shaking, "How the hell did it come to this?" he said with tears streaming down his cheeks. "Start with how you came to be with Mercedes."

Pulling a tissue from his pocket and wiping his eyes, Osborne replied, "I was running the music decks at the club."

"The Master of Sound", cut in the Scottish questioner. "Yeah", replied Osborne looking up with surprise. Then he carried on. "There were a few well known faces there but you couldn't miss Mercedes, she was dancing in the middle of the floor, well pissed, some of the regulars were getting pretty cheesed off." He paused wiping his face and trying to recall the scene. "So what then?" The second man asked. Osborne looked over to him, he had not noticed before but could see he too was a guy who had a military bearing. He wore a well-fitting expensive looking black suit and had swept back blonde hair, but as he made eye contact he noted a coldness that sent a shiver down his spine. He quickly looked back and continued. "Mercedes started an argument with one of the other customers, I stepped in and told her to calm down, I said you don't need to give the press any ammunition, she told me to fuck off. Then stormed off towards the toilets." He shifted awkwardly in his seat before adding. "A little while later she came up to me and apologised, then asked if I could get her out of a back entrance and see her back to her hotel." He looked up and gestured, "I mean Mercedes Johnson asking me back to her hotel, well of course I said yes."

"I bet you did", said the Scottish guy. "Bet you thought your luck was in you dirty little shit. So when did you get the drugs?" Osborne again shifted uneasily in his chair. "I showed Mercedes to a side door where I knew there was a covered area she could stay unnoticed. I told her to wait there while I go get a taxi. On the way back through I saw my usual dealer, he stopped me and said I got something for you, I tried to tell him I wasn't buying but he insisted this is new mate, they call it 'Readymix', he said it was better than cocaine, gave you a great boost, reckoned you could perform all night with this stuff, he said your sex life will never be the same again, but you have to inject it. I told him I'm not into injecting but he said take it and if you don't like it you don't have to pay for it. I was in a rush so I took it slipped it into my pocket and went to get a taxi."

"Hang on", said Blondie, "He approached you, you didn't ask him for anything."

"No", came the reply. "I can't afford the drug scene that often, I do a bit of coke now and then, mostly to get into the right parties."

"I heard you were a bit of a sad wannabe celeb chaser, I take it you got a taxi picked up Mercedes and went to the hotel."

If Osborne was upset at the insult, he didn't show it, he just replied. "Yes I got a taxi almost straight away, went around picked her up and when we got to the hotel I went straight to the lift and up to the sixth floor while she got her key and came up and joined me. She had had a few so I put the kettle on to make a black coffee. Bollocks to that she said haven't you got anything better. I told her about the readymix and what I was told about it. She got all enthusiastic, let's give it a try she said we can have half each, I could do with a good

27

shag." Osborne got emotional again and started crying. " I went to the bathroom and opened the package, as I did her phone rang, I heard her on the phone having a bit of a heated argument, I think it was her father and it sounded as though he was having a go at her. The package contained a syringe with the liquid in, it had a cap on and there were two needles. I took off the cap and put on a needle then pressed it until some of the fluid came out. I then went back into the bedroom. I asked her if she still wanted to do this. More than ever she replied and sat up on the bed holding out her arms. There was a clear vein on her left arm so I inserted the needle." Again he broke down crying and sobbed uncontrollably for a few minutes. Both men let him gather himself together then asked him to continue. He blew his nose then added. "As soon as I pressed the syringe, she immediately gave a little shudder then her body jolted straight and her arms slumped, she was dead as quick as that. I pulled out the syringe and threw it on the bed." He continued sobbing as he added, "The look on her face, it was horrific. I grabbed her phone to ring for help but saw her father's number and rang him. I can't remember what I said just Mercedes is dead. I think I said sorry. Then I panicked I thought I had killed her, so I just ran and came here."

"So what's the name of your pusher?" a sked the Scot. "What?"

"The name of the guy who gave you the drug" he repeated. Osborne looked shocked. "I can't tell you that" he replied, "They'll kill me." Blondie shook his head then stepped forward and struck him with the back of his hand, a blow so hard Osborne nearly fell out of the chair. "You stupid little shit" he said, "he gave you the drug, does he normally let you pay later?"

"No"

"Exactly, no wonder he said your sex life will never be the same again, it wouldn't would it if you're dead? Didn't it sink in to your little brain that that drug was meant for you, they already want you dead now, what's the name of the pusher?"

Osborne wiped a trickle of blood from his mouth and glared at his assailant, but his mind was racing as he realised he had been in such a state over Mercedes that he had not given any thought to the reality of the situation. "Rogers" he blurted, "Ginger Rogers, that's his nickname, he has red hair."

"Really!" came the reply, "I didn't think he was a bloody dancer. Where can we find him?"

"He always hangs around 'Roscoe's' and sometimes the Incognito Club but he lives somewhere on Holland Park Road."

"OK we'll find him", said the Scot. Osborne was still fuming at being struck, "France or not, you can't go assaulting me" he said, defiantly adding. "You know you can't arrest me in France, if I don't want to go back you'll need an arrest warrant."

"I don't recall ever mentioning we were police officers." Said the Scot. "We have no intention of taking you back."

"Certainly not" said Blondie. Osborne turned towards him and was shocked to see him holding a silenced pistol; before he could react there was a single 'phut' as the trigger was pulled, Osborne's head jerked back and he slumped in the chair, blood streaming from a hole that had suddenly appeared in his forehead. Blondie casually slipped the pistol back into his jacket, nodded to the Scot and said "Let's go and tell Mr Rogers we've done the job for him." Without looking back, they both casually left the room pulling the door closed behind them.

CHAPTER FOUR

"Another double whisky" a slurred voice demanded banging an empty glass down on the bar. "I'm sorry sir" the barman replied, "I think you've had enough, why don't you go home?"

"I'll decide when I've had enough, give me another bloody whisky."

"No Sir!" the barman continued. "I'm afraid I'm going to have to ask you to leave." As he was about to argue, the man noticed two doormen heading in his direction. With enough wits left to know when to give in he said "Bollocks to you then" and unsteadily made his way to the door. As he stepped outside and took a first breath of the cold night air, he immediately felt light headed and as he reached out to brace himself against a wall, a voice behind him said "Captain Wood I presume."

"I'm captain fuck all anymore" he slurred turning unsteadily to face his inquisitor. With unfocusing eyes he could make out a tall figure wearing a full-length black coat. "You've not been discharged yet Captain" the man replied, adding "I'd like you to come with me sir," more in the manner of a demand than a request. "Fuck off," Sticky replied. He had hardly finished the 'off ' when a thump at the back of his neck made his legs crumple and he started to fall to the floor.

He was less than half way down before strong hands grabbed him from either side and he was dragged across the pavement and unceremoniously thrown through the open side door of a VW transporter. The men followed him in closed the door and the van sped off.

"Morning Sir", a voice cut through the foggy haze associated between being asleep and awake. Sticky gradually opened his eyes and instinctively swung his legs over the side of the bed until he was in a seated position. Rubbing his eyes with one hand while rubbing his neck with the other, he looked up at the young uniformed man stood by a table across the room. "Where am I?" he asked. "I'm sure the boss will explain that later", came the reply. "There's a toilet and shower to your right and I have put in clean towels, shampoo, soap and shaving gear. There are clean clothes hanging in the wardrobe and underwear socks and boots on the table. Breakfast is in half an hour and the briefing at o nine hundred."

"What bloody briefing?" Sticky asked of no one as the man had swiftly left the room closing the door behind him. For now though he had a more urgent need for the toilet. After relieving himself he stepped into the shower allowing the warm water to run over him and bring him fully awake. After washing his hair and scrubbing himself all over, he switched off the shower and towelled himself down before wrapping the towel around his waist and stepping to the wash basin for a shave. He hardly recognised the face looking back at him from the mirror, his normally alert looking green eyes looked dull, there were bags under them he had not noticed before and his blonde hair looked limp while the two days of stubble on his chin was showing signs of grey. He shaved and combed his hair and decided the reflection looked at least a little more familiar.

In the wardrobe was an obviously new uniform superbly pressed an adorned with the captains rank insignia. He carefully dressed, noting he could see his reflection in the highly polished boots and belt buckle. He had lost a little weight in the last couple of months, but everything fitted perfectly. Someone has been doing their homework he thought to himself, although it was the first time in months he felt smart, he was getting angry as he remembered being abducted off the street, "time to get some answers" he muttered as he stepped from the room. There was the murmur of voices coming from his right so he walked briskly up the passage and stepped out into a large open area where several men were seated around a table either eating or drinking coffee. The conversation stopped on his arrival and all eyes turned towards him. A stocky man, who had been tucking into a large fried breakfast, broke the silence. "Help yourself Captain," he said pointing to a row of hotplates off to the left. "There's plenty to choose from and there's tea or coffee on the end there."

"Thanks" came the reply. There certainly was plenty to choose from, the spread was as good as you would expect in any five star hotel, ranging from continental style croissants yoghurt and cheese selections to every kind of cooked food normally found with a full English breakfast. Sticky took a tray and helped himself to some cereal and milk followed by a couple of slices of bread with which he made a bacon sandwich he then took a cup and the whole jug of black coffee and went to join the others sat at the table.

"Like your style with the coffee" one of the guys laughed, "Yeah well I think I'm going to need it," Sticky replied, " anyone know what the hell is going on here?" he added. "Nowp! I guess we'll find out at nine o'clock", one of the others chipped in. "Let's go around the table" cut in the stocky guy. "I'm Tony Carter and my friend here is Steve Wright both SAS."

"I'm Jim Philips and my red headed pal here is Roy McFadden SBS."

"I'm Robert Campbell and my colleague is Peter Clarke, Royal Marines specialising in demolition and explosives."

"I'm Mike Wood Army Apache pilot."

"And I'm Fred Moore his long suffering bloody Nav and gunner." Sticky spun around to see Pony coming through the door behind him, he jumped up and shook his hand. "Good to see you mate," he said "I thought you'd gone back to Afghanistan."

"I did" came the reply, "but the bloody pilot they gave me kept trying to kill me so I was asked if I wanted to join you. What are we up to this time?"

"Fuck knows" came a reply in unison from all the guys in the room. "We've got a briefing at nine," said Carter "so you got ten minutes to get some grub then perhaps we'll all find out.

Sticky cast his eye over the assembled crew, Carter was about five foot eight what hair he had was cut so short he almost looked bald. He had a round face and intelligent looking eyes, his head seemed to blend in with his neck, while his massive forearms and biceps pointed to the fact he had a body of solid muscle. His companion, Steve, was closer to six feet tall he had dark hair, a thin face with deep-set brown eyes that failed to display any emotion. Although much slimmer than Carter, it was clear he also had a fit muscular body honed by years of SAS training. Both the marines Campbell and Clarke were around six foot and had a slim athletic build, both had dark short cut hair and square cut faces although Campbell had a scar running from his left eye down the whole side of his face. Philips and McFadden were of similar build to the marines although both were heavier built around the shoulders in the typical fashion of professional swimmers. Like Carter, Phillips had short-cropped hair while McFadden had a head of curly red hair and, as with many red heads, a rather pale complexion. Although both were fit, Sticky couldn't help but think that in comparison he and Pony must have looked puny. Finally he said, "Looking around here Mr Carter with all the different specialists and obvious experience, I don't think we've been invited to a bloody picnic."

Just before nine the young man, Sticky had seen earlier, entered the room. "Could you come with me gentlemen?" He said before leading them through to a large briefing room. They all took seats and a few seconds later a tall man entered the room dressed in civilian clothing. He appeared to be in his late fifties or early sixties, his grey hair was cut short and the navy suit he was wearing looked expensively tailored to fit his muscular looking frame. Overall he exuded an air of confidence and had a bearing that indicated a military background. Another man followed him in who was dressed in an army uniform bearing the insignia of a Lieutenant Colonel. This second man was considerably younger, looked fit and sported a head of red hair. No one had stood or attempted to stand when they walked in. The civilian looked around the room and then said. "Good morning gentlemen, you are now part of an elite group." As soon as he started talking Sticky knew this was the man who had abducted him the night before, instinctively his hand went to the back of his head and he glared at the Lieutenant Colonel, thinking if that was you, we will have a score to settle. The man continued, "I'm Geoffrey Hamilton but you can call me sir", he chuckled but was faced with a stony silence, he gave a little cough then carried on. "I represent a part of MI6 that does not officially exist and all of you have been selected because you are the best at what you do. Lieutenant Colonel McGreggor here will have the job of building you into a team." All eyes turned to McGreggor and you didn't need to be a mind reader to hear the collective thought of 'bring it on pal' that was circulating the room. Hamilton continued. "I suppose you are all wondering why you are here and what task you will be taking on."

"It would help." Carter cut in. "Yes well", Hamilton continued, "all of you have come here from different backgrounds and in different ways." He looked straight at Sticky as he said that. "However I hope you will now become the pointed end of an international group we have built up over several years. Throughout the world at this moment in time it would be fair to say that throughout the world at this moment in time it would be fair to say that almost all countries are facing terrorist activity of some type. While in the name of Islam, other terrorists are systematically taking control of country after country on the African continent as well as Pakistan, Afghanistan, Syria, Iraq and now Libya. Alongside these, there are political activists and extremists, all of which are supported by rogue regimes and funded by the drug trade or piracy and armed by unscrupulous dealers or sympathetic governments. All of whom are hiding behind obscure international legal processes or corrupt officials that protect them. Our Government decided that rather like the American 'Untouchables', they needed groups of incorruptible men that would take direct action and were not afraid to shoot first and ask questions after. Well, designated as UN-12, you are to become the latest of these international groups."

There was silence for a moment then Hamilton continued. "Al Capone and his gang might have died a long time ago, but where there was bootlegging there are now worldwide groups of arms dealers and drug barons."

"Drugs!" exclaimed Campbell. "You brought us together to fight the drugs barons, whole bloody armies have been doing that in Mexico and South America for years what are eight of us supposed to do?"

"Nine" cut in McGreggor. "Oh excuse me NINE" continued Campbell. "I signed up for the military not the bloody police force."

"Ok OK!" said Hamilton "Every one of you have lost mates and seen others badly injured in Iraq, Afghanistan and numerous other places we're not supposed to be. Well those poppy fields of Afghanistan, cannabis plantations in Morocco and as Mr Campbell put it, the drugs that pour out of South America and Mexico. All go a long way towards providing the funds for those weapons that are killing and maiming your friends. We have spent years infiltrating these gangs at the highest level and some of my men have already paid with their lives. Now we have people within every major producer and supplier of drugs, as well as the arms trade. It probably won't surprise you to find that a lot of politicians, business men and investment fund managers have a comfortable income from drugs money pouring into every continent on this planet. While peace is the last thing the arms dealers require. As billions of dollars go into research and creating arms and then further billions into creating other weapons to neutralise them. The whole business is self-perpetrating and don't think it's only rogue regimes that are supplying arms. While the Russians were fighting and loosing hundreds of men in Afghanistan, the CIA were happily supplying weapons to the very men who were to become the Taliban, now with the roles reversed, the Russians are returning the compliment. In Iraq, you went in to topple a man put in place by the CIA and mostly armed by Britain. In South America the involvement of the CIA has caused the destabilisation that has led to the rise of the powerful drug lords. Had the major powers stayed out of other countries internal affairs, the world would probably be a much more stable place. However it is what it is and while your mates were dying in Afghanistan, in numerous millionaire hotspots, guys are sipping their champagne on their multi million pound yachts while signing off another arms deal to some militant group or other so they can then sign off another to the poor bastards they're fighting." Carter looked around and could see everybody was contemplating what had been said with varying degrees of comfort. "So exactly where is this going?" he asked. McGreggor nodded to Hamilton "Do you mind sir?"

"No go ahead"

McGreggor continued. "We remain part of the military and will use that as cover and support but we are not an army and we are not going head to head with the drug barons, arms dealers or their financial backers but we will hit them where it hurts. As you heard, several countries have now set up groups such as this. We will share intelligence, but as a group none of you officially exist, so will be able to act with impunity, free from political pressure and legal restraints. Thanks to our network of agents we know when big shipments are due to go out, we know where and how they will be moving we also know who the paymasters are and when arms deals are likely to be done. As a small self-contained cell we will act quickly using terrorist like tactics, we will take and destroy drug shipments and hit arms deals and dealers. Generally we make life bloody uncomfortable. With the help of the inside men we will aim to stir up mistrust in the hierarchy. It will be no bed of roses. Initially we will have stealth and surprise but as they get hit again and again they will tighten security, which in itself will make it more difficult to move large quantities but could also mean they start shooting back. Although our biggest threat will be from the men in power, the politicians, power brokers and money men." Hamilton stepped forward. "That's a lot for you to take in gentlemen coffee is on in the other room. Take a break during which I will speak to you all individually and explain where you are regarding your individual units. Then if you are still here this afternoon. Lieutenant Colonel McGreggor will run through some training and inform you of the first target."

Hamilton and McGreggor left the way they had entered and all the guys stood up and made their way to the rest room where tea and coffee was brewing along with a selection of small cakes and biscuits. As Sticky helped himself to a coffee Pony said "Pour me one while you're at it", adding "not what I was expecting, interesting though isn't it?"

"It's certainly that." 'Sticky replied. Looking around the room he could see several of the others in conversation and from the bits he overheard he judged that they were also bemused but in other ways excited at getting some different action. Clever bastard Sticky thought, Hamilton has picked his men well but considering my recent past why the hell has he picked me? With that the young private appeared, "Captain Wood" he called "Mr Hamilton would like to see you could you come through with me please?" Sticky pointedly took his time to finish his coffee and biscuit then putting the cup down and seeing the young man was getting a little irritated, he said, "Better go before the young lad here pops a fuse." There was mild laughter as he made his way out behind the red-faced young private.

Sticky entered what was a sparsely decorated office, Hamilton stood and came to shake his hand. "Captain Wood or can I call you Mike?" He said. "Mike is fine" came the reply. "Take a seat" Hamilton said pointing to a leather chair by his desk. As Sticky sat down Hamilton went around and sat behind the desk, which was covered with numerous files that Sticky rightly guessed were the service records of him and all those presently in the other room. "Firstly may I apologise for the way you, ah shall we say arrived at this establishment."

"Yes well it was rather sudden I was quite happy getting drunk thank you."

"Something you have done rather a lot of recently I gather," came the reply. "Frankly I was expecting a little more protest from you this morning." 'Sticky looked him straight in the eye and replied. "It did cross my mind but strangely having a shave and putting on this uniform made me feel a little better, besides I wanted to know why some bastard would hit me over the head." Hamilton never flinched he just picked up a file and said. "Your compassionate leave is over and your unit agreed we could borrow you, as your experience on several types of helicopter is something that will be of use to us and as it happens, you and your partner have an exemplary record under fire."

"That maybe so", Sticky replied," but I was happy flying the Apache it's totally different to flying other machines, besides why would I have an interest in bloody drug pushers? Hamilton took out a sheet of paper and handed it to him. "The autopsy report on the guy driving the car that killed your family says he was full of illegal substances, being on the wrong side of the dual carriageway, I'd be surprised if he knew what planet he was on. Those bloody drug pushers killed your family just as much as the shit driving the car".

CHAPTER FIVE

Chief Inspector Penney walked into his office to hear the end of a conversation in French, "What's that all about Charlie?" he asked. Replacing the phone Charlie replied, "It seems the French have got Osborne, our disc jockey, in some back street hotel in Paris."

"Best news I've had today", said Penney, "Are they going to play ball or do we have to go through that European arrest warrant crap?"

"Not that easy boss, it seems someone got to him first, they found him with a bullet hole in his head and definitely not suicide as there was no gun in the room. The French are going to send through some photographs and will keep us up to date with any other information they come up with."

The inspector went to his desk, swung out his chair and flopped into it, he then tilted back placed his feet cross legged on the desk and stared at the ceiling without speaking. Eventually he said. "I don't like this, its messy there are too many questions and no simple answers. Firstly it's clear the drug that killed Miss Johnson was meant for him, now who wanted him dead and why. Secondly did they want him dead so badly that they followed him to France to do it."

"It's possible," said Charlie. "Yes but then that brings up a third question. What was it he did that required him to be bumped off before we could get to talk to him? Everyone we have spoken to so far don't rate him as worth a shit to anyone."

"He was a bit of a womaniser" cut in Charlie "He had a reputation for putting it about a bit maybe he was dipping his wick with the wrong woman. Most of the gangs operating in that area are run by jumped up little shits who think they are latter day mafia godfathers."

"That's possible I suppose" replied Penney, "But fixing him up with dodgy drugs and letting it appear that another junky has overdosed is one thing but tracking him to France and blowing his brains out doesn't fit especially with the publicity going on and the whole of Interpol looking for him. After things went wrong with young Mercedes they knew he was facing manslaughter and their reach into prisons is substantial." While he was talking Charlie had received an email from France and was printing off the attachments, he passed the photographs to the inspector and set about translating the text which was naturally in French.

The photographs showed Osborne slightly slumped in the chair with his head back, another showed the bullet wound and others were of the room. Penney spread the pictures on the desk and said "From these it's clear there was no scuffle or resistance, the room is tidy and undisturbed, I would say he was talking to his killer when he was shot. This looks more like an assassination."

"Killers" replied Charlie, "This report from France says he checked into the hotel at around noon, that's around eleven here. The receptionist saw his picture in the local paper this morning and alerted the police who then found him when they raided the room. However a cleaner saw two men getting into the lift on that floor around seven pm French time. She heard them talking in English and said one had a heavy accent and the other was tall and blonde. There's no record of any other English people at the hotel and no CCTV."

"No other bloody security either by the sound of it" replied Penney, "But at least it gives us something" Charlie was frantically searching through reports, "Ah here it is" he said, "The guys who went around to Osborne's flat said it was a tip he either left in a hurry or someone else had been searching it, a neighbour said she thought the police had been their earlier as she saw two guys leaving."

"Any description?"

"No."

"Christ said Penney "do these uniform guys ever show initiative. Get them back there and get a description and step up the search for the pusher who gave Osborne the drugs I need a name."

Two men already had a name and for the past few minutes had been sat in a black Jaguar XF that was parked in Holland Park Road just outside a small row of shops and opposite some flats one of which had been identified to them as belonging to a certain 'Ginger' Rogers. The Scottish guy finished his conversation on his mobile phone, then turned to his blonde companion and said "Ok Karl let's see if Mr Rogers is home." Both men stepped from the car, locked it with the remote and walked across the road. Although in the middle of the city, this part of Kensington had a tree lined urban appearance with the houses on this side being set well back from the road. All sported tree and bush filled gardens and were a mixture of four and five storey Victorian or early twentieth century buildings. Many came from the 'upstairs downstairs' period and had below street level basements once used by the servants. Most of these had now been turned into flats, which commanded high prices or rental values. The gardens were separated from the street by brick walls topped with white stone pillared affect adornments. Ball topped white painted pillars stood either side of the gates to the properties. The two men passed through one of the gates and walked up the path towards the house. In front of them a flight of steps went up to a large front door, while to the right of that other steps led down to the basement flats. As they started down these steps the main front door opened and a young lady came out and pulled the door shut behind her, she saw the two men and called "I don't think Ginger is in, he normally doesn't get back until about five."

"Thanks" the Scot replied. "We will give him a knock just in case." The girl just shrugged and made her way out on to the street.

They waited a few moments then the man called Karl knocked on the door, with no reply he removed some lock picks from his pocket and very quickly had the door open. They waited again listening intently for any signs of an alarm. Satisfied it was clear they entered. The flat was not what they expected, it was spotlessly clean and sported a nice leather corner unit settee. A fifty-inch flat screen television was mounted above a very modern glass and stone gas fire, while the lounge walls sported copies of paintings by LS Lowry. There was a sound and satellite system to the left of the fire and a glass desk with phone and wireless router to the right. "All very neat" said the Scot. "No alarm system, no CD's for his music and no computer for the Wi.Fi"

"He probably has a laptop he takes with him, doubt he would leave that lying around, as for CD's, it's all digital now he'll probably have all his music on hard disc."

"I'll have a look around the rest of the flat keep an eye out in case he comes home early." replied Karl. The kitchen was open plan with the lounge and was ultra-modern and clean but obviously used. So he moved into the bedroom, which was again exceptionally clean and tidy. The wardrobe was neatly laid out with expensive suits and silk shirts. Every drawer had neatly folded pants, T-shirts and socks several prints of Beryl Cooks oversize ladies were on the walls. The bathroom contained a toilet, bidet, washbasin, shower cubicle and a standard bath, there was a heater cupboard filled with neatly folded towels. Karl placed the plug in the bath and turned both taps on full. Once the water was about ten inches from the top he turned them off and went back to the lounge. "One thing is for sure Mac" he said, "this guy leads two different lives, we saw him in the clubs dressed in jeans and trainers with a scruffy shirt and leather jacket. Well, that's not the guy who lives here. Expensive suits and clothes over the top attention to neatness, even the bloody tins in the kitchen cupboards are all lined up with their labels in the same direction." Karl put his finger to his lip, "Someone's coming," he whispered. Mac stepped into the kitchen area while Karl placed himself flat against the wall on the hinge side of the entrance door.

Rogers was looking forward to getting a shower and something to eat. He had a meeting earlier and was now planning a quiet evening with the young lady who lived in one of the flats above. He had been trying to date her for weeks and had finally won her around so he was in a light hearted mood and looking forward to the evening to come as he put the key in his door and stepped into the flat. "Fancy a cup of tea," said a Scottish voice coming from the kitchen area. Rogers turned to face the source of the question "What the fu.." he started before sensing rather than seeing someone behind him. His reactions were lightning fast as he spun swinging a blow that almost caught Karl off guard, but the big blonde guy parried the blow and catching Rogers arm, twisted it while at the same time kicking his feet away. Rogers hit the floor face first within seconds both men were on him forcing his arms behind his back and placing a set of cuffs on his wrists. "Now" said Mac, "We have a couple of questions for you, be sensible and answer them and we might leave you to enjoy the rest of the evening."

"Fuck off" Rogers spat out. A boot instantly caught him in the side knocking the wind out of him and cracking a rib. "Wrong answer", said Karl. "Perhaps we can start again and just in case you're thinking you can stay silent and wait for a solicitor, that's wrong as well, we're not the police so we're not constrained by any legal nicety there are going to be one of two outcomes to this, tell us everything we want to know and we leave with you still alive, don't answer and you will be meeting up with Mr Osborne again."

Rogers mind was racing and he knew these men weren't joking. For the first time his cocky demeanour was gone and he felt fear. "What's Osborne got to do with this?" he asked. "Everything" came the reply, "we paid him a little visit in France and he gave us your name but as it was clear you wanted him dead we obliged and my friend here lodged a nine millimetre bullet in his brain."

"I heard that on the news", came the reply, "Then you know we're not messing about. You gave Osborne the drug that was used to kill Mercedes Johnson, now we don't think you did that off your own back, so we want to know who told you to give him the drug and why they wanted him dead."

"I don't know what you're talking about, look around I don't have anything to do with drugs" said Rogers. The two men nodded to each other then grabbed a shoulder from either side pushing down at the same time as pulling his arms up against the joint forcing Rogers to call out in pain, they then half lifted half dragged him to the bathroom. Each time Rogers tried to stand or struggle more pressure was put on his arms making it impossible to gain a position from which he could fight back. As they entered the bathroom he saw the water and instantly knew what was about to happen he kicked out more violently but to no avail. Within seconds his head was plunged into the water and he was held under having had no time to take a deep breath, and fighting the pain in his ribs, he struggled and held on as long as he could until it felt his lungs would burst and he had to exhale. As the bubbles streamed from his mouth his head was lifted clear of the water.

"Now don't fuck about again", said Mac. "Each time we put you under it will be for thirty seconds longer, so I reckon by the third time you won't be coming up again. Osborne told us that you told him to try this new drug and that his sex life would never be the same again. So that tells me you knew it would kill him and also you never gave a shit. You weren't to know that he would try it on someone else first, but in the eyes of the law, you killed that girl just as surely as he did."

"No! No!" cried Rogers. "I knew Mercedes and I liked her I never thought she would ever go anywhere with an asshole like him. How could I? Given a chance, I would have shot the bastard myself."

"So who wanted him dead and why?" asked Karl. Rogers hesitated and was instantly plunged towards the water again. "Ok Ok", he called "It was my supplier, he had some of the top European dealers over here and took them to a club to impress, he was trying to chat up one of the girls but she brushed him off and then put her arms around Osborne, so Osborne turned to him and said you've either got it or you haven't, you obviously haven't. Well he couldn't let Osborne dis him in front of the others and get away with it. He had to be seen to deal with it, nobody could have seen it would go so wrong."

"Maybe it hasn't", said Mac. "Osborne's mug was splashed all over the European press and so is the fact that he is now been shot perhaps your man can claim responsibility and be seen as a guy not to mess with. All you need to do now is give us his name."

"Bollocks" came the reply; "He has connections everywhere in the Police, Home Office even Parliament, I don't want to end up like Osborne."

"Well that's the rub," said Karl "You don't give us his name and you're going to end up like Osborne anyway, bit of a catch 22 eh." They allowed Rogers to slump on the bathroom floor then Mac said. "Look lets level with you after Mercedes death, I had every intention to kill you son, but It's clear from your set up here you're meticulous with detail, my guess is that you're well up the supply chain. The fact is we'll shortly be in possession of a lot of top class gear, and your man won't have to worry about importing them as we'll take care of that. What we don't have is a supply chain, so we need to meet to set up a deal. When your boss hears what we're offering he'll want to kiss you not kill you."

Rogers thought for a moment then shook his head, he was not convinced he was not about to die so figured he needed to give them something to ensure he was more use alive, "Look there's no way I can give you a direct in," he said, adding "He's not the sort of guy where you can just turn up and knock the door, let me talk to him first I'll get him to set up a meeting." A mobile phone's ring took them all by surprise. It was clearly in Rogers's pocket, Karl reached in and took it out pressing the answer key as he did so. "Hi" he said. A woman's voice asked "Is Ginger there?" Karl replied "Sorry he is in the bathroom at the moment, can I take a message?"

"Yes ok" came the reply "Please tell him I will be about fifteen minutes late I'll see him at quarter to eight."

"Will do" Karl replied then switched the phone off. "It seems your date will be a bit late tonight", he said as he reached into Rogers's pocket and removed a second phone he'd noticed earlier. "No" Rogers cried as he tried to sit up but was pushed back to the floor by the heavy boot of Mac. "One of these might have a number we want", said Karl as he switched on the second phone, once it had come to life he pressed the 'contacts' button and only one number came up. "Sloppy very sloppy Mr Rogers" he said as he hit the call key. A few minutes later a voice said. "Why are you calling?" "I was hoping to set up a distribution deal", said Karl. There was a few seconds of silence then the voice asked, "Who is this?"

"I'm the guy who dealt with Mr Osborne for you and I'm importing a multimillion pound shipment of consumer goods and need a distribution net-work Mr Rogers recommended you."

"I'm not into distribution" came the reply "Goodbye."

"You retain eighty percent of street value" Karl quickly cut in. Again there was silence then "Keep hold of that phone, I'll contact you."

"Well Mr Rogers it seems we don't need your help after all" said Karl putting the phone in his pocket. "You do," said Rogers, "I run the distribution in this area." "Maybe", said Karl. " But I don't like the fact you're a bit sloppy, occasionally acting as a dealer yourself, gives you a buzz no doubt but that led us to you and will probably lead the Police here as well." He nodded to Mac and together they lifted Rogers by the arms and plunged him into the bath. He kicked and struggled furiously as the two men held him down, then gradually the struggling ceased and he lay still. Mac removed the plug as Karl removed the cuffs. They then walked out of the bathroom leaving his lifeless body face down in the bath.

CHAPTER SIX

Pony came out of Hamilton's office and joined Sticky who was sat talking to Carter; he was the last one to have been seen. "Well" he said, "Are we in then?" Both Carter and Sticky looked up. "Just been discussing that" said Carter. "Thought we might see what McGreggor has in mind this afternoon before we commit ourselves, it all seems a little odd, I mean is Hamilton for real?" cut in Sticky. "Oh I reckon he is," said Carter "I have worked on a few specialist jobs before with the increment."

"The what?" asked Pony? "A special SAS group" replied Carter. "We operated in friendly countries and took out people on behalf of the Government, while they denied any knowledge and protested at such outrages. In the last few years I've been a Taliban fighter, Somali pirate, instigated an uprising and even been one of the paparazzi."

"Jesus", said Pony "I'd heard rumours but didn't think these things were for real." "Well they are" replied Carter. "And now we are about to become another one of those units that don't exist." A couple of cooks entered the room each pushing a trolley, which they started to upload to the hotplates that had previously held the breakfast food. One turned and addressed the men sat at the table. "Lunch is served gentlemen, please help yourselves, I'm instructed to tell you the next briefing will be at fourteen hundred." One by one the men got up and made their way to the hotplates, after surveying the various dishes Pony said. "Blimey if the food is like this every day I'm definitely staying."

"Me too" said Phillips. The men all finished their lunch while recounting various tales of places they had served. Then just before two they all made their way into the briefing room. A screen had been pulled down at the front of the room and an overhead projector was throwing an image of the western Mediterranean. "Looks like we are headed for some sun" quipped McFadden as they took their seats.

LT Col McGreggor entered the room, "Good afternoon gentlemen" he started. "It is important that we get to work as a team, you all have individual skills but we need to bring them together so you're able to operate knowing everyone will be doing their bit. For that reason we will be undertaking a couple of small operations in the Med to get you used to one another and to the way you will be moving around." All the men sat impassively with just the odd glance at one another. McGreggor continued. "Your first trip will be easy, there's a military transport leaving here at 07.00 tomorrow flying to Gibraltar, you will travel in civilian clothing and will only carry the wallets and passports that we provide you with, any other items that can identify you or of a personal nature will be placed in locked bags and placed in a safe until you return. Look at the passports and cards and ensure you learn the details off by heart."

"I take it we're not using our own names then" said Philips. "No" replied McGreggor, "and that is an important point, this is for use when travelling so travel separately so you don't inadvertently use your normal names and don't tell each other of your new identity, that way you won't be able to identify your travelling companion. When on military transport or when you're alone together there's not a problem. For radio communications on operations you will use code names. Phillips and McFadden will be 'Wet 1 & Wet 2', Carter & Wright will be 'Ground 1 & Ground 2', Campbell & Clarke will be Dem 1 & Dem 2 Wood & Moore will be 'Air 1 & Air 2'."

"Even I can remember that," said Pony raising some chuckles.

 "Settle down" said McGreggor as he pressed a remote and a picture of North Africa appeared on the screen, he then zoomed in until they could see a small harbour created from a natural cove with a long outer wall stretching from a headland out to the west. "El Jebha, Morocco, gentlemen a small port town situated in the Rif Mountains." A closer view showed a small town with houses of the Mediterranean flat roofed style and a port protected by a large cliff at the Eastern end. Again the screen changed and this time a picture of a motor yacht appeared. "A Jeanneau Prestige 42S and for those of you technically minded it is of GRP construction, is forty three feet in length and has twin Volvo diesel engines giving a total of three hundred and seventy horse power. It has one interesting feature which is a tender garage." He changed the screen again and a picture of the stern of the boat appeared with a hinged section opened revealing a large stowage space. "When this leaves port" he continued, "it will not be carrying a tender I am expecting this space as well as the under seat stowage's to contain four hundred and fifty kilograms of Moroccan Black with a street value of around one hundred and twenty pounds an ounce, that makes this cargo worth approximately two million pounds. Its destination is Marbella on the Spanish coast, it will be met by a local pleasure boat and the cargo transferred before it makes port. Only we are to see it never makes it that far."

"I know two million is a lot," said Phillips, "but surely this is peanuts in the scale of things."

"You're right," replied McGreggor. "However there will be two men on the boat one of whom will be Ahmed Zawahiri." A photograph appeared on screen. "He is travelling under another name and is a wanted leader of a Somali terror group. Intelligence believes he is heading for Britain where he is intending to organise an atrocity similar to the Kenyan shopping Mall incident. This job is intended to see how well you work together and fulfil the objective."

"What is the full objective?" asked Sticky. "One you eliminate all on board and sink the boat leaving no trace and two, you recover the drugs." There was silence for a moment, and then Carter said. "So this is an assassination."

"I prefer elimination," came the reply. "At this point we want to create doubt, and ensure there is mistrust between the drug dealers and the terrorists. When you get to Gibraltar tomorrow you will join your boat in accordance with the instructions you'll find in your rooms, all the equipment you need will be on the boat, and at that stage the full details of the operation will be communicated. Your planned interception is in forty-eight hours' time. I suggest you get some rest, good day."

Silently they all got up and left, some stopped in the rest area and grabbed a coffee while Sticky returned to his room where he found new clothing hanging in the wardrobe and a barrel bag containing spare underwear, shirt and toiletries there was also a passport in the name of Michael Baker and a wallet containing five hundred Euro, a debit card and credit card both again in the name of M Baker. A sealed envelope lay on the table, which he picked up and opened. The message inside confirmed he was to travel as Baker gave the pin number for the cards which were to be used for flights, hotels and any necessary expenditure. There was no specified limit but all spending was to be accompanied by receipts and would be strictly audited. The instructions also confirmed the seven a.m. flight in the morning and that only the items provided were to be carried. On reaching Gibraltar he would be met and transported separately from the others to join a ship called the Minerva. He re-read the instructions, noted the pin number then tore up the letter and flushed it down the toilet. As he finished, there was a knock and Pony walked in and flopped onto the bed. "Yes I know", said Sticky.

"Know what?" came the reply. "You're worried about this set up, I agree it's a bit odd, but we have done a lot of odd things before." Pony just looked up, knowing his friend had read him well. "It's just this assassination bit that bothers me, I mean when someone is shooting at me then I'm happy to shoot back but to just bump them off it doesn't feel right."

"Look at it another way", replied Sticky. "If he is heading to Britain to commit mass murder then we're saving innocent lives. Besides, my guess is Carter and Wright will have no problem taking care of that side of things." Pony smiled, "Yeah evil looking couple of bastards aren't they." They talked for a couple of hours, then agreeing they had an early start, Pony said his goodnights and went back to his room.

The following morning, the group of men found themselves looking like smartly dressed business men and seated on the A320 transport plane along with an assortment of uniformed personnel and other civilian dressed civil servants. The flight took just over two and a half hours, before the pilot brought it in to land on the tricky Gibraltar runway, which had the bay of Cadiz at one end and the Mediterranean at the other. As he left the aircraft, Sticky was immediately stuck by the temperature in relation to that he had left just a couple of hours before. With the time difference, it was now ten thirty in the morning but already it was thirty degrees and with clear blue cloudless skies it would soon be even warmer. He found himself waved through arrivals with only the minimum of formalities and with just the barrel bag to carry, was soon walking through the arrivals area.

"Mr Baker" a voice called before repeating "Mr Baker", Sticky suddenly realised the man was addressing him. Shit he thought I'm going to have to sharpen up on that. "I'm sorry" he said, "I was miles away there for a moment, must be the sudden heat." The man smiled "You'll soon get used to it", he replied. "I'm to transport you out to your ship, I believe they are sailing around noon." Sticky studied the man as he led him out to a parked van which had 'Johnson Marine Industries' painted on the side, along with local phone numbers. He doesn't look like a marine engineer to me he thought although casually dressed he was smart, his shoes well-polished, slacks neatly pressed and his hands certainly showed no signs of ever been in the vicinity of oil. He climbed in the passenger seat, and as he dropped the bag behind him, he noted how clean, and empty, the interior of the van was. Not a very convincing cover he thought, let's hope the rest of the operation is better thought out.

As they left the airport Sticky noticed they were on Winston Churchill Avenue as they drove along he could not help being struck by the "Englishness" of it from the occasional post box to the police officers he saw entering one of the shops. The driver noticed him looking. "Not been to Gib before?" he asked. "No" Sticky replied, "I thought I was still in England for a minute." The driver chuckled. "Everyone's first thought" he said, adding "The Spanish do a bit of sabre rattling now and then, normally when there is some bad political news at home but they could never really change it." Sticky noticed they had turned onto Corral Road then over a roundabout into Waterfront road. A short distance later they entered North Mole Road. In the distance he could see a large cruise liner that was tied up near a quay. They were clearly now in one of the harbour areas as the buildings became more industrial. Just before a security gate, which clearly led to the cruise ship embarkation area, the driver turned left onto a small pier and pulled up beside a ship that was tied up alongside. "Here you are sir, have a good trip." Sticky thanked him, took his bag and whilst he looked up at the ship. The driver spun the van around and was quickly heading back the way they had come.

He watched him turn right back towards the town and then took a good look at the ship. The words 'MINERVA' Glasgow were painted on the stern, at least it's the right ship he thought. He was not much of an expert on ships, but this one didn't look like anything he'd seen before. It looked like the illegitimate offspring of a Cruise ship and a luxury yacht. The raked bow gave the impression of a ship capable of high speed. A two storey superstructure ran from just short of the bow right through to the stern. The forward part of which was raked back with beautiful smooth lines that curved around to blend with superstructures sides. On the second level was what Sticky assumed was the bridge and the sides ran as a continuous span, interspaced with panoramic windows. While on the first level the sides had four cut out sections showing the cabins set back forming a walkway on either side. Above the bridge was a funnel or mast holding radar domes and several aerials while the almost flat stern appeared to contain a door? The ship was painted white with a blue and gold stripe running from bow to stern.

A voice called "Are you going to stand there all day?" Sticky looked up to see Carter standing by the rail; he waved and then made his way up the open gangplank. On entering through the open doorway, he felt as if he had entered a luxury hotel. There was a thick maroon carpet, several armchairs and a polished oak table at which McGreggor was seated. Carter was pouring a coffee, "Want one Capt.?" he asked "Yes thanks" came the reply. Over the next thirty minutes all the others arrived "Right gentlemen" announced McGreggor. "Now you're all here we will be casting off in about thirty minutes in the meantime you'll find cabins down the passage to the left, with your names on. I suggest you freshen up and put on the uniforms provided. One thing all the crew are military and have the highest clearance, however do not discuss details of any operation with anyone. Once we put to sea I will take you on a guided tour. Then we'll go over the details of the operation and you'll start running through practice drills and you Mr Wood, will need to get familiar with your helicopter."

"What helicopter?" asked Pony "Have a good look around I'm sure you'll find it Mr Moor" replied McGreggor. "I'll see you back here at thirteen hundred."

CHAPTER SEVEN

Sarah Thomas was running late, but had showered and changed and was only about ten minutes behind the time she had told Ginger. At least she hoped the message had been passed on. Leaving her flat, she went down the front steps of the building and then down the further set to the basement flat. To her surprise the door was open, she knocked anyway and then on entering she called out, "Hi Ginge it's me, sorry I'm late." There was no answer; again she called "Ginge are you here?" Again no reply, then she noticed his bag on the floor and some footprints left by wet shoes that were leading from the bathroom, cautiously she went forward and pushed the door open. For a second she was frozen to the spot at the sight of the body face down in the bath, then with her hand to her mouth in an attempt to stop herself from being sick, she fled out of the flat pausing at the bottom of the steps and with her body trembling, she fumbled in her pocket for her phone and dialled 999.

Inspector Penney was sat at his desk reviewing some reports of possible drug suppliers on the club scene. Charlie had just opened an E-mail. "Ah" he exclaimed, "We have a description of the two men seen at Osborne's flat. One is described as six foot, stocky with a possible Scottish accent, the other tall with blonde hair and wearing a long dark coloured coat." As he was talking, a uniformed officer had entered the office. "That fits the description of the two guys seen at the Holland Park murder" he said. "What Holland Park murder?" snapped Penney. "Sorry guv", replied the officer that's what I was coming to tell you, they've found the body of a guy called Andrew Rogers face down in his bath. Local boys called it in as a suspected murder and a witness had seen two men answering that description, entering the flat at around four thirty." Inspector Penney got up from his desk, "We'd better get over there Charlie, hope you had no plans for this evening." Then he stopped and fumbled through some of the reports on his desk, picking one up he read out loud "Ginger Rogers full name Andrew Joshua Rogers, one caution for possession but believed to occasionally deal in some of the more expensive night clubs. I don't like this "he added throwing the report back on his desk, "I don't like this at all."

With siren blaring and lights flashing, Charlie expertly guided the police vehicle through the London Traffic and was soon pulling up behind two others outside the building housing Rogers's flat. The Inspector had not spoken a word during the whole trip so neither had Charlie, knowing that the inspector was piecing together things that had not even crossed his own mind. He also learnt a long time ago when it was best to keep his thoughts to himself. Unclipping his seat belt, the Inspector said "Right then Charlie let's see what we have here, if this is the guy I think it is then these bastards are one step ahead of us and as I said earlier, I don't like that." They walked up the path in silence, showed their ID to the officer positioned at the top of the steps and then went down to Rogers's flat.

A forensic team was already at work and Dr Stuart was just packing items back into her bag as the Inspector entered the bathroom. Immediately he noticed the red hair on the body. "Think that confirms it's Ginger Rogers" he said to Charlie. Then turning to Dr Stuart he said. "We meet again doctor, you do seem to frequent the nicest of places. What have you got so far?" The doctor replied. "Well inspector didn't you know, I only come to these places to meet you." Charlie couldn't resist a smile as he noticed Penney blush, good on you girl he thought. The doctor continued. "From preliminary examination I would say he drowned, there is some indication of bruising on his shoulders and from the marks on his wrists I would say he was handcuffed" "Handcuffed" repeated Charlie. "Yes" continued Dr Stuart pointing out the red marks on each wrist. I would say he was handcuffed with his hands behind his back, they then probably pulled his hands up and pushed his shoulders down forcing his head under the water."

"What makes you come to that conclusion?" asked Charlie. "The marking is more noticeable on the front of the wrists", replied the doctor, "Indicating that more pressure was applied to that area." She put her hands behind her back in a mock demonstration. "When he was found the cuffs had been removed as had the plug so the bath was empty."

"Thank you doctor that is very precise, do you have a possible time of death?" asked Penney. "No more than three hours ago" came the reply, "but it's difficult to be precise at the moment as I don't know how long he was in the water and whether it affected his body temperature. I might be able to narrow it down later. By the way the Mercedes Johnson thing, she had a lot of alcohol in her blood but also some of the same chemical that was in the syringe but no one has been able to identify it yet, every test has come up blank."

"I think the first two was fairly obvious," replied the Inspector. "But really have none of the labs got any idea?"

"None as of yet" she replied. "Perhaps you should send a sample to her father" said Charlie. "He's supposed to be the top chemist in Britain."

Having both left the bathroom they took a look around the flat. "For a bachelor pad it's a bit too tidy for my liking" said Charlie. "This from a guy who lines up the pencils on his desk" laughed Penney as he went to speak to one of the scenes of crime officers. "Have you turned up anything?" he asked "Not a lot" came the reply. "There was a bag on the floor which contained a laptop and two sets of keys, one of which wouldn't fit anything here, there was also a mobile on the body but it was wet and dead."

"OK" replied Penney. "Get the laptop and mobile down to the lab boys and see if they can recover anything, especially look for encoded files on the computer and see if we can pinpoint where the phone has been used. I've a feeling this pad is a front, he's got another place somewhere, hence the keys. If he was a drug pusher he definitely wasn't doing it from here. One other thing" he added, "the guys seen in Paris, Osborne's flat and here don't seem to be making any effort to cover their tracks, so get as many prints as you can and compare them with any taken from Osborne's place let's see if we can pin these two bastards down a bit."

"Who called this one in?" asked Charlie. "Some girl from one of the flats above", the officer replied adding. "There's a WPC up with her now, flat three."

"Thanks" Penney replied "let's go and have a word with her."

The two men left and made their way up to the second floor flat. Their knock was answered by the WPC. "How is she?" asked Penney "A bit shook up" came the reply "but you shouldn't have a problem, she's called Sarah." Penney nodded and entered the room. The girl was sat at a table, she had a crumpled tissue in her hands, looking up, she flicked back her long dark hair revealing the smudged makeup around her striking grey blue eyes. "I'm Detective Inspector Penney and Charlie here is a detective sergeant, are you up to answering a few questions?" She nodded, "Yes I'm fine, please sit down."

"Thanks" said Charlie as he and the inspector sat in the chairs opposite her. "Had you known Mr Rogers long?"

Penney asked. "Not really, in fact until just now I didn't know his last name was Rogers, I always called him Ginger."

"I see," replied Penney. "So how was it you were at his flat and found him this evening?" Sarah wiped her eye with the tissue and replied. "I bought this place about six months ago and a few weeks later Ginge moved in downstairs. I was going out as they were moving his furniture in and he said hello and introduced himself as Adam no, that's wrong," she said with a frown as she was trying to recall. "Andrew" cut in Charlie. "That's it Andrew" she smiled "but then he pointed to his hair and said everyone calls me Ginger, after that I started calling him Ginge. I saw him a few more times and he asked me out once or twice, but I always made excuses, then yesterday he asked me down for a quiet drink and I said yes."

"Why the change of mind?" asked Penney. "I was intrigued" came the reply, "every time I saw him he was always immaculately dressed, then I was at a club and saw him dressed down in jeans and a leather jacket, and he was talking to a politician."

"Which one?" cut in Charlie. "The one that was on telly recently had that fight with his boyfriend in Stringfellows." Charlie and the Inspector exchanged knowing glances. "Ginger didn't see me, but I mentioned it to my friend and she said you've got to find out what he does now, so when he asked again I said OK."

"Do you live here alone or share with your friend?" Asked Charlie "Alone." She smiled. "Getting back to this afternoon", said Penney, "you told the officer here that you saw two men going down to Rogers's flat."

"Yes" she replied, "I was going out at about four thirty when I saw them just about to go down the steps. I told them that Ginger doesn't normally get back until after five. The Scottish guy replied thanks but we'll just check, so I just shrugged and carried on."

"You're sure he was Scottish?" asked Charlie "Oh yes I spent some time at St Andrews University, he had a strong west coast accent like Glasgow may be."

"Did you study dialects?" asked Penney. "No" she laughed "Finance, I'm currently a finance director with a small medical company but we are expanding into the States, which is why I was going out for a telephone conference due to the time difference it had to be early evening."

"That explains how you could afford one of these flats" said Penney. "But what about the accents."

"It's something that has always fascinated me" she replied. "You Inspector are probably from west London, while your sergeant is probably from Dorset."

"Right on both accounts" replied Charlie, "Ever thought of joining the police force?"

"I couldn't afford the pay cut."

"You're right there as well," replied Penney, adding. "Well thanks for your help, you will need to make a formal statement and you could be asked to give evidence in the future, I'm sorry you have had to go through this and the

WPC will advise you of any help or counselling if you need it."

"Yes thank you Inspector, she has already been very helpful and I'm going to spend the night at my friends."

"That's probably very wise" Penney replied, "Make sure the WPC has the address and for the record our current enquiries leads me to believe you are in no danger from the men you saw, and that if you had got to know Rogers, he would not have been someone you would have liked at all." With that they both left

They walked back to the car and were about to get in when Charlie said, "Hang on a minute Guv, across the road there that shop has a CCTV camera, I wonder if it could have picked up anything."

"I doubt it," replied Penney "It's probably covering the front of the shop certainly not this side of the road."

"True Guv, but the only legal parking is that side of the road and if they had parked there it might have caught them." Penney replied in an irritated manner "Go take a look then but don't waste too much time on it, I'll wait in the car." Charlie crossed the road and entered the shop, it was a small newsagents which also sold sweets, cigarettes and cold drinks but little else. The counter was near the door and behind the man serving, there was a monitor showing four small screens, three of the shop interior and one covering the pavement area. Immediately Charlie could see that it gave very little coverage of the road. He showed his warrant card and introduced himself to the assistant. "I was hoping your CCTV might have been of some assistance to us, does it pan at all?"

"No" the man replied, "It just covers the shop front and the ATM, we had a bit of bother with youngsters at onetime hanging around upsetting customers, you know trying to get them to buy cigarettes for them and the like, or coming in and nicking sweets, I don't know if it's the camera or if they have moved but we don't seem to have seen them recently."

"Well thanks anyway," said Charlie as he made to leave. "Rumour is someone has bumped Ginger off, is that right?" asked the assistant. Charlie replied, "Did you know him?"

"Only to speak to he came in for a paper and the occasional coke, shame though, but I did see a couple of guys come out of the gate over there as I came to work."

"What time was that?" asked Charlie "About quarter past six, I do six thirty to eleven but normally get in a bit earlier."

"Can you describe them?"

"Didn't take a lot of notice but one was a big guy with longish blonde hair, he was quite noticeable, they got into a Jag and drove off."

"Did you notice what colour Jag and which direction they went?"

"Yeah, it was a black XF, always wanted one of them, they stayed this side of the road, but there's a junction about fifty yards up so they could have gone in any direction, I had come in the shop by then."

"Thanks for your help" said Charlie "Would you be prepared to make a statement if required?"

"As long as it won't take all day," replied the assistant. "I'm sure it won't," replied Charlie as he left and made his way back to the Inspector who was waiting impatiently in the car.

"Well" snapped Penney, "Was it any use?"

"No" came the reply "It only covered the shop front and ATM."

"Knew it would be a bloody waste of time." replied Penney. "Not exactly" Charlie came back and then he related the information the assistant had given him. "That ties down the time of death I suppose, but how many bloody black Jag XF's are there in London?" Asked Penney, adding "Get the local boys to take a statement from your man back there and circulate a description of the two men and the car, but keep it low key, I don't want their descriptions in the press just yet."

"You sure?" asked Charlie. "Yes, it bothers me that these two are not even trying to be discrete. It's as if they are looking for publicity and until I get my head around this I don't want to play that game. Let's see where it goes from here, I have a hunch these two will pop up again before too long."

CHAPTER EIGHT

Sticky found the cabin with his name on and entered, the thick maroon carpet continued into the room maintaining the feeling of luxury. There was a wardrobe, desk and chest of drawers to his right, which were fitted as one fixed unit. The desk held a phone and a laptop computer. There was large picture window running across the width of the room, with a single bed placed beneath it. To his left was a door leading to an en-suite bathroom. He threw his bag on the bed and went into the bathroom and took a shower. Once towelled off he looked in the wardrobe and found the uniform, which consisted of a black shirt and trousers, there was also a bomber jacket and a bulletproof vest. In one of the drawers he found a leather belt and a holster containing a loaded Glock 19 nine-millimetre pistol and two magazine pouches each containing a fifteen round magazine. Although used to these and having previously proved to be a very good shot, he hated using them, preferring to fly the aircraft and let someone else do the shooting. Never the less he got dressed, noting the shirt had American style patches on the upper sleeves showing entwined letters U and N in red and the number twelve underneath. The epaulettes contained his Captain's insignia and his name was on an embroidered strip above the left shirt pocket. He had just finished tying the laces on his boots when there was a knock on the door and Pony entered.

"What do you think then?" he asked as he struck a pose. Sticky laughed. "Don't give up the day job" he replied, adding. "A bit American looking isn't it but you do look presentable for once."

"Thanks a lot" came the reply. "Have you switched on the laptop at all?"

"No, Why?"

"Take a look at this" said Pony as he switched on the computer and waited for it to boot up. "There's a lot more to this ship than it appears on the surface." He said as he clicked on a video icon and a picture of the ship appeared on the screen, it rotated and then the camera angle gave a view from above, as they watched the roof of the rear cabins separated and slid back to the left and right, then a helicopter appeared being raised up on a hydraulic platform. "I'll be dammed," declared Sticky. "That's not all" replied Pony "but it's one o'clock, so we had better take the tour don't want to keep McGreggor waiting."

"After you then" said 'Sticky as they left the room and made their way back to the main cabin. The rest of the group were already there and dressed in the same uniforms. As Sticky and Pony entered the cabin, McGreggor entered via steps from the forward end.

"Right gentlemen" he barked, "time for you to get acquainted with your floating office. This ship was built for a Russian millionaire however he then decided that at four hundred and sixty feet in length, it was not big enough. So it was bought and taken to a shipyard in Glasgow where it was refitted. As you have already seen, externally it has the appearance of a super yacht and indeed the forward end retains all the super yacht features and luxury fittings. Down the stairs there to the forward end is the dining area you will be using, there are also cold drinks and snacks available at all times, there's a gym and a TV room with games consoles for when you relax, or should I say if you get time to relax."

"No pool table?" asked Phillips. "It was tried but every time we hit a wave the balls rolled to one end," replied McGreggor. Everyone laughed at this unexpected humour. Then McGreggor continued. "The main crew all eat and sleep on the level above, other than helping with equipping the boats and launching or retrieving the helicopter you will not normally have contact with them. I will let you explore the forward end later, for now we need to go to the stern, which you'll see is far more of a working ship so please follow me."

McGreggor went to a door at the stern end of the room, flipped open a key pad and typed in a code, the door slid open and one by one they all entered and then the door slid shut behind them. Sticky was amazed to find himself in what could only be described as a well-lit hangar, with a helicopter sat on a white painted 'H' in the centre. A couple of men had just finishing refuelling and as one removed the fuel hose, the other disconnected the earthing strap. The machine was painted matt black and its two bladed rotor was strapped in the forward and aft position, which was just as well as there would be no room for it to rotate in this closed space. "Have you flown one of those before?" asked Carter. "If it's what I think it is, then yes," came the reply. "But it seems to have one or two additions to the last one I flew." McGreggor cut in, "A Jet Ranger with an uprated Allison 250C20 400SHP engine, it has a two bladed main and rear rotor and is equipped with a Bendix audio panel, a Bendix Navigation and Communications system a KY96A Transceiver, KT76A Transponder and GPS. It has rupture resistant fuel cells. However this one has also got titanium engine covers and fuel tank protection. The screens are bullet proof and as you can see there is a machine gun mounted below the main fuselage, which can be operated from the right hand seat." Sticky looked at McGreggor and then realised he was reading from a clipboard he was carrying. McGreggor looked up and said, "Well you didn't expect me to know that off by heart did you Wood?" adding; "Do you think you'll be able to fly it?"

"No bother" Sticky replied "but taking off and landing back on the ship again is another matter."

"Well you're going to get a couple of hours practice later now follow me down here gents let's see where the rest of you will be working."

They went down a further set of steps to the deck below. Again they were all taken by surprise. It was clear the rear end of the ship was in twin hull configuration with an open moon pool in between. The forward part held a dock which contained four twin seater Jet Skis and two fourteen foot Rigid Inflatable Boats or RIB's, which each had a forward mounted machine gun and twin seven fifty horse outboard engines. "I take it the SAS and SBS amongst you are familiar with these craft" announced McGreggor. "With the ship in this configuration the divers can exit and return via the moon pool undetected, while with the rear door lifted any of the boats can be launched."

"Impressive" remarked Carter. "Indeed it is" replied McGreggor. "To the left is the armoury, everything you need can be found there, I will outline the mission, you decide what you need to take. Behind us is the briefing room, I suggest we make our way there and go through the details of what's expected from you in the next twenty four hours."

They entered the briefing room in the centre of which was a large table, McGreggor flicked a switch and the whole of the table lit up revealing it to be effectively a television screen. "Gather around gentlemen" ordered McGreggor. As they did so they could see the screen was displaying a picture of the Mediterranean and coast of Morocco, similar to that seen the day before, this time though there was a moving icon on the screen that signified their position. "As you can see, this is our position and the port of El Jebha is here" said McGreggor using an extending pointer to mark the relevant positions. "If our intelligence is correct the target boat will leave port at around 06.00 tomorrow morning. Depending on the speed they will be travelling we intend to intercept it about here." He continued again pointing to a spot in the sea. "The Med is a big bit of sea", cut in Carter, "how sure are you of the course they will be taking?"

"Pretty certain" came the reply, "however a couple of weeks ago a visiting boat 'accidentally' damaged the target boat, the visitor apologised profusely and arranged immediate repairs, part of which involved concealing a transmitter which we will turn on just after they leave port. Then we'll know exactly where they are Mr Carter. Perhaps that might help you understand that you are now part of a highly organised group. Our security ensures no individual unit is aware of the others part in things but each groups actions will contribute to the success of the others mission and I intend our first mission to be a success."

As professionals, the group understood exactly what was expected of them although each had a hundred thoughts racing through their minds. McGreggor looked straight at them all and knew then he had them fully with him. "Right", he continued. "Around three miles from the expected intercept point we will launch the RIB's with Carter, Philips and Campbell in one and Wright, McFadden and Clarke in the other. On reaching the line of interception you will turn and make a head on approach to the target boat. Wood and Moore will make the first interception in the chopper and order them to heave to and prepare to be boarded."

"And if they don't?" asked Pony. "Then I suggest you use your thirty millimetre cannon and persuade them otherwise." replied McGreggor, adding. "Remember there are to be no survivors so they will stop one way or another. Once boarded you will eliminate both occupants and use weighted body bags to ensure they don't float back to the surface. Campbell and Clarke will place charges to scuttle the boat, but please don't blow it to bits and leave debris all over the sea."

"Seems your reputation precedes you Clarkey" said Campbell. "To continue," said McGreggor. "We need you to recover the drugs so you'll take a cargo net with you then Wood will use the choppers under body winch to lift it off and fly it to another ship which by then should be about twenty miles astern of us." Carter looked up with a surprised expression. "What?" exclaimed McGreggor; "Did you expect a pot party when you got back?" Carter just shook his head then looked quizzically at Sticky. McGreggor continued, "The operation will commence around six thirty AM tomorrow. So I suggest you all have lunch, then use the rest of the day to make yourselves familiar with your equipment, by the way the door code is UN12 as it's on your shirt I guess Mr Moore will be able to remember that as well."

They went to lunch but not before some had stayed for a further look around the docking area and Sticky and Pony had stopped off for a further look at the chopper. They noted the under body winch and hook that was placed centrally to the body and aligned directly below the rotor head allowing the maximum lift without upsetting the aircraft trim. They also noted a rope and hook above each of the rear doors which was attached to a winch mounted internally above the doorframe. They had both seen similar set ups before which could be used to lower or recover a person or item into or out of an area where landing was impractical. To assist with this, the rear doors were modified so that they pushed out and slid to the rear. The rear seating was designed for three people but could take four at a push. They each climbed into their respective seats and Sticky turned on the power, all the instruments lit up and as they ran through them both felt confident they could easily operate everything although were pleased they would get a little practice before going into action. Pony found that the machine gun was operated via a joystick with top mounted firing button, which was protected by a safety lock. When the 'weapons on' switch was selected, a sight with crosshairs was projected on to the windscreen and as he moved the joystick up, down or left to right, the sight moved indicating the selected target. Satisfied they could do no more at this point, they left and joined the others for lunch.

As at the base the day before, there was a generous selection available for lunch and each selected their choice then sat at the table with the others, several conversations struck up and Sticky noticed they involved football, formulae one racing and some of the recent television programmes, no-one mentioned anything about this morning's events or the proposed mission. As soon as both men finished, they made an excuse and went straight back to the aircraft as they were keen to do as much as possible while there was still daylight. On entering the hangar, they were met by a short overweight man who had dark sweptback hair, beady little eyes and a rather long pointed nose. Pony immediately christened him Pinocchio. "Are you ready to give it a go?" the man asked in an unexpectedly posh voice. "Now is as good a time as any", replied Sticky. "Then if you go to room one over on the left there, you will find your survival suits and helmets, as soon as you're ready we will get you launched." On entering the room, their suits and helmets were hung up with their names both on the helmets and on the suits. "You've got to give it to them for organisation", remarked Pony. "It was only yesterday they 'Invited' us to join them but uniforms boots everything fits and is labelled, even the bloody rooms, that's some going."

"Or they knew we'd be here long before we did", replied Sticky.

Once dressed, they re-entered the hangar and went over to the chopper where Pinocchio was waiting. "A couple of things gents"' he said. "As soon as you're settled in we will raise the deck, when it locks into place we will remove the rotor straps and release the skid clamps. Now about those; they release and shoot back about four feet either side of the skids, they go in and out in less than a second, bloody things would take your foot off if you get in the way. When you land, bang the machine down on the deck the weight activates them and will instantly lock you down. Remember to bang it down and keep it down, don't bounce, the locks can cope with about a foot of bounce but it will be more comfortable for us all if you land once. Today is fairly calm so good for practice it's more fun when it's rough, wouldn't like you to drown like the last crew."

"Thanks a lot", said Pony, "very reassuring I'm sure."

They settled into their seats, connected and checked their communications then gave the thumbs up. Immediately additional light flooded into the hangar as the roof panels parted and slid open. Three hydraulic lift posts on either side of the deck then whirred into action and the whole helipad lifted up and locked into place. The complete process taking around one and a half minutes. The rotor straps were released then after going through the pre-flight checks the engine was started. The turbo jet roared into life and seemed a lot noisier than either man expected. With the gauges showing the engine up to speed, Sticky engaged the rotor, which slowly started to turn and then with a 'whoomp' 'whoomp' rapidly increased speed. Sticky gave the thumbs up and immediately there was a hiss and slamming noise as the skid locks were released. Increasing power he lifted off allowing the aircraft to move backwards before increasing height and swinging away from the ship and out over the sea. They flew around for half an hour ensuring they were happy with the instruments and the communications. Sticky then called up the ship and requested landing permission. With the request granted, the ship slowed and Sticky lined up with the stern and brought the aircraft to a hover just above the helipad, adjusting his forward movement to that of the ship. He then dropped the last few feet to the deck. With the ship rising on a swell there was a bit of a jarring and bounce but the skid locks did their job and they were down. The process was repeated several more times before he was satisfied. Then with the engine shut down and the rotors secured, the deck was lowered and the roof again closed. "Well let's hope it is still calm in the morning," said Pony.

CHAPTER NINE

With the blonde wig removed and his short cut dark hair
exposed, Karl looked more round faced than previously, his
dark eyes showed no emotion and appeared to be set deep
into his face. He was idly playing patience while Mac was
talking on his mobile phone. Putting the phone back in his
pocket he turned to Karl. "It seems everything is going well
in the Med, and as expected, Pakistan has confirmed capture
of their shipment."

"That gives us some bait", replied Karl, "now we need the
bite."

"And the American contribution" added Mac. The phone,
they had taken from Rogers, lay on the table and as if on cue
it rang. Karl picked it up and answered, a voice on the other
end said, "You didn't have to kill my man."

"We did," replied Karl "He was sloppy, if we could get to
him so could the police." There was a few seconds silence
then the voice asked. "Are you still in London?" "Yes."

"Ok be by the gift kiosk outside Westminster tube station at
four o'clock, a white limo will pull up get in it." With that the
phone went dead. "Well it seems we have him on the hook"
said Karl. "Maybe" came the reply, "but I think we will have
to be careful how we reel him in, one mistake or wrong word

and we'll be left empty handed." Karl nodded knowing that the next step would be make or break.

With the Jaguar long since returned to the hire company, a battered white Transit van was now parked outside their apartment in Paddington, however they elected to walk the short distance to Paddington station where they descended the escalators to the circle line. To Karl there was always a smell about the tube that he never particularly liked. After a short wait they boarded the first tube train heading for Bayswater. Unusually it was not packed and they both immediately found seats. Mac looked up at the underground map positioned on the curvature of the train ceiling opposite him and noted there was eight stops prior to Westminster. Neither spoke as the train set off, it was a strange thing Mac had noticed on many occasions, there was seldom any conversations overheard on the tube, people either sat or stood holding the overhead straps either looking down or blankly at the passing walls. It was something that continued even as people alighted the carriages, just hurrying through the stations and up into the daylight without speaking to one another. After Bayswater came Notting Hill Gate, High Street Kensington, Gloucester Road, South Kensington, Sloan Square, Victoria then St James Park. Mac nudged Karl, "Next stop" he said, they both stood and made their way to one of the doors, the train pulled in and with a hiss the doors slid open and they stepped onto the platform, following other people towards the exit, they then took one of several very long escalators to the surface.

As they exited the station Mac noticed Big Ben was showing three fifty, "we're a little early Karl," he said. Several Japanese tourists were buying items at the kiosk while others were photographing the Houses of Parliament. They idly watched the flow of people and traffic as they waited, both pulling their coat collars up and placing their hands in their pockets as a cold wind blew straight in from the River Thames. As the bells of Big Ben started to strike four, a white stretch limo pulled up. "Punctual" remarked Karl as they both quickly stepped forward, opened the rear door and got in. As soon as the door closed the driver pulled away, turning left onto the embankment road. They travelled along the embankment before turning onto New Bridge Street and shortly afterwards right into Charter House Street before turning left again down into an underground car park. Mac had known they had turned unto the embankment but the rest of the journey was lost to him as the Limo's blacked out windows had made it impossible to see. The inside the limo was fitted out with blue buttoned velour seating with a long seat on one side with drinks cabinets on the other a partition between them and the driver blocked any forward vision. As soon as the car came to a halt they heard the driver get out and shut the door. Mac went to open the rear door when a voice said, "Stay there gentlemen, help yourselves to a drink if you wish." Both men turned to face the front as the partition behind the driver's seat lit up to reveal itself to be a television screen.

A figure of a man appeared on the screen sitting in a large office style chair and holding what appeared to be a glass of wine in one hand. The lighting was such that his face was totally in shadow making him impossible to identify. Speaking in a very educated and deliberate manner the man said. "You gentlemen went to a great deal of effort to get my attention, so what is it you have to offer." Mac cleared his throat, irritated that he felt at a disadvantage. "We have and are currently in the process of acquiring four hundred kilograms of pure Cocaine and Two hundred and fifty kilograms of Heroin, which is coming to us as, shall we say a by-product of other operations. Once cut to twenty five percent purity this will have a total street value of over one hundred and sixty million sterling. We're offering you the lot delivered to an address of your choosing for thirty million."

"On the face of it very generous", came the reply. "But why should I trust you or even deal with you?"

"We have trusted you so far," replied Mac. "After all you know we dispatched Osborne and Rogers so you could have turned us over. I think you're aware our offer is genuine." There was a moments silence and then. "I have considerable risks and distribution costs to take into consideration, as well as replacing Mr Rogers's operation, dispatching him as you put it has put me to considerable expense. I'm afraid I could not go above twenty million and then only if the quality of the goods is of an excellent standard."

"I can assure you they will be of the highest quality", cut in Karl. "We have also taken risks and incurred considerable costs," said Mac, "You know this is an exceptional offer, currently you're paying up front, to middlemen and rip off merchants, every delivery is a risk that can be confiscated at any number of borders and your money has gone down the proverbial pan. With us there's no risk, it will be delivered directly to you, in Britain with payment on delivery. We'll throw in an extra four hundred and fifty kilos of Moroccan, so make it twenty five million and we have a deal."

"That would be acceptable" came the reply. "If the goods are of the standard you have stated, and I decide to go ahead I take it payment will be by wire transfer and not cash, dealing in notes is so offensive."

"Wire transfer will be fine", said Mac "Two weeks from now we should be in a position to deliver, if you wish, we'll courier you samples to a place and at a time of your choosing."

"That won't be necessary because if they are not as you say I will be doing some dispatching of my own. For now keep hold of that phone gentlemen I will be in touch." With that the screen went dead and shortly after the driver returned, Karl noted the car was driven forward and they were quickly back into the traffic and retracing much of the previous route.

From a window high above, the man watched the car pull out into the traffic. He was aware of shipments going missing on route from Mexico and Afghanistan, for which he was due to pay fifty pounds a gram. He had now got them for around thirty. The way they had been taken was very professional and would have been an expensive operation. So why was he being offered them cheaply? These men were well informed and had no qualms about dispatching Rogers, they also seemed to know that he never allowed drugs from his operation to be sold at less than twenty five percent pure. His operation was at the top end having built a solid reputation. All his dealers were employed and got a monthly salary anyone caught trying to cut items further were ruthlessly dealt with. Rogers had organised that very efficiently and they were now working to take street dealers out altogether. Using the dark web, drugs could be ordered online and delivered by post taking the face-to-face risk out of the operation. This was now accounting for thirty percent of sales and was growing so rapidly it would soon be seventy five percent, the plan was for one hundred percent within twelve months. Avatar was in the process of being converted to a mail order centre and computer experts had been recruited in the Dominican Republic to handle sales. Rogers was a loss but would have soon been redundant in his current role. What concerned him was, who was behind this deal? His old friend Hamilton was running units of MI6 which were capable of pulling it off. Perhaps one of his units had decided to cash in. He made a mental note to speak to the minister at next week's get together, a couple of grams of cocaine usually produced useful information. For now he wanted to know more about the two men he had just spoken to, but it would be up to his man at the station to provide that.

Mac and Karl sat quietly in the car, rightly assuming that any conversation they had would have been recorded. Suddenly it came to a halt and the driver called, "Please step out quickly I appear to be holding up the traffic." Mac opened the door and stepped out onto the pavement immediately next to Big Ben or to be more accurate, 'The Elizabeth Tower.' They watched the car drive on with Mac making a note of the registration. It was now approaching rush hour as they crossed the road back to the tube station, a tall thinly built man dressed in denim was casually looking at a magazine next to the kiosk. As the two men entered the station, he folded the magazine and followed them in. To Mac, there was a noticeable increase in the number of travellers and the train, when it did arrive, was packed to the doors with standing room only. Some form of sixth sense made Karl look around the carriage where he noticed a man who appeared to be watching them, he shifted his position and from the corner of his eye could see this man staring at them. As the train pulled in to the next station he grabbed Mac and said, "We're getting off." As they stepped onto the platform he saw the man push his way forward and get off through the next door along. "What's up?" enquired Mac.

"We're being followed, I don't think our new friend trusts us." They crossed to the next platform and waited, noting the man follow and wait a few yards further up. The next train pulled in and they waited for passengers to exit before stepping on, positioning themselves right by the doors. The other man got on further along the carriage and was followed by several other passengers who effectively blocked his exit. Mac and Karl waited and just as the doors were about to shut, they jumped back to the platform. Mac's timing was slightly off and his arm caught in the door, he watched as the doors re-opened and then closed, cursing he thought he had blown it but then noticed their pursuer trying to push his way out but he'd left it too late. They watched the train leave and then crossed back to the other platform and continued the journey back to their apartment pausing several times and taking a roundabout route to ensure no one else was following them.

Back in the apartment, Mac made a phone call and reported on the recent events and agreements. The conversation continued for a while, during which time Karl had made them both a coffee; passing one to Mac he sat down drinking his and waited for the conversation to finish. Finally, Mac put the phone down. "Well?" asked Karl "He's happy with the arrangement and will provide us with an account number for the funds to be paid into."

"What about the tail?" asked Karl. "Don't worry in our next conversation with 'shadow man', I'll make it clear what we thought of that. It's up to the others to pull off their particular bits now. If all goes well we'll be able to deliver in less than two weeks and relieve our man of his twenty five million." Karl laughed, "I note he insisted on top quality, so the bastard can cut that stuff at least twice, a hell of a return for a twenty five million outlay, and that's without the cannabis"

"The boss is counting on him cutting it," replied Mac. "That's key to screwing the drug scene and that bastard completely.

For the fourth time, Charlie was going through the reports and statements both from the French investigation and their own with regards Osborne and Rogers. "Well" asked Penney, "Have you anything for me?"

"Not really" came the reply. "We know Osborne gave the drug to Mercedes and the likelihood is that Rogers gave the drug to Osborne and I would bet the idea was to get rid of Osborne. Mercedes was unfortunately in the wrong place at the wrong time." Penney was irritated. "We've gone through all that several times, it doesn't tell us why someone wanted him dead, or why they followed up by killing Rogers."

"Mercedes father would have a good motive for killing both of them", said Charlie; "He has a reputation for being ruthless."

"And emotionless by what I saw of him" added Penney. "I can see he might want Osborne dead after his daughter was killed, but he had no reason to want him dead prior to that."

"Unless we're looking at two unrelated incidents," replied Charlie. "The original attempt at Osborne could just be related to the drug scene, it was a bit hit and miss, but the two actual killings were done by professionals." Charlie shuffled through some of the papers. "Ah here" he announced, "The French report says Osborne had some bruising to the left cheek and a cut inside his mouth."

"He'd been slapped about then" replied Penney. "Probably to get Rogers's name out of him."

"Exactly "replied Charlie "and they would not have needed that if they were the ones that wanted him dead originally."

Penney sat back in his chair and stared thoughtfully at the ceiling as he twiddled a pencil in his fingers. "How would Johnson have known about Osborne?" asked Charlie. "Those two guys were at the flat in the middle of the morning and we didn't release his name until lunch time at the earliest, it was only you and I that had that information until then."

"Not quite" replied Penney as he flipped through an address book on his desk, finding the number he wanted he picked up the phone and dialled. It was quickly answered. "This is Chief Inspector Penney" he announced, "Can you put me through to John Greenhall?"

"I'll try for you sir" a young lady replied. The phone went quiet and then he could hear it ringing at the other end.

After a few seconds it was picked up and a voice said "Greenhall."

"Hello John, Inspector Penney here, I just wanted to check something with you." "Sure" came the reply "What do you want to know?"

"On the morning of Mercedes death, was there a chance anyone told her father about Osborne."

"Osborne the DJ guy" queried Greenhall. "Yeah, as far as I'm aware it was you, your hippy mate and myself that knew about it. Did you or the hippy speak to Johnson or the press?"

"No" replied Greenhall, "Henry wouldn't have said anything and I never speak to the press and didn't speak to Johnson other than when you were there."

"Ok" replied Penney. "It was just a thought, thanks anyway."

"Hang on a minute." Greenhall cut in. "I just remembered, as you left a guy called to me, turned out to be ex-army intelligence, he was with me when I lost my leg, did his best to hold it together. Turns out he is now head of security for AJ associates Johnson's companies. He knew Mercedes, said he thought she was desperate for affection but was surprised she'd used drugs. I think I mentioned Osborne to him, sorry."

"That's ok, no one could have predicted what happened. Do you have a name for him and a description?" Penney listened for a while then said "Thanks John, most helpful goodbye." The Inspector replaced the phone on the hook and looked at Charlie. "Well what do you know?" he proclaimed, "It seems

Johnson did know about Osborne almost at the same time we did, or at least his head of security did, who happens to be a Glaswegian called Mac McCrae who's ex SAS and army intelligence and described as six foot and of a stocky build."

"Bingo" said Charlie. "Shall we pull him in?"

"No not yet, I still have a feeling this goes deeper, if it is him, he's made no effort to conceal his identity and being ex intelligence he must have known that at some point we would put two and two together, and as he's based north of the border there's too much paperwork for something that at this stage is circumstantial. If he was SAS and ex-army then get a warrant to pull his military record there should be a photograph let's see if we can get a positive ID from Miss Thomas, then get to know our man before we possibly make fools of ourselves."

CHAPTER TEN

Sticky had already been awake for a while, listening to the dull thud of the ships engines and feeling the vibration as it cut though what felt like a gentle swell, when his phone rang informing him it was time to get up. He looked at his watch, which read 05.00am. He swung out of bed and grabbing a towel headed for a shower after the usual wash and shave. He put on his uniform this time adding the leather belt, complete with holster, Glock 19 and the two magazine pouches. He also put on the bulletproof jacket and then picked up his helmet and headed up for some breakfast.

Pony was already there as was Carter. "Couldn't sleep either," enquired Sticky. "No not that well", Pony replied. "Me either" added Carter. They took a light breakfast of cereal, toast and coffee and were rapidly joined by the rest of the group who also avoided the fried food on offer. McGreggor popped his head around the door and called "Briefing room in five minutes." Quickly drinking down the last of the coffee, the group left and headed for the briefing. McGreggor went over the plan as highlighted the day before, he then placed a tablet style computer on the table, "Each of the boats and the helicopter has had one of these fitted," he said. "When switched on it is programmed to pick up the squawk signal from the target boat, keep the signal on the centre line of the screen and you will be heading directly towards it. When you confirm mission completed, select option one on the screen and you will pick up Minerva's signal bringing you back to the ship. You fly boys will need option two to direct you to your cargo drop, then option one to bring you home, understood." They all nodded. McGreggor then went to each group in turn ensuring they were happy with their equipment and had everything ready to go. When it came to Sticky, he brought up the question of the ship he was supposed to fly the recovered drugs to. "For a secret operation and effectively assassination", he said, "there seems to be a lot of external people involved, the crew of this ship for a start and now another vessel where are they supposed to assume the drugs have come from?"

"I must confess" added Carter, "That question had been keeping me awake last night."

McGreggor looked at each man in turn and could see they all wanted an answer. "Ok" he said. "As far as the crew of this ship are concerned, they are all navy and have the highest clearance. To them, you are a special marine group training for covert operations, they have been told nothing and not to ask questions. What they will see today is you leaving on a training exercise and then returning to the ship. We will be too far from the action for them to see anything else. As for the 'Coastguard' ship, they won't assume anything Mr Carter as they have been told to expect the delivery and they know what to do with it. I thought I made it clear previously, Each UN group has its own task the success of the whole relies on each group completing the task allocated yet not knowing of the others existence. Now you have a mission to complete and I suggest you get on with it."

All the men got up and made their way to their stations, McGreggor stayed seated and stared after them as they left. On the lower deck the two RIBs were floating in the moon pool, each team had donned black lifejackets over the bulletproof vests, which especially for Carter restricted movement. They climbed into the boats and double-checked the equipment, their hand held rapid-fire machine guns were loaded and the belt feed for the thirty millimetre front mounted guns was stowed. Both boats had a net and two body bags in case one boat was compromised. Satisfied all was correct, Carter called in for clearance and as the ship slowed to a virtual halt, the rear door opened and with all four outboards started the RIBs exited the stern and immediately opened up turning left and right running along either side of the ship before opening full throttle rapidly hurtling through the water leaving a wake that quickly disappeared into the distance.

Pony and Sticky had run through their own checks and with both boats confirmed away, the roof opened and the hydraulics raised them up ready for departure. The rotor straps were removed and with confirmation the deck was clear, Sticky started the engine. Once up to power the rotor was engaged and quickly started to pick up speed. He radioed ready for take-off and immediately heard the skid locks release. He increased power, raised the cyclic and lifted into the air again dropping back before swinging left and running parallel to the ship and setting off after the fast disappearing boats. Within ten minutes he had caught the boats and swooped overhead, slowing his pace to keep station four or five hundred yards ahead. The Mediterranean was supposedly a busy shipping area yet they could see no other craft in any direction.

Their ship had just disappeared from view when Pony announced he had picked up the signal from the target craft. It was clear the others had as well as he watched them turn to the right for a head on approach. Increasing speed, Sticky headed towards the blip, noting the quickly decreasing distance between them. "There they are" shouted Pony, "Dead ahead."

"I see them," came the reply "Call them up and tell them to heave to for boarding." Pony did that but there was only static in reply. He was about to try again when a heavily accented voice said; "We are in International waters, you have no authority to board us and we have no intention of stopping." Swinging the chopper to approach side on Sticky said. "Put a couple of shots across the bow." Pony flipped the safety and a burst of fire stitched its way across the water. "I say again heave to" called Pony. In response a figure appeared on the foredeck with a machine gun, which he fired directly at the aircraft. Sticky swung to the right but heard a couple of pings as a few bullets found their mark. Pony immediately returned fire, as he did so the boats pilot had noticed the RIB's heading directly towards them and swung his boat to the right, putting himself directly in line with the helicopter. Pony watched as the burst of fire from his thirty millimetre cannon cut down the figure on the foredeck, the gun flying from his hands and falling into the sea as his body was flung back through the now shattered windscreen. The burst had also caught the pilot throwing him back into the cabin to disappear in a bloody mess onto the cabin floor. Sticky was shocked by the brutal swiftness with which both occupants had been dispatched, "Someone takes a little shot at you and you get right nasty Pony do you know that." He said. "Guess it's my weakness" Pony replied.

The boat began to slow but continued its turn to the right Phillips brought the RIB up alongside the damaged craft and matched its speed as Carter deftly leapt on board. At the same time McFadden pulled along the opposite side and Wright boarded giving Carter cover as he moved forward into the cabin to shut down the engines. They quickly confirmed there were no other occupants and with Wright and Carter photographing the bodies and placing them in the body bags, Campbell and Clarke set shaped charges either side of the engines with the intention of blowing holes in the stern and hoping the engines weight would sink the boat in one piece. Having tied the RIB's securely, Phillips and McFadden forced open the rear 'garage' door and started loading the blocks of drugs into the net. Sticky and Pony ran through all the aircrafts systems and did a quick visual to satisfy themselves that no serious damage had been done by the hits they'd taken. With all the drugs loaded, the four corners of the net were brought together and Sticky was signalled to come in for the pick-up. Pony lowered the hook so they would spend as little time as possible over the boat. Bracing themselves against the helicopters down draft Phillips caught the hook and with McFadden managed to feed the four corners onto it. They then signalled Sticky the all clear and he lifted off adjusting for the extra weight before pulling some five hundred yards away. After a quick search and with the bodies located in the forward cabin, all six men returned to the RIB's and pulled away. Campbell then remotely detonated the charges; there were a couple of muffled thuds and the boat lifted slightly in the water before slowly the stern started to submerge. Then the pace quickened and just over fifteen minutes from first being sighted the boats bow lifted clear and rapidly slipped beneath the water.

By the time the boat had sunk, the helicopter was over a mile away and heading towards the new signal on their screens. Pony spotted what appeared to be a container ship about three miles over to their right, but as they were passing the stern, he hoped no one would have been looking in their direction and wandering what a small helicopter was doing in the middle of the Med with a net dangling beneath its belly. After ten minutes of flying, they spotted a low-lying ship directly ahead. "That's our target," said Pony, "Looks like a fast patrol boat."

"It is" replied Sticky, "But not the usual navy grey." In fact the hull was dark blue and the superstructure an orange colour very much like the RNLI lifeboats. As they approached, the craft slowed and turned its open stern deck towards them. Several figures appeared on deck, and both Pony and Sticky noted they were wearing uniforms very similar to the ones they wore themselves. Sticky brought the helicopter in over the stern deck and guided by one of the ship's crew lowered the net unto the deck. As soon as it was released from the hook, Pony called "All clear" and started winching the hook back in. At the same time Sticky pulled the helicopter away and watched as the ship lurched forward in the water and sped off at an amazing rate of knots. "Must have its original engines," said Pony, "Or something better", replied Sticky. "Did you notice any markings Pony?"

"No nothing, did you?"

"No, but I thought I made out a faint or painted over word on the stern which is interesting."

"Come on then" said Pony "What word?"

"Glasgow" came the reply. After another fifteen minutes of flying and with the fuel tanks down to a quarter, they spotted the Minerva and radioed in for landing permission. On the return to the ship the skies had got perceptively darker and it was clear the waves were beginning to pick up. The Captain slowed the Minerva and turned into the swell but even then, as Sticky brought them above the ship it was clear the heli-deck was rising and falling at least three metres. He knew he had to time it just right and as the ship rose he banged it down on the deck. The skid locks slammed into place and they were secure just rising and falling with the ship. He shut down the engines. The deck crew appeared and secured the rotors. Then they dropped into the hangar and the overhead roof closed. With the lighting in the hangar it was now brighter than it had been on deck. They finished the shutdown checks and stepped down out of the flight deck. Pinocchio was there to meet them. "Can you give it a good check over, I think we upset a couple of fisherman and they took pot shots at us." Pinocchio just gave a knowing look and replied, "It'll be as good as new next time you need it don't worry."

"We won't" Pony replied.

The two men made their way to the briefing room where the rest of the team was already seated. "Ah gentlemen. All went well with the delivery I hope" said McGreggor. "Very efficient and straight forward." Pony replied. "As was the whole mission gentlemen, you'll be pleased to know that Mr Carter's photographs confirms the demise of Ahmed Zawahiri. So a lot of people in Britain will sleep easier. Our agents will spread rumours that he's done a bunk with the drugs and stir up unrest between the factions within his group. Several are ready to take his place and while they're killing each other they're not trying to kill us. Our next stop is Monaco, where we will be visiting an arms dealer. For now gentlemen get cleaned up and back in your civvies and by then I'm sure you will be ready for lunch. Enjoy the cruise; I'll speak to you tomorrow."

CHAPTER ELEVEN

As Charlie was walking towards his office, a young policewoman called to him. "I have a report here for you sir, it's on the laptop they recovered from Rogers." Charlie took the folder with a thank you to the young woman, then watched admiring the way she looked as she walked away. Turning he saw an old colleague of his smiling at him. "Tut! Tut! Charlie" he said. Charlie laughed. "Good to relive your youth now and again Sid, be fair there aren't many that can make a police uniform look good." Still smiling he walked in to his office. "What you grinning about?" asked Penney. "Private joke," came the reply, "but I have the report on Rogers's laptop" he added passing the report to the inspector.

Penney took the offered file and started reading as Charlie went to his own desk and started checking his emails. After a few minutes silence, the Inspector sat up "This is interesting", he said, "It appears there were a couple of encrypted files on the laptop, one of a bank account in the name of Roger Andrews, with regular deposits from a couple of hundred to several thousand"

"Drug income," queried Charlie. "No doubt" came the reply, "but there are three regular payments out of the account, two vary but one is a set monthly amount." , "Property rent perhaps?" Charlie cut in, "could be where he was operating from."

"You could well be right, hang on, see note one," Penney flicked through the pages, "Where the fuck is note one?" He mumbled, followed by "Ah", he read on for a few moments then with a flick of the file said. "Good boys", adding, "the IT guys have tracked the payments, one goes to an account held by Andrew Rogers, the other to a numbered account and the third to a property agent JM Properties in Beauchamp Place."

"That's off Brompton Road I think", said Charlie pulling up Google maps on his computer. "Shall I give them a ring?"

"No" came the reply. "I need some fresh air, we'll take a trip down there. But go and get the keys that were found at Rogers's place I've a feeling we might need them."

As Charlie left the office, the inspector kept reading. One of the files contained lists of names, followed by numbers and running total amounts. Each of the names was listed in a separate spreadsheet which recorded dates and presumably amounts paid. Penney was staggered by the amount some of these people had regularly paid, some added up to more in a month than he earned in six. Well he thought if nothing else, Rogers was efficient and clearly it was not only his flat that he kept fastidiously tidy. He was sure the names weren't real but tags Rogers used for each client. He hoped that some of the numbers might be traceable though so picked up his phone and asked one of the other detectives to come up to his office. Charlie came back with the keys, just as Penney was briefing the detective that he wanted the numbers checked to see if the phone companies can put names to them, and he wanted the amounts checked against the payments into the Andrew Rogers account to see if there was any match. Making it clear he wanted this done as a priority, the detective took the file and promised to get the information ASAP, then acknowledging Charlie he left. "What was that lot?" asked Charlie, "I'll brief you in the car, have you got the keys and know where we're going?"

"Yes," said Charlie. "Then let's go." Came the reply.

After leaving Scotland Yard, Charlie headed for the Mall and up towards Buckingham Palace before turning right in front of the Queen Victoria memorial statue and on to Constitution Hill. On the way the Inspector told Charlie about the names and spreadsheet. They discussed the possibility, but both felt that Rogers's killers were unlikely to be amongst them although they may be able to establish another link to Osborne. Charlie made his way around Duke of Wellington Place before entering Knightsbridge and carrying on past the controversial Park Casino Tower then taking the second left into Brompton Road. The Traffic was quite heavy as he made his way up the road to the left turn into Beauchamp Place. Parking was always going to be a problem but luckily on the right hand side of the road a car was pulling out so Charlie quickly took its place. "Where about are they?" enquired Penney. "I'm not sure," came the reply, "but it's not a long street and I'm not likely to get another space." The Inspector undid his seat belt and got out of the car slamming the door behind him. Charlie chuckled to himself as he knew Penney was not one for doing much walking. As it happened there was an estate agents only fifty yards or so up the street so they thought that would be as good a place as any to start. The shop was double fronted and had 'Domans Estate Agency' painted on a board above the windows. Both windows had rotating displays that held details of the properties for sale in the area. As they entered Charlie noticed one proclaiming a one bedroom flat in a tower block at almost four hundred thousand pounds. How anyone managed to live in London amazed him and he was thankful that he had inherited his own house after the untimely deaths of his parents while sailing off Africa.

Inspector Penney showed his warrant card to a young lady sat at one of the five desks spaced around the office. "Detective Inspector Penney." he announced. "Do any of you know of a company called JM Properties in this area?" A man looked up from a desk situated at the back of the room. "That will be us now," he said, "How can I help?" The Inspector raised an eyebrow and looked around noting all advertising sported the 'Domans' logo. "I'm looking for the address of a property that you had let to a recently deceased client." The man stood up showing he was only around five feet six tall of small build, although very smartly dressed in a typical estate agents suit and tie. Charlie guessed he was in his mid-thirties even though he was obviously going very thin on top. "Perhaps you would like to come through to my office." he said, adding, "Would either of you like a tea or coffee?"

"Tea white, no sugar." replied Penney "Same again" added Charlie. "Mandy would you fetch in two teas and I'll have a coffee." Mandy got up from her desk adjusting her very tight skirt and looked less than pleased to be relegated to being a waitress. The man showed both detectives into an office at the back of the room, which contained a desk with the obligatory computer, four armchairs and several filing cabinets.

"Please take a seat gentlemen; if I can explain. I'm Charles Doman."

"Does everyone call you Charlie as well?" asked Charlie. "No Charles" the man replied in an indignant tone Penney smirked to himself as Charlie felt a slight flush to his cheeks. "As I was saying." Doman continued. "JM Properties used to operate from here but I bought them out eighteen months ago. All new lets are with Doman contracts but we still have almost a hundred in the JM name. Who was it in particular you were interested in?"

"A man called Andrew Rogers although I think his contract would be in the name of Roger Andrews" said Penney. "I see and you say he is deceased."

"Murdered actually," cut in Charlie. "Oh dear!" exclaimed Doman, "then I can see why you need information, let me see what I can find." As he tapped away at the computer, Mandy came in with the teas and coffee. She handed the Inspector a mug then placed the coffee on Domans desk before handing the final mug to Charlie, who looked up noticing the girl was only around twenty and was very pretty with dark hair and bright blue eyes. "Thank you" he said, adding, "I'm sorry, I hope you weren't too inconvenienced." This time the girl blushed realising she must have shown her displeasure. "No not at all" she said, adding, "Enjoy your tea." As she made her way from the office. "I have nothing in the name of Roger Andrews or Andrew Rogers," said Doman. "Are you sure that was the name used?"

"That was the name on the bank account that made payments to JM Properties." Penney replied. "I wonder…." said Doman as he got up from the desk and went to one of the filing cabinets and spent a few moments searching. "Here we go" he announced. Pulling a file from the top drawer. "Roger Andrews, it was a commercial property he was renting, a one thousand nine hundred square foot warehouse in Stewart Road, that's in the Covent Garden area." He handed the Inspector the file. "Not exactly what I was expecting" said Penney, "Can I have a copy of this?" "Certainly" Doman replied, "I'll get one of the girls to photocopy it for you."

"Allow me", said Charlie, taking the file and walking out into the main office. "Could one of you ladies make a copy of this for me please?" he asked. Mandy got up "I'll do it, how many copies?"

"Two please." Charlie replied. Mandy took the file and within moments came back and handed over the original and two copies. "Thank you so much," said Charlie before adding, "You have the most beautiful eyes." Mandy blushed again and went back to her desk as Charlie returned to the office.

Doman agreed to accompany the two detectives to the warehouse and took with him a bunch of keys one of which he hoped would fit. With the Inspector sat in the back of the car, Doman guided Charlie through the numerous side streets before crossing the river via Chelsea Bridge. They then wound through numerous other streets before entering Stewart Road from Wandsworth Road and pulling up by a little set of warehouses on the left. A sign on the entrance proclaimed 'Warehouses to Let' they quickly found the one they wanted although it had no signs or indication of ownership and all the four, marked parking bays were empty. The front of the building had a large roller door, which contained a personnel door on the left. All three men alighted from the car and Doman began searching the keys. "If I'm correct, I think we may be able to help there", said Charlie, pulling the keys obtained from Rogers out of his pocket, and walking to the door, The ring held a car key, a Yale type key, which was clearly for the flat, and a secure lock key that appeared to match the warehouse door. He selected this one and placed it in the lock; immediately it turned and the door opened. Charlie stepped in and looked around for a light switch. On finding an industrial style one to his left, he twisted the knob and with a flicker, the overhead florescent tubes came to life flooding the room with light. "Bloody hell!" he heard Penney exclaim, which reflected his thoughts exactly. The room contained several cars, including a black Porsche Boxster, a red Ferrari 308, and a blue Audi TT. Near the doors was a small white Renault van. Charlie pressed the remote on the car key and with a beep the lights flashed on the Audi. "Guess that must have been his everyday car," quipped Charlie.

Inspector Penney said "I would appreciate it if you didn't touch anything Mr Doman."

"No I won't, do you mind if I wait outside," he replied hastily stepping back through the door before receiving a reply. There were no windows on this level, but to the right was a staircase leading up to offices, which had windows overlooking the small estate. While the inspector looked around on the lower floor, Charlie made his way up to the offices. This level contained a small kitchen, a bathroom and an open plan office. It was immediately clear that someone had already been there and been less than careful in removing any evidence of the use the office had been put too. All cupboard doors were open and empty, an empty desk and filing cabinet drawers were scattered on the floor. A computer monitor was lying on a desk but from the wires left dangling from that and laying on the floor, it was clear the main box had been removed. Touching nothing Charlie went back down the stairs and advised the inspector as to what he had seen. Penney relayed that as well as this area there was a small room on this floor that ran along the wall under the stairs. It contained a table, a couple of chairs and two wardrobes' full of clothes and several pairs of trainers. This one didn't look as if it had been touched. "Must be where Rogers changed into his drug dealer role" said Charlie. "Yes well I think this is one for the forensic team" announced Penney. "Call it in and get them down here, there have to be traces of something around the place, as for the computer hopefully Rogers had backed everything up on his laptop, so that may not be too much of a loss." The two men waited for around forty-five minutes before two police cars and a van arrived. Penney briefed them of the situation, thanked Mr Doman and arranged for him to be taken back to his office. Then he and Charlie made their way back to Scotland Yard.

CHAPTER TWELVE

The tramp steamer 'Maria de Quainta' was docked in the port of Odessa on the Black Sea, with the dockyard cranes loading large pallets of crates into her hold. All the crates were marked in Russian and listed on the manifest as humanitarian aid destined for Syria. In fact, most of the crates were packed with rocket launchers, Kalashnikovs, grenades and ammunition destined for the Al-Qaeda factions fighting the current regime, although the Russians were supporters of the regime. Enough money had changed hands at the docks, to ensure the cargo was loaded with the minimum of inspection. The contents of the crates had travelled from legal and illegal arms manufacturers throughout eastern Russia and from the rebel stronghold of Chechnya. It was in the war torn confusion of Chechnya that agents of a group designated UN07, had planted explosive devices in several of the crates. These were now firmly in the hold of the Maria de Quainta' with several tons of grenades and arms neatly stacked on top.

The ships boson was a hard drinking disciplinarian who appeared to hate everyone and everything. He was around five foot six tall with massive shoulders and a baldhead that seemed to disappear into his neck Currently he was overseeing the loading of the crates, as well as several vehicles, which seemed to entail screaming unnecessary orders at everyone that entered his line of sight. In his pocket, his wallet bulged with notes he had gratefully accepted while out drinking the night before. With the last of the cargo loaded and tied down, he signed the manifest and went back to screaming at the crew to close and seal the hatches. Once they were all secured to his satisfaction and at least one crew member had been physically abused for failing to properly close one of the hatch clamps, he reported to the Captain and just less than an hour later, the rusty old ship cleared the port and headed across the Black Sea destined for the eastern Mediterranean. Around an hour into the journey, the ship passed an even rustier trawler slowly heading in the opposite direction. The trawler captain watched it pass and when it was around half a mile astern, he reached down and popped open a safety cover then flicked the switch underneath. Almost immediately there was sound like a huge clap of thunder, and he watched as one of the ship's hatch covers flung itself twenty feet in the air before falling into the sea. Unseen to him the bottom of the ship was ripped open and with the engines set at full ahead, the ships screw drove it forward pushing the ship below the waves and down to its watery grave. Without stopping or turning to look for survivors, the trawler continued its journey to an unknown destination.

Two days before, a similar quantity of arms had travelled through North Korea, this time with the full knowledge of the regime. At almost the same time as the Maria de Quainta was being loaded in Odessa, 'The Kim Un Sun' was being loaded in South Pyongyang intending to set sail for Gwadar Pakistan, where the weapons would be unloaded and shipped to the Taliban. For the members of the group designated UN04, this time there was more at stake: the possibility of getting to the arms in front of the fanatical army in North Korea was very remote. Also if the ship were to explode anywhere near the Korean peninsula, the North would undoubtedly blame the South leading to an escalation of tensions between the two. Therefore, when the ship had made a previous delivery to Pakistan, the group had managed to sabotage the engines and consequently get access to the ship during the repairs. It was then that explosives were hidden in casings near the propeller shaft in such a way that it would shear the shaft and damage the hull to such an extent the ship would inevitably sink and with luck, a faulty propeller shaft would be blamed. Once loaded with the arms, the ship set sail. Travelling around the coast of China, past the island of Taiwan and was just heading towards Vietnam, when an aircraft flew overhead. Almost immediately the ship shuddered and the engine note changed followed by a massive vibration through the ship as the propeller shaft tore itself to pieces. The engineer ran forward and quickly shut down the engines then with escalating panic in his voice, he reported to the bridge that the ship was taking on water at a rate they could not contain. Already the ship had lost-way and the Captain could feel it rapidly settling by the stern. He ordered a 'May Day' to be broadcast and all hands to the lifeboat stations. Knowing the dangers of trying to release the lifeboats when the ship started to angle badly or even worse, capsize, the crew wasted no time in lowering them to the water. Within minutes the waves were rolling over the rear deck of the ship. And with the angle of the deck getting steeper by the minute, the captain fought his way to his cabin grabbed a coat, lifejacket and the ship's log then ordered abandon ship. All the crew managed to get clear, although some had to jump and swim to the lifeboats. By the time the rescue boats and helicopters arrived, much of the cargo had broken free pushing the stern deeper into the sea. Sat in the lifeboats, the men watched in awe as the ships bow increasingly pointed skyward and then with what sounded like a last sigh she slipped beneath the water.

That same afternoon In Lash Wa Juwayan Afghanistan, Ahmed was sweating in the heat of the Afghan sun, and was glad to see the last of the bags loaded into the rusting tarpaulin covered truck. Harvesting and preparation had been difficult with officials to pay off on one side and Taliban threats on the other. Now he was looking forward to payment, knowing it would be a pittance compared to the millions it could fetch on the streets of Europe. The driver complained that Ahmed should be providing this free to help the Taliban, but eventually he paid and still muttering got into the truck and turned the key, although externally battered, it was clear there was nothing wrong with the engine, as it started immediately and the truck quickly headed off towards the border with Iran. Ahmed watched it go and then pulled a mobile phone from his pocket confirming the shipment was on its way. "The Taliban doesn't pay the bills my friend", he called after the already disappearing truck. "But the infidels do" he laughed patting his pocket. Forty kilometres ahead, a Taliban commander put his phone away and in English said "Ok guys take positions we're on."

After deftly steering the truck over several kilometres of unmade road, the driver turned off and was now picking his way through a gorge, bouncing over rocks and cussing as time and again he banged his head on the doorframe. Rounding a narrow bend, he was forced to brake heavily as two figures appeared in front of him, one was dressed in the normal manner of a Taliban commander and the other, wearing two bullet belts around his shoulders, was pointing a Kalashnikov directly at the truck. "My friends" the driver called, "please don't delay me I have to get this to a ship, my load will pay for your weapons." The commander walked around to the driver's door. "You have the Heroin on board then enough to keep the infidels in permanent sleep eh!"

"Yes" came the reply. "Then join them my friend." The driver had no time to react as he saw the pistol in the commander's hand, neither did he hear the shot that killed him, his body arching back before slumping across the steering wheel. "Get him out and out of sight", barked the commander, who was in reality the leader of the group designated UN02. Instantly four other men appeared and between them dragged the driver from the truck and carried his body up the side of the gorge, where they concealed it in a small cave. With the commander and his original companion now driving the truck and the others following in a military four by four, the vehicles continued through the gorge before altering their route to cross at a prearranged spot into the Sistan and Baluchestan Province of Iran. Several miles later, they pulled into a dilapidated barn that stood next to a small-disused farmhouse. The heroin was quickly transferred to a box van with markings more like the many others normally travelling Iran's main roads. With the original truck and four by four abandoned, the six men changed clothes then set off with two in the front and the other four seated around the sacks of heroin in the back. After a long and uneventful trip to the coast, they arrived at the harbour at Ramin. Confident the guards had been well paid, and using false papers, some of which were carried by the original driver, they passed through the harbour gates and pulled up next to a different ship than the one their cargo was originally intended for. Once the sacks were transferred, the six men boarded the ship and a short time later, it carefully manoeuvred out of the port leaving their vehicle on the dockside. By the time the ship reached the Red Sea, the six men had been transferred to a naval vessel, all Iranian markings on the ship had been removed, the funnel was sporting the blue and white flag of the Saltire Shipping line and the Red Ensign was flying from the sternpost.

In a warehouse on the outskirts of Ciudad Del Carmen Campeche Mexico, members of the Pacific Cartel or GLO, were packing four hundred kilograms of pure cocaine into a torpedo shaped waterproof container. This was to be transported to Puerto Pesquero and attached to the bottom of a container ship due to cross the Atlantic. At a prearranged spot off the coast of Britain, the container would be released into shallow water, where a local dive boat would later retrieve it. This was a process that had been repeated many times so with most of the local Police on the payroll the small band of men were relaxed as they chatted and joked. For years the Mexican drug gangs had been fighting one another for overall control of the billion-dollar drug trade, at the moment the GLO felt they had the upper hand, with only one main contender left which was the Gulf cartel. Over the years, individual members were killed on both sides, but to date, neither side had launched a full-scale attack on the other. So the men were taken completely by surprise when an armed group smashed through the doors spraying bullets in all directions. Several men were cut down immediately while others dived for cover, the gun battle that ensued was totally one sided, with the attackers in bulletproof vests and firing machine pistols, it was soon over. All eight men that had been in the premises lay dead. One other body also lay on the floor, but the attackers had brought this one with them.

The cocaine was quickly loaded in to a small van and after a quick search of the warehouse; all the equipment on the premises was destroyed. The attackers then left heading away from the docks before turning back and taking a route down to the marina at Arroya Grande Puntilla, where a thirty-five metre high-powered motor yacht was moored in one of the berths. The van pulled up alongside and less than two hours after the attack, the cocaine had been loaded, the yacht had left its berth, manoeuvred under the Ciudad del Carmen to Villahermosa bridge and was heading across the gulf on its way to the Atlantic. Designated UN03, the group of men who carried out the attack stayed behind knowing the body they left in the warehouse belonged to a well-known member of the Gulf Cartel. If all went to plan, the GLO would blame them and seek redress for the lost cocaine and equipment, sparking an escalation of the violent war between the two cartels. One the men of UN03 hoped to exploit at every opportunity.

CHAPTER THIRTEEN

Pony knocked on Sticky's door and announced he was going to lunch. Agreeing to join him, Sticky got up and with the two of them now dressed in deck shoes, slacks and open neck shirts, they made their way to the forward dining area. Carter was already there. "Hey Pony" he called, "Next time leave us something to do other than pack up your mess."

"Sorry about that", came the reply. "But like the Captain here says, I get real mean when someone shoots at me." Sticky cut in, "Next time we'll hold back and let you go in first, the sound of bullets hitting my copter always causes bad smells on the flight deck."

"Don't look at me" replied Pony with a laugh. Sticky took Carter to one side, "Seriously though" he asked. "What's your impression of this operation so far? I noticed you were also surprised at the fact we had to drop the gear off to another ship."

"You're right about that," Carter replied. "What was it?"

"Looked like a converted fast patrol boat, certainly had a hell of a turn of speed. It was painted more like an RNLI ship than military, but the crew wore uniforms very much like ours but dark blue rather than black."

"Interesting." Carter said, adding "I can understand that in case of capture or foul up, not knowing anything can be a bonus and protect the other groups, but in all my operations I have always felt there was an eventual purpose, damned if I have worked out what the current one is."

"Me either," Sticky replied, "Although I've noticed there seems to be a Scottish element McGreggor, McFadden, Campbell, even this ship is registered in Glasgow and I'm sure the patrol boat had Glasgow painted out on the stern." Carter thought for a minute then said. "Come to think of it, McGreggor made sure McFadden was in one boat and Campbell in the other, might just be coincidence but I think I'll play safe and for now at least, say as little as possible to those two."

"Yeah and until I'm more comfortable with things I think Pony and I will do likewise."

One by one the others joined them and it didn't go unnoticed that McFadden and Campbell came in together. As usual the food was of five star quality, and after the relatively small breakfast they all ate well. Then some settled down by the television, others went back to their cabins while Pony and Sticky sat with coffees and made small talk over a game of cards. After a while they went out and stood in one of the walkways and just took in the fresh air, feeling the gentle rise and fall as their ship cut through the waves. After another freshen up and yet another evening meal, they went back to their cabins and settled down for the night. Recently for Sticky going to sleep was often a problem as it was proving to be tonight, reliving the events of the day and the sudden and brutal death of the men on the boat. He reflected on how dreams and life can end in a second. Lying there on the bed his thoughts were of Sally and Peter, he could see her short dark hair, sparkling brown eyes and infectious smile. Other times he could see Peter playing in the garden trying to kick a ball and falling over. He thought that somehow by now it would have gotten easier, but it never did, tonight he could even smell her perfume, eventually he drifted off to sleep with tears dripping onto his pillow.

When he woke, light was streaming through the window and although he could still feel the rise and fall of the ship, something was different. It took him a second or two to realise it was quiet, the hum and vibration of the engines had ceased. They had stopped and were at anchor. Looking out of the window, he could make out other luxury yachts of all sizes and he could just make out the shore and buildings. Monaco I presume he thought to himself before heading for a wash and shave. He had just finished dressing and was combing his hair when there was a knock on the door and he heard Carter shout, "Come on Captain, time for breakfast." One last glance in the mirror, then he made his way to the dining area. He took some cereal and made up a bacon sandwich then, adding a mug of coffee, he went and sat down with Carter, Wright and Clarke. "Since I joined this outfit" he said, "All I've seemed to do is eat, I'm going to have to start using the gym or I won't be able to get the chopper off the ground." Pony and Phillips came and joined them, having overheard the previous comments, Pony said; "Thought you were getting a bit of a belly on you but didn't like to say."

"Where's McFadden and Campbell?" asked Carter. Phillips replied, "McGreggor had a job for them apparently they've already eaten." Carter and Sticky exchanged glances, which didn't go unnoticed by Pony.

After a while McGreggor appeared and announced that as soon as they had finished he wanted them in the briefing room adding that as they were now in Monaco, they should remain in civvies all the time they were at anchor. Swigging down the last of the coffee, they all got up and made their way through the lounge to the security door and then down the two decks to the lower deck briefing room. McFadden and Campbell were already there with McGreggor when the rest of them entered and took their seats at the table. "Right" said McGreggor, "while you lot have been sat on your backsides and filling your stomachs some of our other groups have been busy." Once again the table top screen came to life, this time displaying a ship. "A Russian freighter" announced McGreggor. "Yesterday she left Odessa heading for Syria, carrying 'humanitarian aid'. In fact it was carrying rocket launchers, Kalashnikovs, grenades and ammunition destined for the Al-Qaeda factions. It appears however that the ship exploded and sank while crossing the Black Sea. Another ship, also loaded with weapons but this time destined for Pakistan and the Taliban sank shortly after leaving North Korea."

"What a coincidence." Muttered Phillips. "Even more of a blow to them," continued McGreggor, "Is that a shipment of heroin with a street value of around forty million has disappeared en route from Afghanistan. While four hundred kilograms of Cocaine was taken from under the noses of the GLO or Pacific Cartel in Mexico these drugs were to provide the funding for the arms shipments and was to travel by sea to Britain. I can confirm it is now on its way by sea, but as with the cannabis we recovered yesterday, it's now under our control."

"So where do we fit in?" asked Carter. "I'm coming to that" came the reply. "These arms deals were set up by Simon Houghton." The screen changed to show a picture of Houghton, "he is supposedly a well-respected businessman who contributes to a particular political party in Britain. Rumour has it that he's likely to be knighted in the next round of honours." They all suddenly looked up as they felt the engines start up and the now familiar hum and vibration resume throughout the ship. "Ah we obviously have clearance to enter the harbour." McGreggor announced. "We intend to tie up alongside Port Hercule. But back to Houghton, the loss of those ships and the payments has not only hit him hard in the pocket, but also pissed off his clients. When we tie up his yacht will be tied alongside Quai Antoine almost directly opposite." Again the screen changed and a picture of Houghton's yacht appeared. The hull was painted green with the two storey upper superstructure in white, it had swept lines with the hull line dropping around two thirds of the way along the ship revealing the third deck. McGreggor continued, "Built in the USA it is two hundred and eighty feet in length, has a forty seven feet beam, thirteen feet six draft and is just short of three thousand tonnes and is driven by twin screw diesels. Our information is that Houghton will join the yacht this afternoon where he will meet with Mohamed Hussiad; He is already on board and is one of Al-Qaeda's chief moneymen. I would imagine the meeting will be somewhat fraught."

"Considering what you've told us so far, I'd guess you're right" cut in McFadden. "Indeed" continued McGreggor. "The Yacht is due to sail at sixteen thirty and is due to transfer Mr Hussiad to a freighter off the coast of Libya. Our job gentlemen, is to ensure it never makes that transfer and that Mr Hussiad and Houghton are removed permanently. This morning, Mr Campbell set up some charges connected to suction and magnetic mines later, Mr Phillips and McFadden will attach them to Houghton's yacht. As soon as we're tied up some of the ship's crew will go ashore and collect some fresh supplies, we'll also refuel and make it appear we are making a normal re-supply stop. In the meantime, Phillips and McFadden will slip out via the moon pool and attach the mines." A line drawing of Houghton's yacht appeared on the screen and Clarke pointed out the best places to place the mines in order to ensure the most damage and rapid sinking. "We don't want to give them time to launch a boat" added Campbell, "Shouldn't be a problem as there's enough explosive to blow it out of the water." Phillips cut in saying. "I have placed these before but to be honest I don't like carrying the bloody things."

"I assure you" replied Clarke. "That unless someone presses the remote or you're still holding them at twenty one hundred, you will be perfectly safe."

"Twenty one hundred?" queried Pony. "Yes", replied Campbell "We intend to remotely detonate them, but as a backup they will be set to explode at nine this evening."

"Let's hope their departure is not delayed then", said Carter, "Or they might need a new map of Monaco."

"Be serious gentlemen," snapped McGreggor. "We intend to depart around thirty minutes after Houghton then when clear of land and when we can confirm they are clear of other shipping we'll detonate the charges."

"Nothing for us or the fly boys this time then", said Carter. "On the contrary" replied McGreggor. "Prior to detonation I want the helicopter in the air to confirm there are no small boats in the area, the radar should cover the rest. I also want Phillips, Carter and Wright in one of the boats to immediately launch and search for survivors." The screen changed again and pictures of both Houghton and Hussiad appeared. "These two are not to survive" declared McGreggor. "But no bullet holes, if they happen to be floating in the water I'm sure you can find a way of neatly dispatching them."

"My speciality" said Wright. "This time of year it starts getting dark around eight thirty, so I would like things tied up well before then."

"What about other survivors?" asked Sticky "There probably won't be any, but if there is, I certainly don't want them brought back to the Minerva. It's getting on for eleven now, so I suggest you all go and check your equipment, the sooner those mines are in place the happier I'll feel. Oh one thing, remain in civvies, with concealed weapons. If you're seen you're just men working for Johnson Marine who are going to a ships assistance."

They all left the briefing room and stepped out into the moon pool area that seemed to Sticky like a breath of fresh air. The ship had stopped again and he assumed was now tied up alongside. The reality was the air smelt of a mixture of the sea and oil. Phillips and McFadden had donned wet suits and flippers and had a full helmet style mask in their hands. "Give me a hand with this will you Sticky?" asked Phillips, picking up a large backpack, which was encased in a streamlined fibreglass shell. Sticky held it up while Phillips slipped the shoulder straps in place and buckled it across his chest. Before attaching a weight belt. "Not the oxygen tanks I was expecting", said Sticky. "No" replied Philips, "this is a re-breather, which allows you to stay under longer as well as preventing bubbles giving away your presence." Attaching breathing tubes to the especially designed helmet, then checking the valves and air supply he gave Sticky the thumbs up and slipped into the water. Campbell and Clarke had each loaded three mines onto battery-operated sleds, which were now floating in the water. The divers took one each then holding the handles the motors silently whirred into life and they moved forward adjusting the dive planes they slowly disappeared from view. Sticky stood watching the empty water for a moment before he heard Pony say "Hey I'm talking to you." Snapping out from his thoughts, Sticky replied. "Sorry mate, miles away for a minute."

"I was saying do you want to give the chopper a check over before lunch?"

"Yeah why not, looks like we're using it this evening."

The two men made their way up to the hangar and were taken aback when they saw the aircraft. It was still matt black but now had a "G-JHNA" registration in big white letters on the tail spar and below the doors was a green and white flash with Johnson Marine emblazed across it. Underneath the fuselage where the machine gun was mounted, was a pod covering the gun and resembling a camera assembly. Pinocchio walked towards them. "You've been busy", said Pony. "Just one or two mods we were asked to make, apparently the next time you take it up you're civilians."

"That next time will be this evening, probably around seven" said Sticky. "She's ready anytime you like." Came the reply. Pony asked if he found any damage after the last trip as they'd had a bird strike. He was told there were a couple of dents on the bulletproof casing of the engines and a chip on one rotor blade that had now been replaced. They thanked him, and Pinocchio walked away muttering that he wouldn't like to meet the bloody bird. They then did their own walk around checks and flight deck instrument checks. Happy with the results they decided it was time for lunch. Deciding it was better to have a decent meal now, as they were unlikely to feel like eating prior to the mission.

Having left the Minerva, the two divers checked their heading and then made their way across the hundred and fifty yards of water that lay between them and Houghton's yacht. With only thirteen feet of draft, they knew they had little room for error, and the possibility they could be seen from above, although thankfully the harbour water was not as clear as that along the coast. They approached the boat near the stern and while McFadden dived under and went up the port side Phillips stayed to starboard. Selecting one of the mine positions just forward of the propeller tubes, he was expecting the hull to be of fibreglass and was shocked as the magnet slapped into place with a clang he felt could have been heard all over the harbour. Almost immediately he heard a second clang as McFadden's mine was slipped into place. On the yacht and from the dock there was a sound no more than the normal slaps and groans from the sea and mooring ropes. Waiting a few moments and happy there were no reaction, both men flipped over the suction seals for added security and then started the timer. Moving along they placed all four of the other charges with each man convinced the clang as they connected got louder with each mine fitted. Inside the yacht an engineer running checks on the engines prior to their afternoon departure, heard one of the clangs on the hull and on stepping around to investigate, noticed a wrench lying against a bulkhead and assumed this had fallen after being left on the engine.

McFadden appeared from under the hull and gave Philips the thumbs up then with the sleds electric motors on full power, they headed back to the Minerva. Surfacing in the moon pool some forty minutes after they'd left. McGreggor and Campbell were waiting for them and helped to recover the sleds and remove the re-breathers. Then, after the two men had confirmed to McGreggor, that everything had gone as planned, McGreggor and Campbell left while they removed their wet suits and after taking a shower in the changing room, dressed back in civvies and went to join the others for lunch.

CHAPTER FOURTEEN

Back in the office, the Inspector was reading through the report on Rogers's laptop again. "One thing bugs me Charlie" he said, "There's not one personal item on this no documents, letters, emails, nothing."

"He was obviously very careful" replied Charlie, "Unless this was just a backup, all the personal stuff might have been on the other computer and somebody has had that away." Stabbing at the paper, Penney said, "What about this numbered account, wasn't there a recent international agreement about these things and the sharing data for tax. There must be some way of finding out who holds it."

"To be honest, I don't know guv," replied Charlie, "but I know a man who might. I'll give him a ring."

"While you're at it, where have you got to with the army records?"

"Nowhere yet" came the reply. "I checked again earlier but I seem to be hitting a brick wall." As Charlie picked up the phone, there was a knock on the door and the detective tasked with tracing the numbers, found on Rogers's laptop, entered the office. "Thought I'd better let you know what I've got so far guv" he said. "There are one or two things I think you might want to know. Unsurprisingly, most of those numbers relate to pay as you go phones that are not registered and some are now not in use."

"I expected that Dave" replied Penney, adding. "As soon as it came out that Rogers had been murdered, I expect more than one got stepped on and binned."

"Probably", replied Dave. "But quite a few are still operating and I have names for a dozen of them which I thought you'd want to see." He handed Penney the paper who read the names then exclaimed. "This for real?"

"Yes" came the reply. "Has anyone else seen it?" Penney continued. "No just me" said Dave. "I'd appreciate it if you kept it that way for now, this would be press gold but if it leaked we'll be road sweeping next week." Charlie had finished his call and looked up inquisitively. Penney passed him the list as he read through it he muttered, "Bloody hell, Jesus and bugger me", then looked up and said. "These idiots didn't even try to disguise their identity then."

"Doesn't look like it", replied Dave, "The couple of so called pop stars are not really a surprise, but that list contains a Cabinet Minister, High Court Judge, a well-known Politician and leading TV personality. You'd of thought they'd have had more sense than to use their registered phones to contact their dealer. Ordering a Pizza is one thing but a wrap of cocaine beggars' belief" said Charlie. "One other thing" added Dave. "If you take the amounts listed between the days amounts are deposited, they add up to the penny. Rogers appeared to bank everything into the Andrews account, then live off the Rogers account."

"That's what I was expecting." replied Penney. "He was meticulous with detail, hopefully that will prove to be the key to cracking this. Great job Dave see what else you can pull out of those numbers. But whatever you do make sure no one sees that list or gets involved with what you're doing, keep all the info on your own secure part of the computer. If it becomes a problem I'll second you into this office."

After Dave left, Charlie reported on his phone conversation. "It seems the IT guys had already asked the same question regarding the numbered account. Their contact at revenue and customs has traced the account to an offshore company, which in turn seems to be just another front company. Apparently this is common and the money moves around from one to another sometimes a dozen times or more. They have passed it to their specialist team and are confident of pinning it down in the next few days." The inspector's phone rang, he answered it and listened for a few minutes then said. "Thank you," and hung up. "Preliminary report from the forensic team" he said. "The white van came up with traces of Cocaine as did one of the office cupboards there were also traces of heroin in one of the drawers as well as on scales in the kitchen. So we can show that the unit was used for the supply and distribution of drugs, and we can show that our friend Rogers used it and rented it in the name of Andrews. What it doesn't do is give us any clue as to who was his supplier, who killed him or why. We need to put a name to that numbered account; that'll give us the supplier. But I don't think it was them who bumped him off, although I think they do have a link to the drug that killed Mercedes. It's time we took a quiet look at Johnson's operation. In the meantime Charlie I want you to go and retrieve Rogers's laptop and make sure there are no other copies of that report around. I'm going to have a word with the Chief."

The Chief Constable and the Inspector had known each other for many years, so although getting to see him was a problem for many, for Penney it was no more than a twenty-minute wait. As he walked into the office the Chief said "Sorry to keep you waiting Pincher." This was a nickname going back to when they were young officers. As well as being good at catching criminals; Penney had a reputation for being a bit tight hence 'Penney Pincher'. These days, other than the Chief no one else dared to utter it. "Sorry to bother you Keith," Penney replied. "But I've got a potential time bomb here, a local drug dealer called Andrew Rogers was murdered in his flat on Holland Park road."

"Oh yes" replied the Chief, "I saw the report."

"We recovered a laptop from the flat which had some encoded files" continued Penney. "The IT boys have cracked it and pulled off a list of phone numbers relating to some of his clients, and we have managed to track some of the phones owners." He handed the Chief the list, who took it and started reading. Sinking back in his chair, the Chief looked up. "This for real Paul?" he asked using Penney's actual name. "Looks like it" came the reply. "I've sent Charlie down to recover the laptop and ensure no other copies of the report exists. It was young Dave Williams that tracked the numbers."

"Don't think I know him," replied the chief. "A good lad." said Penney. "I made it clear to him if it leaks he'll be sweeping roads. We found the warehouse Rogers operated from but someone had been there and other than for a couple of vehicles they'd cleared it and taken another computer from the premises."

"So another copy of this exists" said the Chief. "Possibly" Penney replied. "But I would imagine it's more so they can continue supplying rather than expose the users."

"Even so," the Chief cut in. "It certainly opens people of this calibre to blackmail, I think it might be worth looking at the Judges cases to see if there are any irregularities."

"Two other things." Said Penney. "We had the forensic teams go over the warehouse and I'm expecting the drug squad to be knocking on my door demanding the laptop."

"Leave that to me" said the Chief. "I'll hold them back for now, what's the other thing?"

"The Murder of Rogers and Osborne was linked to the death of Mercedes Johnson. I have reason to think that Johnson or his security officer are possibly involved in both the murders, and would like to make arrangements to speak to them in Scotland."

"Shit, Paul, throwing that list in is one thing tackling Johnson is another. There are some pretty powerful people involved here, go ahead but keep me informed and for God's sake tread carefully."

"I will," replied Penney, adding, "Johnson's security officer is ex-army intelligence and SAS. I would like access to his army record but have not had much luck so far."

"That's three things" the Chief quipped, "Send me the details and I'll see what I can do."

To close friends and all his colleagues in the Army he was known as Mac, but when he started working for Johnson, all those working for him either called him sir or Mr McCrae. On this occasion there was a smart salute and a welcome back sir as he drove through the first of two gates leading to Johnson's estate. The interior of his car and the boot was checked as the first of the gates were closed behind him. Once satisfied, the second gate opened and he drove through. He had instilled in the men that regardless of who came through, whether or not it was Johnson himself, they were to do a complete check, as the person may be at gunpoint or under threat. He was pleased to see that there had been no slacking while he was away. He drove the half-mile up to the house, noting Johnson's helicopter was on the pad. On reaching the house, he parked in his allocated bay and went up the front steps and into the foyer. He was met by Jim Connelly, his deputy and ex-army colleague. "Hi Mac, good to have you back."

"Yeah it's a long drive," replied Mac. "Anything to report while I was away?"

"Nothing of importance," came the reply. "A deer set off the alarms in section eight again and one of the factory workers had a bad acid burn on his hands when a glass broke. But he'll live. Johnson's in the library said go to see him as soon as you're ready."

"I'll go now," replied Mac turning towards the library door. He knocked and without waiting for a reply walked straight in. Johnson was sat behind a large oak desk with a buttoned red leather top. He was working on a computer, tapping away on the keyboard with considerable speed and dexterity. To his right was a tray with a decanter of Whisky and several glasses. He looked up and without any break in his typing he said. "Ah Mac take a seat and pour yourself a drink, I'll just be a second." Mac poured himself a good slug of Whisky and held the decanter towards Johnson "No not for me thanks." said Johnson as he finished typing and pushed the keyboard to one side.

"So how did it go?" he asked "Much as I told you on the phone, he then gave Johnson the full details of Mercedes demise as told by Osborne. "So it was meant for him," Johnson said thoughtfully, "and she goes and picks that moment to decide to try the drug scene."

"Looks like it" replied Mac, "but he led us to Rogers and that has got us in with the money man. It was him that ordered the drug be given to Osborne and at some point I'm going to make him pay."

"I'm sure you will", said Johnson, adding "Any idea who we're dealing with?"

"Not yet", came the reply "The plates on the limo are registered to a Renault Clio. He was definitely a toff, spoke in a very well educated manner and clearly knows his way around financially. I would imagine he has a lot of contacts in high places."

"So have we," Johnson replied. "It seems someone in the Met is interested in you and is trying to obtain your military record."

"Interesting" said Mac, "Have they got hold of it?"

"No, and I've asked Mr Hamilton to ensure they don't."

"How's his side of things going?" asked Mac. "Very well I understand, two shipments are already en route and the third was collected yesterday. I should have it all by Monday."

"Then we can ensure the shit really hits the fan," said Mac.

"Indeed" came the reply. "I think I'll have that whisky now."

CHAPTER FIFTEEN

The last of the six men had just collected his lunch and was about to sit at the table when Philips and McFadden walked in. "Enjoy your swim?" asked Wright. "If you like swimming in oily harbour water it was Ok." replied Philips. No more was said about their exploits as all the men ate their lunch and carried on with general conversation and banter about various football teams. There was general mirth when Clarke recalled having to blow up a damaged truck in Iraq and managed to spread it over a five hundred yard area and blow a crater two foot deep in the road they were trying to clear. "That explains Campbell's remark about the boat then," laughed Pony. "Yeah." replied Campbell. "It was like the Michael Caine scene from the Italian Job."
"You're only supposed to blow the bloody doors off", they all said in unison. They sat chatting a little longer, but the talk tailed off as all the men had the events scheduled for the rest of the day on their minds.

Unseen by the team, a van had pulled up alongside the ship and members of the crew were unloading the fresh food and drink while towards the stern a bowser was refuelling the ships large diesel tanks. By four in the afternoon all the jobs had been completed and calmness had returned to the dockside. Like all the others, Sticky had returned to his cabin, had checked personal emails and started making a few notes, planning a sort of story board in the hopes of piecing some of the recent events together. Checking the clock he saw it was about four thirty and feeling a little more than curious he made his way out to one of the walkways where he had a clear view of Houghton's yacht. He was surprised to find Pony already there and a few seconds later they were joined by Carter. "Checking on the departure then?" asked Carter. "Thought I'd just get some fresh air and enjoy the view" replied Sticky. "Didn't we all", mocked Pony. Just after four thirty, the three men watched as a Bentley pulled up behind Houghton's yacht. The driver got out and opened the rear door for the occupant. A man wearing unfashionably long dark hair, an open necked white shirt and pale blue slacks, hurriedly stepped from the car and went straight up the gang plank and boarded the yacht. Immediately the gangplank was removed. "Looks like Mr Houghton has arrived" said Sticky. In less than a minute the crew had cast off the mooring lines and the sound of the engines throttling up carried across the harbour as the big yacht made its way out to sea. "It's a pity the crew will have to pay a high price for the deeds of their boss," said Pony, before adding; "well they're on their way, I suppose we'd better get ready." Silently they all left and headed back to their cabins.

Twenty minutes after Houghton's yacht had departed, the engines on the Minerva came to life and all on board felt the now familiar vibration and hum as the mooring lines were released and the Captain reversed away from the dock before deftly swinging the bow around and setting off in pursuit. Fifty minutes later, the phone rang in Sticky's cabin and McGreggor ordered him to the hangar in preparation for take-off. Remembering he was to appear as the pilot of a civilian helicopter, he dressed in the blue flying suit that had appeared in his wardrobe, put a lifejacket over the top and after picking up his helmet and goggles, headed for the hangar. Pony arrived shortly after him and after running an external check and signing the aircrafts log Pinocchio had handed him, the two men settled into the flight deck and started the pre-flight checks. The roof panels opened and once again the hydraulic lift took them up into the open air. They were well out to sea now and Sticky was relieved to see the waves were no more than three or four foot swells. Looking around, neither man could see any sign of the land they had recently left. Up on the bridge McGreggor and the Captain were looking intensely at a radar screen. They were maintaining the distance between themselves and Houghton's Yacht, ensuring they were close enough to operate the detonation, but not so close they could be visibly identified. The only other blip appeared to be a large ship about four miles to their starboard and travelling slower than they were. This meant they would probably see the explosion but not be close enough to arrive before their RIB. Down in the moon pool area, Wright, Carter and Phillips were preparing one of the RIB's. Dressed in civilian boiler suits and life jackets, they'd stowed weapons in the under seat lockers. McFadden and Clarke had prepared the other boat in case it was needed, while Campbell was busy checking and double checking the remote detonation device.

Sticky's radio crackled and he was given a heading and permission to depart. With the rotors unfastened and the deck clear, he started the engines, engaged the rotors and once up to speed signalled the skid locks release. Now getting used to the ship and machine he waited until he judged they were on top of a wave and then lifted off. Sweeping along the port side of the ship, they quickly put it behind them before Sticky started to gain height. At six thousand feet they could see Houghton's yacht ahead of them and what appeared to be a cruise ship off to their right. Other than that, there was nothing else to be seen. Unknown to Sticky, Carter had already launched his boat and was on the same heading as him. So when he radioed in that the sea was clear, other than for the yacht and cruise ship. Both Pony and he were shocked to instantly see the explosion in front of them. Flames leapt fifty feet into the air, followed by parts of superstructure and decking. Within seconds the shock wave hit them throwing the light helicopter into a side slide and spin. Sticky quickly regained control and turned the nose back towards the spot where Houghton's yacht had been. As the plume of water and smoke settled, there was no yacht to be seen; only floating debris. "Looks like Clarke has done it again" said Pony. Regaining a professional attitude, Sticky radioed 'Mayday' 'Mayday' and reported that he was piloting a Johnson Marine helicopter and had seen a yacht explode in front of him he added the co-ordinates and reported that he was heading in to search for survivors. The cruise ship also reported seeing the explosion and was altering course to assist.

At that moment Carter sped beneath the helicopter in the RIB, intent on finding Houghton and Hussiad before any unwanted assistance arrived. Sticky and Pony arrived over the scene, and saw several bodies floating in the water amongst small pieces of what was once a luxury yacht. Over to the right, Pony spotted what looked like a woman in a bikini, clinging on to the remains of a floatation aid. Sticky brought the helicopter in as low as he dared and Pony lowered one of the ropes attached to the winches above the rear doors. He then signalled to the woman to grab the rope, but it was quickly obvious she was too badly injured or weak to hold on. He quickly outlined a plan to Sticky, then with an "Ah well, in for a penny in for a pound." He opened the door, which hinged from the front, and carefully climbed out onto the skid, holding the rope with one hand, he then closed the door and jumped into the sea. Pulling himself alongside the woman he could see she was probably in her mid-twenties and although conscious, was losing a lot of blood from a cut on the top of her head. One of her legs was also at an awkward angle and appeared to be broken. As Sticky brought the helicopter forward, he managed to take hold of the rope, and fighting against the downdraft of the

THE THISTLEDOWN CONNECTION

rotors, he held the woman face to face passing the rope under both of their arms and clipped the hook to the rope behind her back. "When he takes our weight this is going to be painful and uncomfortable he told the woman but hold me as tight as you can and we'll get you across to the cruise ship and medical attention.

Carter was weaving his way through the debris, and had already found four bodies and identified Hussiad as amongst the dead. "Over there," called Wright pointing to a piece of debris with someone clinging to it. They motored over and immediately could see it was Houghton. He was barely alive but muttering, "Help me, I think I'm dying." "Yes, not your lucky day is it?" said Wright, lifting Houghton's head from the water and snapping his neck so quickly that he was dead before his head hit the water again. Phillips pointed out Pony getting lifted from the water strapped to a bikini-clad woman. "Look at that", he said. "Typical bloody fly boys" replied Wright "Pick up the birds wherever they go."

"Looks like they're heading for the cruise ship" said Carter. "Makes sense as they have medical facilities," cut in Phillips, "also saves us any problems with visitors." Working hard to keep the aircraft stable, Sticky couldn't winch Pony and the girl in so had to let them dangle in mid-air. They were two thirds of the way to the cruise ship when the girl fell unconscious. Pony's arms were killing him and pointlessly apologising to the woman he was forced to grab her buttocks to prevent her from slipping. Like many modern cruise ships, this one had a heli pad and Sticky was able to swing in and hover above the pad, lowering Pony and the woman to the deck. A medical team and other crew members quickly untied them and placing the unconscious woman on a stretcher, swiftly whisked her off to the infirmary. Sticky lowered the machine to the deck and although uncomfortably wet and aching from the strain, Pony confirmed he was ok, and climbed back into the flight deck, once given the all clear and watched, filmed and photographed by hundreds of the passengers, Sticky took off and headed back to the Minerva.

Pony relayed the message to the Captain of the Cruise ship that their RIB had confirmed they could find no other survivors, and as their own ship had suddenly lost power it was looking to return to Monaco. The Cruise ship Captain thanked them for their help and confirmed they would conduct another search and remain in the area until the main search and rescue arrived, which would be fairly quickly for as Sticky was dropping back onto the deck of the Minerva, he could see search and rescue helicopters a mile or so in the distance heading for the 'disaster' scene. While out of view of the Minerva a coastguard lifeboat was also en route. Safely back on the deck and with the skid locks in place, the engine was shut down and the deck started dropping into the ship even before the crew had finished stowing the rotors. Within a few minutes they were in the hangar with the roof closed. Ten minutes later Carter and the crew of the RIB were secure in the stern of the ship, which for a craft that had lost power, suddenly burst into life and was surging off away from Monaco and on a course towards Gibraltar. After completing the shutdown checks, Sticky and Pony left the helicopter to be met by Campbell who informed them McGreggor wanted them in the briefing room immediately. Descending the stairs, the two men reached the room at the same time as the crew of the RIB. On entering it was clear McGreggor was less than happy.

"What the hell were you two playing at?" he stormed. "There are probably dozens of photographs and videos of you playing the heroes going to every bloody television station in Europe."

"As we were both wearing helmets and dark goggles no-one would be able to identify us." replied Sticky. Pony cut in "I don't mind bumping off arms dealers and terrorists but not young women, anyway we were just employees of Johnson Marine weren't we?"

"That's as maybe" replied McGreggor. "But I don't want too many questions asked about us or this ship." Carter interrupted with, "Hang on a minute boss, wouldn't it have looked a bit odd if we'd just turned up pottered around and then disappeared back here, surely more questions would have been asked then especially after an explosion of that magnitude." McGreggor thought for a minute and then said, "Ok I'll give you that." Then he turned to Carter and asked if the targets were confirmed dead. Carter replied they were but Houghton needed a little assistance. "Then that's another mission completed," said McGreggor. "I'll let Hamilton deal with the flack, time the bastard did something."

The group then left and headed back to their cabins to freshen up. However Sticky was still fuming inside and threw his helmet on his bed in anger before thumping his wardrobe door in frustration. Having failed to close the door behind him Carter was walking past and said, "Whoa steady on Captain, don't want you breaking your hand."

"Didn't like McGreggor from day one," Sticky replied. "I already owe him a slap and he is going the right way about getting it, that outburst was well out of order. You can't blow a bloody great yacht to smithereens in front of a cruise ship of two thousand passengers, put your men in to ensure your target is dead and then expect to disappear unseen."

"You really are pissed off, aren't you?" replied Carter, "If it's any help, there are things about our operations so far I feel uncomfortable about too. Don't know what it is but just a feeling. We know we're not getting the whole picture, that's a given but maybe it's just McGreggor, he does have the sort of face you want to smack." Sticky smiled, "Yeah and maybe it's just me" he replied, "But I appreciate what you said, keep thinking that way and if anything else comes up let me know."

"Will do." Came the reply. "See you later."

Later that evening, the group were having a few drinks and watching the television when the international news came on. There was a headline report on the explosion, which destroyed a yacht belonging to a well-known businessman and political fundraiser Simon Houghton. The report continued that it was rumoured, but never proved, that much of Houghton's money came from International Arms deals and there's speculation that his yacht was illegally carrying arms when it exploded. Further to that, besides finding Houghton's body amongst those of the crew, the French police also found and identified the body of Mohamed Hussiad; who was wanted in several countries and believed to be one of the top money brokers within Al Qaeda. The television then cut to a shaky video of the rescue of the only survivor and showed the helicopter landing Pony and the woman onto the Cruise ship. "See you had a good hold on her ass" laughed Clarke. "I was afraid she'd slip", replied Pony feigning a hurt expression. The announcer went on to say that the woman had been identified as Samantha Houghton, the twenty eight year old daughter of Simon Houghton, and that doctors reported she had a broken leg, burst eardrum and concussion as well as several other minor wounds and was now stable after being transferred to a hospital in Monaco. It was believed she had been sunbathing on the upper deck, which saved her from the main blast. A spokesman for Johnson Marine said that a rigid inflatable boat belonging to one of their small vessels had been recovering some scientific recording equipment when the explosion occurred and were first on the scene; their ship had also dispatched the on board helicopter and was delighted to have been able to save Ms Houghton. Naturally though they continued the crews were traumatised by what they found and would remain at sea, so would not be available for interview. A photo of a Johnson Marine ship was displayed on the screen, complete with helicopter. Whatever ship it was it certainly wasn't the Minerva.

CHAPTER SIXTEEN

The Chief Inspector walked back in his office to find Charlie already there with Roger's laptop on his desk. "See you got it then," said Penney; "Yeah but they weren't too happy at releasing it, apparently Chief Super Reynolds from the drug squad had requested it so he'll probably come in here ranting at us before long."

"I've sorted that," came the reply. "I have spoken to the Chief and he's going to call him off for a while but I don't know how long we can keep this under wraps. Has anything else come up while I was out?" "Yes, I got a preliminary report from the team at the warehouse. As we thought, the Audi was registered to Rogers at his Holland Road address, as was the Porsche. But the Ferrari is registered to a Mark Harris at Campden Hill Road."

"That's Kensington isn't it? Queried Penney, "Not far from Holland Park either, perhaps we should speak to Mr Harris. But first see if we have anything on him."

"Will do" replied Charlie, adding "All the cars other than the Audi had their keys in the ignition and neither of Roger's cars have shown any traces of drug residue, but the Ferrari has given a positive result for cocaine in the glove box and they've also had several positive readings from the van, and some of the clothes you saw and the upstairs offices. It will be a couple of days before we have the full report."

"Well that doesn't surprise me" said Penney, "Got to give it to Rogers though he certainly kept the two parts of his life neatly separated."

"There's one interesting thing about the van though" continued Charlie. "It was reported stolen shortly after Rogers was found dead."

"Now that is odd," replied Penney, "It's clear it'd been in the warehouse well before Rogers was murdered, my guess is it was the one used for normal deliveries. Looks like someone trying to cover their backside. Who's it registered to?" Charlie looked through the paperwork then announced "A company called Avatar Imports."

"Ok get everything you can on them use your financial pal if you have to, might be interesting to know exactly what they import."

"Blimey guv" replied Charlie, "Anything else you want me to follow up." Penney just stared at him. "Sorry if it's too much for you, just chase up Avatar, I'll run a check on Harris and as we've traces of cocaine in his car, I'll get the beat boys to bring him in for questioning. Can you manage that?" Charlie didn't answer; he just picked up the phone and started chasing down the owners of Avatar.

The Inspector started searching the police database for a Mark Harris, and was presented with a long list of names, refining his search to Campden Hill he was left with just the one. Mark Harris, aged forty-four, was arrested for possession of cannabis when fourteen years old, charged and acquitted of living off immoral earnings when nineteen. Then there was nothing on him until three years ago, when he was cautioned for possession of a small amount of cocaine. Intelligence said he was now a city shares dealer and suspected of insider dealing although there was no evidence to support it. His address was given as a flat on Campden Hill Road. Penney remembered that when he first came to the 'Yard' he had actually looked at flats there himself. He recalled a terrace of mostly four but some five-storey houses. He looked at one basement flat but didn't like being below road level and remembered it was quite dark. In another house he had looked at a second floor flat that was quite large with high ceilings but had arch topped windows split into three with large dividing pillars that again made the room quite dark. Snapping out of his reminiscing, he picked up his phone and ordered Harris to be brought in for questioning, and arrested if necessary.

Charlie was not having a lot of luck in tracing the owners of Avatar Imports; he had established that they had a registered operating address in Dover. But a call to the local police, confirmed this was just a convenience address used by many instant start-up companies. A call to Companies House, established that Avatar Imports, was owned by another company called International Avatar Imports. In turn, this was owned by a financial investment group based in the

Dominican Republic. He then spoke to his contact in the finance and fraud unit, and had his first break, when it was confirmed that International Avatar Imports was one of the front companies they had so far traced in trying to link to the account number found on Rogers's computer. He then turned to the report regarding the van being stolen and noted the name and address of the person reporting the theft and after discussing it with the Inspector, they decided that it would be worth having a word with him. Penney was sitting back in his chair in his familiar thinking mode of staring at the ceiling. "Did you ever see the film Avatar Charlie?" he asked. "Yes" came the reply, "Quite liked it in an odd sort of way."

"I caught it one evening on satellite when it was raining and I had sod all to do" continued Penney. "Not my sort of thing normally and a bit long but found myself getting quite into it." Charlie raised an eyebrow; it was unlike the Inspector to talk of anything outside of work. "Thing is" said Penney, "When those characters went to sleep in a cocoon in one place, they became something else, an Avatar in another part of the world."

"I see where you're going," said Charlie, "This company Avatar is out there moving the drugs about, while the real power is safely cocooned somewhere away from the action."

"Exactly Charlie, all we have to do is smash that bloody cocoon."

As if on cue, Chief Superintendent Reynolds, knocked the door and without waiting to be invited, barged into the room. "Ok Paul, what the hell is going on, I know you got a murder on your hands but the warehouse and items you recovered should be handed over to us, it could help with an investigation we've been running for two years. Then the Chief Constable tells me to back off. I'm not happy Paul, not happy at all." "Charlie go take a tea break and check on young Dave will you" said Penney, without saying a word Charlie got up and left. "Sit down Jack," Penney said indicating to a chair. "Before I go into the details have you heard of Avatar Imports?" He could see immediately from Reynolds face that he was well aware of the name. "Not sure I have" came the reply. "For Christ's sake never take up poker Jack, It's obvious you have."

"Ok, Ok, yes I have, it's a front company which we think is being used to move the majority of drugs in and out of London. We have got no-where so far in tracing the money men behind it, all we've been able to do is pick off the odd dealer, one of the ones who recently came to light is your guy Rogers and from what I've been able to get out of your team so far he was a major distributor."

"It does look that way," confirmed Penney. "There was a van in Rogers's warehouse registered to Avatar which strangely enough, was reported stolen after Rogers was found murdered. Someone cleared the place of any drugs or equipment but seems to have overlooked the van. Look Jack, I'm sorry if we appear to be holding out but Rogers kept a

client list encrypted on his computer and although we have
not been able to identify all of them, the ones we have
confirmed include two politicians, one cabinet minister, and
a head of a prominent bank, several well-known celebrities
and at least one high court judge."

"Fuck me!" exclaimed Reynolds, "No wonder the bastards
are so well protected and we often fail to get search warrants
or prosecutions."

"I suggest if you've had one or two particular judges blocking
you, you mention their names to the Chief, he's seen the list"
replied Penney, adding. "Look Jack we don't want to
obstruct you and anything we come up with regarding
Avatar we'll keep you informed but until we can get close to
the main man. I think the less people who see that list the
better, because once you know the names it's difficult to
approach them impartially."

"Point taken, Paul" replied Reynolds "what you've told me
stays with me. If anything else surfaces about Avatar I'll keep
you informed."

After Reynolds had left, Charlie came back in the office,
"What was that about?" he asked. "Psychology" replied
Penney, "I know Jack, and he's full of shit really, over
promoted in my view, so asking you to leave was to make
him feel what I had to say was more important." Charlie just
looked at the Inspector and shook his head, "Every time I
think I have you worked out, up comes something like that."

"Keeps you on your toes then Charlie, has young Dave got any further?"

"Yes he's tracked another half a dozen names but as far as we can make out, no-one of significance although a couple have convictions for possession and one for dealing."

"Tell him to pass those names on to Reynolds," replied Penney "Shows we're cooperating and should keep him quiet for a while." The young policewoman, Charlie had seen earlier, entered the office. "Sorry to bother you sir but there's a Mark Harris in interview room four, I believed you wanted to see him."

"Yes thank you," Penney replied, "I'll be down shortly." As she turned to leave, she looked at Charlie and blushed. Either she fancies me, or that bastard Sid told her I was eyeing her up thought Charlie. Then after another moments thought, he decided it was the latter and a payback was on the cards. "Oi! You still with us." Charlie realised that Penney was talking to him. "Sorry Guv miles away for a minute."

"Yes I bet you were," smiled Penney adding, "Grab that file of yours and lets go see what Mr Harris has to say for himself." This time Charlie blushed as he followed the Inspector out of the office.

As they got to the interview room, the constable that had been looking after Harris stepped out. Penney asked him if Harris had been arrested or came in voluntarily and if he had been informed of his rights. On receiving a reply, he thanked him and entered the room. Harris was not exactly what the

Inspector had been expecting. He looked a lot younger than his forty-four years and his brown hair was neatly cut in a short style, which was gelled to give the top a spiky but neat appearance. He was wearing an expensive looking grey Saville Row suit with white silk shirt and grey tie. He stood up when Charlie and the Inspector introduced themselves and held out his hand in a formal greeting. The Inspector shook his hand and noticed he had blue eyes that seemed to exude a deep intelligence. "Thank you for coming in at such short notice Mr Harris" said Penney, "I'm sorry if it has caused you any inconvenience, as you are aware, you have not been arrested nor I gather has anyone informed you of your rights, is that so?"

"Yes," Harris replied, "I was asked to come and see you and as I was free I could see no reason not to, however, I do have an important meeting at five so if we could conclude by then I would appreciate it."

"I'm sure we will be finished well before then, I intend to keep this informal so there will be no recording at this stage, nor will I read you your rights so you are free to go when you wish. But I would like you to answer a few questions if you would" said Penney, keeping a very relaxed and laid back approach was something Charlie was used to with Penney and often led to people being off guard and giving slightly more information than they otherwise would and at this stage they were not interested in getting an arrest for possession or use.

Penney started with, "I believe you know or are an acquaintance of Andrew Rogers know as Ginger."

"I thought this might be about that," replied Harris, "But until I read it in the papers, I thought he was called Andrews not Rogers." Then suddenly appearing shocked, Harris added; "I didn't kill him, though I'd liked to have at times."

"It's ok we know you didn't kill him," said Penney trying to keep Harris calm, "we think we know who did but we are not sure why yet. So tell me why you could have killed him then?" Harris shifted in his chair. "That was a figure of speech Inspector, he pissed me off over my car."

"A red Ferrari 308." said Charlie. Harris looked surprised, "Yes" he said eagerly adding. "Do you know where it is?"

"Indeed we do Mr Harris" Penney replied, "Currently it's here in the compound, forensics have been taking a look at it, so perhaps you can explain why we found it parked in a warehouse being rented by Rogers."

"The bastard did have it then" stormed Harris, "He told me it had gone abroad."

"That doesn't tell us why he had it," said Charlie. "Or why there are traces of cocaine in the glove box." Harris sat back and looked at the two men. "This is off record" he said "Currently" replied Penney. "Ok I'm sure you already know I've had one caution for possession, well after that I quit," seeing the look Penney gave him he continued, "I did honestly, but the game I'm in is high pressure, you can make or lose millions a day and about six years ago I had a really good week and made a mint, I bought some mining shares that had been steady for a couple of years, intending them to be a safe holding. Then they announced a major gold find and they went through the roof, I managed to off load them right at the top of the surge. Some people accused me of insider dealing but honestly it was just pure bloody luck. Sometimes though it pays to be at the right parties keeping your ears open and other times it pays to provide a little stimulus, if you know what I mean." Charlie and Penney nodded, and invited him to carry on. "Well that's when I met Andrews or Rogers whatever he called himself. He provided the occasional bag of stimulus."

"Cocaine," clarified Charlie, "Yeah well a couple of months ago I owed him about five grand, when I got really stitched up on a deal and lost a bloody fortune, it took me over a month to move funds and get what I owed him, but during that time my car disappeared."

"Did you report it stolen?" asked Penney, "No, Ginger let me know he had it and said it would cost me twenty grand to get it back. Well when I had my windfall six years ago I bought the car, always wanted one and this one was mint, it's still worth thirty grand plus, but I wasn't going to pay that bastard twenty for my own car. I told him that for a couple of grand I could get his legs broken, I said I'd give him six, the five I owed him plus one for the delayed payment. He replied too late I've arranged for it to go abroad. I'll be honest with you inspector, I was fully intending to get him done over, but not killed, I wanted the car."

The Inspector sent Charlie to check on the car and confirm when it could be released. "I suggest you be a little more careful at these parties you attend, did you ever see Rogers with anyone in particular, or was he at any of the parties?"

"Mostly I saw him at some of the top spots in town, he only seemed to operate amongst the high rollers he wasn't a street dealer. I think most of his clients had an account as did I," replied Harris. "Can you let us have the number Rogers contacted you on?" asked Penney, "He kept them on a computer it would help if we can eliminate yours." Taking a pen and diary from his pocket, Harris scribbled down a number, tore out a page and handed it to the Inspector, adding "if some people knew he had them on computer they wouldn't be sleeping so well." Penney thanked him for his help and asked him not to spread that information around. Charlie came back and informed them the car was finished with and forensics could see no reason for keeping it, so he offered to take Harris down to sign it out. Harris could not conceal his delight at the thought of getting it back. "One good turn deserves another inspector", he said. "I did see Rogers talking to a guy on a couple of occasions, and it was clear he was not dealing but taking orders."

"Could you identify him?" asked Penney. "Better than that I can give you a name" replied Harris, "Courtney or to be precise Sir James Courtney, now that's a man you don't want to cross."

Inspector Penney made his way back to the office, while Charlie took Harris down to the compound and signed the car out. Harris walked around it and his smile got even larger after seeing there was no damage and that the car had obviously been cleaned of any fingerprinting or other residue. "You love that thing don't you?" said Charlie. Harris nodded then shook Charlie's hand got in and with a throaty roar from the engine he drove off. After watching him go and with mixed feelings as to whether Harris was a crook or not running through his mind, Charlie headed back to the office. Penney was on the phone when he arrived asking for everything they could find on Courtney. On putting the phone down he turned to Charlie and told him to get back on to the finance guys to track all of Courtney's business interests and any companies he owned. I have a feeling he said that Avatar will appear somewhere. "Harris gave me another snippet while we were going to the car," said Charlie. "Apparently some DJ put down Courtney in front of some of his business colleagues, Harris reckoned that if looks could kill the DJ would have been dead on the spot, he then noticed that Courtney called Rogers over to him and they spoke briefly before Rogers left. Apparently the DJ called himself The Master of Sound." Penney banged his desk that fills in the bit that's been bugging me. Charlie I think we may have found the cocoon."

"Could be" replied Charlie, "But I have a feeling smashing it may take a little longer." Penney thought for a moment then said, "That might be the motive that inadvertently led to the death of young Mercedes, however, the death of the other two points to a completely different motive and I feel Mr Johnson may well be involved there. I spoke to the Chief and he has given approval for us to speak to Johnson and his Head of Security. Have you had any luck with those army records yet?" Charlie checked his emails and intranet notices, "No" he replied, "Still being blocked by the look of it," "Ok, we'll manage without, get the guys started looking at Courtney's interests, then army records or not we'll make arrangements to go up to Scotland and speak to Johnson on Monday."

"I'm afraid you won't gentlemen," came a voice as a man strode into their office. "You will be going nowhere near Mr Johnson or his staff." Penney was furious with this abrupt interruption and sprang from his chair to face the man, noting he was around six foot tall had a military bearing with grey hair and was wearing a long navy coloured coat and white scarf. "I'm conducting a double murder investigation and will interview whomever I bloody please. Who the hell do you think you are barging into my office and telling me who I can and can't speak to?"

"I'm sorry gentlemen, let me introduce myself. I'm head of a special unit of MI6, we have an ongoing operation that would be put in serious jeopardy should you go ahead with your enquiries. My Name is Geoffrey Hamilton."

CHAPTER SEVENTEEN

On the Minerva, the men found themselves once again sat around the table in the briefing room. "Our next mission was to disable the ship Mr Hussiad was intending to meet," announced McGreggor, "however it has been confirmed that it's not carrying weapons or persons of particular interest. The powers that be also felt that another ship exploding in the Med might start one or two people asking awkward questions. It was confirmed last night that the large quantity of cocaine, recovered by our group in Mexico, is now well on its way to Britain and as hoped, the incident has sparked off an escalation of the war between two of the largest drug cartels." Sticky intervened. "There's one aspect of our operations that has been bugging me from the start", he said, "Ok" replied McGreggor, "get it off your chest." Sticky looked around at the others and then continued. "The ship loads of arms and the corrupt dealers, I'm happy to see the back of, but it's the drugs. Firstly the cannabis that was on the boat we sank, could have stayed on and gone to the bottom of the sea. Then you mentioned the heroin from Afghanistan and now the cocaine from Mexico all of which is now on its way to Britain. Why? What are we doing sending sixty or seventy million pounds worth of drugs to Britain?" McGreggor looked around at all the group and could see the majority were also interested in an answer.

After a pause, he said, "Let me assure you we're not about to start dealing on the streets."

McGreggor went to stand up, when Carter said, "Is that it? Is that your answer we're not about to become dealers, well I for one don't find that very reassuring." McGreggor sat down again. "There are certain things we wanted to keep from you, it's true, mostly because the less you knew the less of a security risk you all become. But I can see that this causing some of you concern and I can understand why. Also in the past few days I have got to know more about you all and have seen you in action. So I think there'll be no harm or risk in clarifying this part of the operation. It can't have gone unnoticed that on more than one occasion, the name Johnson Marine has surfaced." Several of the group nodded. "Well Johnson Marine is a subsidiary of AJ Associates who own dockyards, shipping, electronics companies and chemical plants. AJ stands for Albert Johnson, the internationally renowned chemist who owns a pharmaceutical research plant in Scotland."

"Isn't he the father of Mercedes Johnson who died of a drug overdose recently?" asked Wright. "Yes he is," continued McGreggor "so you can see that he has no interest in seeing these drugs out on the streets, they are in fact going to his research plant in Scotland, where it is hoped the heroin will be turned into Morphine and Diamorphine for medical use in civilian and military hospitals. I am told that cannabis resin, as compared to leaf, can have substances extracted from it and turned into tablets for use of people suffering from Multiple Sclerosis and that cocaine can also be manufactured into tablet form as pain killers. I also understand that they're researching ways of producing a tablet or injectable substance designed to combat the addictive element of these drugs."

"So shipping this stuff to him is a thank you for the use of equipment" said Carter. "More use of the name", replied McGreggor. "We paid a lot of money for this ship but I can also confirm any drugs we come across in future Carter can blow to hell. We'll be concentrating on arms and the bastards dealing in them."

The group sat back and thought about what had been said, it seemed to make sense and was as good an answer as any although there was something about the demeanour of both McFadden and Campbell that left Sticky feeling a bit uncomfortable. But if that was the complete truth, then he felt he could sleep a bit easier tonight. Pony broke the silence that had descended around the table, "So with no ship to blow up, what are we going to be doing next?" he asked. "We'll shortly be docking back in Gibraltar and then the Minerva will be travelling up to Glasgow for a little maintenance work." Came the reply. "I don't see any need for you all to stay on board for that, so I hope to arrange for you to get a flight back to HQ, then you can all have ten days leave reporting back to the ship in Glasgow by lunch time on Monday week. For now go get some lunch and I'll confirm the flight details and see you in the dining hall later with the details"

"That'll do me" said Phillips, "I've got a little red head to renew acquaintances with in Southampton." A bit of banter was thrown back at him as they all left and made their way back up the stairs to the main reception room. Most of the men went to their cabins to freshen up but Carter followed Sticky into his cabin, "What did you make of that?" he asked, "Not sure, it made sense to a degree but seems a lot of gear for research purposes." "Yeah but if they are converting it as well it could add up." Pony walked into the Cabin, "What's with you two?" he asked, "I've noticed the little looks between you. You're not coming out of the closet at last are you?"

"You're going the right way for a slap", laughed Carter, adding, "I'm getting a wash, see you two at dinner." As Pony made himself comfortable on the bed, Sticky had a quick wash and told him about the things that had been on his mind and his mistrust of the Scottish element. "Wish you'd said something earlier." Pony replied. "As it happened I decided to stretch my legs this morning and saw Campbell and McGreggor together on the outer deck, they didn't see me but McGreggor passed him a piece of paper. I heard him say something about Hamilton and getting something at Thistledown."

"Thistledown?" queried Sticky. "Sounded like that" replied Pony, I stayed out of sight so only got snippets."

"Well I was feeling better about this set up five minutes ago" said Sticky. "Now you've given me another conundrum."

It was late afternoon when the Minerva entered the Bay of Gibraltar and headed back to its previous berth in the harbour. Sticky and Pony were stood on the outer deck and admiring the beauty of the bay and the rock itself towering over it. Dozens of boats were lazily swinging on their moorings. A British frigate was anchored in the bay and a cruise ship was alongside the same harbour wall where the one had been when they first arrived. This one though rose up like a giant block of flats and appeared at least twice the size. As the captain manoeuvred the Minerva into her berth, crewmembers jumped ashore and with the skill honed from years of experience, they swiftly tied the bow and stern of the ship to harbour side bollards. With not much else to see, the two men went back inside and down into the dining area. Crew members were just finishing laying out this evening's offering on the hotplates, so they poured themselves a coffee and then as other members of the team arrived, helped themselves to the offerings and sat with Carter and Wright at the table. A few minutes later McGreggor arrived and confirmed that he had arranged a flight for them on a military aircraft at ten this evening. They were to travel in civvies and use their alternative identity taking only what they arrived with. Vehicles would collect them at eight to allow them time at the airport. He reminded them that once they arrived back at base they would be officially on leave but were to report to the Minerva in Glasgow on Monday week. He finished by saying he hoped they would make the most of the break and gesturing to Phillips, passed his commiserations to the young lady in Southampton.

Each man went back to their cabins and packed their bags, with the minimum items they had travelled out with. Sticky got out the passport for Michael Baker and just before eight, several cars arrived and taking one each. Sticky, Pony, Carter, Wright, Phillips and Clarke got in to them and headed for the airport. Neither the driver nor Sticky said anything as they drove through the Gibraltar traffic although Sticky was fascinated by the buildings and the occasional stunning views and vowed that he would ensure he visited the place in the future. On arriving Sticky stepped from the car and thanked the driver then made his way to departures. After passing through security, he made his way to the departure lounge set aside for the military transport plane, and joined army personnel, sailors and an array of various civil servants. Looking around he saw Pony talking to a young blonde woman near a drinks machine, Carter was sat reading a paper, and Wright was nearby reading a magazine, while Clarke appeared to be sleeping in one of the chairs. Looking around further, he noticed Phillips who was stood looking out of the window at the aircraft. Sticky smiled to himself, knowing Phillips was a nervous flyer. After waiting a few minutes, and seeing no one else he knew, he sauntered over and sat next to Carter and pretended to search through his bag. He noticed the front of the newspaper Carter was holding, had a photograph of his helicopter lowering Pony and Ms Houghton onto the cruise ship. "Odd thing that," he said, "a beautiful yacht like that blowing itself to pieces." Carter quickly caught on. "Yes" he replied, "but according to the paper here it was carrying arms and ammunition for Al Qaeda."

"Really" replied Sticky feigning shock, "then it's no loss, but I thought he was supposed to be a big fish in political circles and going to be knighted. Just shows you can't trust politicians, I wonder if they found everybody, I had two friends that went missing at sea once, couple of Scots blokes."

"Really" replied Carter. "That's not good is it?"

As they boarded the plane and took their seats, Carter looked around and confirmed to himself that McFadden and Campbell were indeed missing. Sticky took his seat and smiled as he noticed Pony was sat next to the same blonde he had seen him talking to earlier. The flight back was uneventful and with no thoughts of missions or killings on his mind, Sticky managed to get some sleep. He was jolted awake as the plane touched down and braked hard before turning off the runway and taxiing to a halt. As each person left the aircraft, they either headed for the car parks and their journey home, or as with the six men of UN12, they headed for their barracks with the intention of collecting their personal items and heading off on leave. Sticky was gathering his things together when Carter and Pony entered. "So what do you make of that?" asked Carter. "Perhaps they stayed on board for the trip to Glasgow," cut in Pony. "No doubt they did" replied Sticky, "But the question is why? And, what is it that McGreggor has still not told us? For now I'm going to enjoy my few days off, but if I don't get answers when we get to Glasgow I'm quitting this and going back to my unit."

CHAPTER EIGHTEEN

"I don't care if you're called Hamilton or fucking Hamlet" ranted Penney, "you don't tell me how I run an investigation or who I can and can't interview."

"I'm afraid that on this occasion I do," replied Hamilton in a smug manner. "I think you'd better check with the Chief Constable, he has a document on his desk signed by the Attorney General that forbids you from approaching Johnson." The Inspector grabbed his phone and rang the chief, after a five-minute rant and with the Chief offering the occasional platitude, Penney calmed down. "Look Paul," said the Chief, "we're effectively banned from directly interviewing Johnson or his staff or going near his premises. Having seen the list you had earlier I'm sure strings are being pulled and debts being paid. Now that hasn't stopped you before Paul and I don't think it should now, but you'll need to go at it from a different angle. Nobody's going to commit a cold blooded murder in my city and be protected by drug taking bent politicians." The Inspector put the phone down and looked at Hamilton. "For now I'm going to hold off" he said, "but I promise you one thing, the guys who committed the murders are going down and if that means bringing down you and the bent bastards that pull your strings, then that's what I'll do." The smug smile vanished from Hamilton's face and he turned and walked out of the office.

Charlie had sat quietly throughout the confrontation and as Hamilton left he turned to the inspector and said, "Bloody hell guv that's a new one, can they really do that?" "Looks like they have," came the reply, "but the Chief's not happy, I can tell you that we're going to need to be a bit clever and I'm going to need to think about this, but it's Friday and my weekend off so I'm going fishing, I suggest you see how they're getting on with the investigation into Courtney's company structure and I'll see you Monday morning." Charlie knew that fishing relaxed the Inspector and if past experiences were anything to go by, he would be in on Monday all guns blazing so after wishing him a good weekend Charlie left and went down to the financial investigation department.

The following day saw the boat, Sticky and Pony had transferred the cannabis to, tied up alongside a deep water harbour wall on the west coast of Scotland having its cargo unloaded into jeeps, under the watchful eye of armed guards. Once unloaded, the jeeps made their way through the double gates and up towards the laboratory. As this ship was preparing to leave, less than a mile away another ship, was heading in carrying the heroin previously recovered from Afghanistan. Mac was there to meet this one and as soon as it docked, he leapt aboard and went straight up to the bridge. After greeting the captain and confirming everything was in order, he handed the captain a large envelope of money to pay off the crew. The UN group having been dropped off en-route. A lorry came through the double gates to the dock and reversed up alongside the ship. Watched by Mac and the captain from the bridge, the crew transferred the bags of heroin in less than fifteen minutes. The ship was scheduled to arrive at the Johnson Marine docks in Glasgow, so after saying his goodbyes, Mac left and climbed into the passenger side of the lorry. The driver then passed through the outer gate and once closed the lorry was checked, then the inner gate opened, the driver then took a route up past the main house before turning onto a narrower road that led down through the woods to the scientists' accommodation and main laboratory. Several men dressed in long white coats were waiting for them and took only ten minutes to unload the bags into four wheeled hand trolleys and push them into the laboratory.

Mac got out of the truck and followed them in. This part of the lab was just a goods inward area and contained racks of containers marked with the names of many chemicals and symbols marking them as poisonous flammable etc.: These bags were taken straight through to the next area where they were to be prepared before going into the chemical manufacturing plant. This was divided from the rest of the building by a large triple glazed wall and a sterilization air lock. The workers entered the first part where they stripped naked placed their belongings in lockers and then passed through a metal and chemical detector unit before going to other lockers and dressing in their chemical protection suits. Further along was another glass wall enclosed sterilization lock, this was protected by a retina identification unit, and only selected staff were allowed to enter. At the far end was the dispatch area, where finished items passed by conveyor from the manufacturing plant for packaging and distribution. Mac stood for a while watching the twenty or so men the other side of the glass, who were working on the automated lines producing various tablets and bottles of medicines. To the right were new lines especially prepared for the three types of drugs shortly to be processed, already two men had started to process the cannabis. Not long now he thought to himself. The crackle of his radio, brought him back to the present, and on answering it he was informed the shipment from Mexico was scheduled for arrival in just over thirty minutes. He acknowledged the call and went back out to the truck and ordered the driver back to the docks.

By the time they had driven back, and passed through the security gates, the dock was empty. The driver was ordered to pull up on the quay facing out to sea. Some ten minutes later the yacht came into view. It was sporting a completely different name from the one it wore while anchored off Mexico. Its powerful engines having propelled it across the Atlantic in a little over five days. Mac was pleased to see this vessel as it was actually Johnson's own yacht and had been used for this trip against his advice. Some forty minutes later it was alongside and the containers had been unloaded and were now in the truck heading towards the lab. As they passed the front of the main house Mac had the driver stop and he got out. The driver then continued on as Mac strode up the front steps and into the house. As usual, Johnson was in the library, Mac knocked the door, and again without waiting for a reply walked straight in. Johnson was sitting at his desk and was staring at his computer screen while scribbling notes on a pad in front of him. "Everything has arrived and by now is safely in the lab" announced Mac. "Excellent", Johnson replied without taking his eyes off the computer, "I think you should ring our friend and arrange delivery. I will check myself later and run some tests, but I'm certain it will all be ready for delivery by first thing tomorrow morning." Mac acknowledged that he understood and agreed to make the call from his office and pass on the details later.

Having made his way to the top of the house Mac entered his own office come sleeping quarters and found Karl waiting for him. "All Ok?" Karl asked "Yeah" came the reply "I'm just going to ring now and hopefully arrange delivery." Rogers's old mobile was on charge on Mac's desk. Noting it was reading fully charged, he unplugged it and dialled the stored number. It rang several times before it was answered. "I'm just confirming that all your goods have been safely imported and its quality checked" said Mac, "I would like a delivery address."

"I see," the now familiar voice replied, "when do you wish to deliver?"

"Tomorrow if possible," replied Mac, "I don't really want them hanging around."

"Very well, I will text you the address and postcode which will be in North London, I'll have someone there to meet you to double check quality."

"Fine" replied Mac, "but if it's North London make it around six in the evening, we have a long trip."

"Actually seven to seven thirty would be more suitable for us, although its Sunday it will still be a little quieter then. Should everything be satisfactory you'll need to text me the account details for transfer of funds."

"It will be and I will." Mac replied before shutting off the call. "Looks like we have a bit of a drive tomorrow Karl" Mac joked. "Make sure you're up early and suitably equipped."

At precisely six thirty the following morning, Mac and Karl passed out of the main security gates, driving a plain white Ford van loaded with boxes containing the three different drugs with a street value of over seventy million and a lot more once the dealers had cut them by adding various powders and chemicals. Initially they made slow progress along the 'B' and 'A' roads that led from Johnson's estate, so it was already past nine before they reached the outskirts of Glasgow, and a further forty minutes before they finally picked up the M74 and managed to pick up and maintain a reasonable speed. Travelling close to eighty miles an hour they started to eat up the miles but the undulating road slowed them on the uphill sections some of which were fairly steep. Eventually the M74 gave way to the A74M and there were more dual rather than three lane sections. At around twelve they pulled into a services, topped up with diesel, had something to eat and took a toilet break. Then after changing over drivers, they were back on the road by one and heading down the M6. They followed this all the way to the outskirts of Birmingham where the volume of traffic slowed the pace to around forty. Once clear of this they continued on the M6 eventually joining the M1 and headed towards London. They had been lucky in not coming across any accidents or major hold ups although the M1 was now proving to be a series of sprints, between sections of slow moving traffic. It was past five in the afternoon when they pulled off into another services. While Karl went to get some drinks and snacks, Mac set-up a portable satellite navigation device, mounting it by rubber suction to the windscreen. He then entered the postcode he had received by text and pressed go. After a few seconds, the device connected to the GPS signal and the screen lit up showing their position and the slip road back to the M1. Karl returned and after taking an eager swig of coke and devouring a chocolate bar, Mac resumed driving and they headed back onto the M1. As they approached Edgware, the device told them to take the next exit from the motorway, and then the third exit at the roundabout. This they did followed by a left at some traffic lights and a second right three hundred yards along. A few seconds later, the device announced. "You have arrived at your destination."

It was five minutes past seven when they pulled up and they appeared to be at the back entrance to some old brick built factory buildings. A few yards along was a large roller door and Karl nudged Mac and gestured towards it as it started to open. When it was about five feet from the ground, a man ducked under it and stepped out into the road. Both men instantly recognised him as the one who had tried to follow them on the tube. He waved them forward and indicated they should drive in. Mac started the engine and drove slightly past the entrance, then, with the door now fully open he reversed in. Immediately the door started closing again. Instinctively they both placed their hands by their shoulder holsters more as a self-reassuring gesture than to actually draw the weapons. "Haven't I seen you before?" Karl said as he stepped from the van. There was no answer just a scowl from the man that brought a smile to Mac's face. Two other men approached, one of which was dressed in a smart blue suit, and a white open necked shirt. He had a tanned appearance, short neatly cut black hair and his fingers sported several gold rings. The other was an older man who was wearing a white coat and was pushing a small trolley on top of which was an array of testing equipment. "Not going to trust us then?" quipped Mac "Not in this game" came the reply. "That's fair enough" said Mac as he unlocked the rear doors and climbed up into the van. "What do you want first?" he asked. "Cocaine." Mac opened one of the boxes. "From the top, bottom or middle?" he asked, "Middle", "You're a man of many words," joked Mac as he reached in and pulled out a kilo bag of powder from the middle of the box. The man took a sample, ran some tests and nodded, "Hundred percent." He said addressing the man to his left. "We promised you no rubbish," cut in Karl and that's what we deliver. The second man jumped into the van, opened another box and removed another pack "Test this"; he said throwing it to the chemist. It was duly tested and came up with the same result. The whole process was repeated with the heroin and the cannabis. "It seems you're as good as your word," the suited man said as he took out a phone and sent a pre written text.

A minute later the phone bleeped indicating a returned text. He read it and announced, "The funds have been transferred." Then calling to the man from the tube, he said, "Help these guys unload this gear."

"Just a minute", said Mac reaching for his own phone. A few seconds later a text came through confirming receipt of the money. "Ok" he said, "now you can unload." "Not going to trust us then?" called the suited man. "Not in this game" came the reply. With the van unloaded, the roller door was re-opened and Karl and Mac drove out and headed into London. By the time they had dropped off the van and made their way to the London apartment, it was gone eleven and both of them were exhausted. After they had had a quick shower and a coffee it was past midnight so they made their way to their rooms, and were asleep as soon as their heads touched the pillows. Back in Scotland, Johnson was enjoying a whiskey and wondering how long it would be before the first fatalities would be reported, he guessed a week but had underestimated the speed with which drugs are distributed. His answer would come in less the forty-eight hours.

CHAPTER NINETEEN

About seven the following morning, Charlie was walking into the police canteen. As he lived on his own, it was easier and cheaper to turn up for work early, have a good breakfast and have no cooking or washing up to worry about. He selected his breakfast, added a black coffee and paid, before looking for a table. As he made his way to one he spotted by the window, he was surprised to see Dr Stuart sat at one of the other tables, drinking a coffee and reading a large file. "Mind if I join you" he asked. "No not at all Charlie, take a seat."

"I've never seen you in here before Doctor" replied Charlie. "Oh I do use it a lot, but mostly these days it seems to be in the middle of the night, what about you?"

"Its easy meals for me Doctor, I live alone so it saves on shopping and washing up," smiled Charlie. "Really" came the reply, "I always thought of you as the sort of man that's settled, and married with two point four children." Charlie laughed. "Never understood the point four of a child, knowing my luck I'd get the dirty bit, I never seem to have found time for a wife and no one I've met has ever been happy with the sort of hours I keep and the number of times I have to cancel dates, how about you Doctor, are you married?"

"Nobody will have me either," she replied. "That I can't believe" said Charlie, "you're beautiful, smart. Intelligent, I'd have thought they'd be queuing up, I'd love to meet a woman like you." As soon as he'd said it, Charlie cursed at himself. The Doctor blushed and said. "That's sweet of you Charlie, but I think like you I'm wedded to the job."

Quickly changing the subject, Charlie asked, "Did you ever send that sample to Johnson?"

"Yes I did, he was not an easy man to speak to but agreed to try and analyse it, I had a preliminary report yesterday, which said they had developed a similar chemical that is inert and almost undetectable in substance, but when mixed with certain other elements it can act similar to strychnine causing almost instant death, but his lab had not been able to separate it for full spectrum analysis."

"Wow" replied Charlie, "It would be a bit of a blow if the chemical that killed his daughter was one developed in his own laboratory."

"My thoughts exactly" replied the Doctor looking at her watch, she added, "sorry Charlie I've a meeting in ten minutes so I've got to go, I'll let you know if I get anything else."

"Thanks" he replied, politely standing as she got up to leave. She went to walk away and then turned and said, "Charlie, when we're not in a formal mode its Lucy, 'doctor' is so boring." Charlie smiled as he watched her walk away, then returned to his seat and finished what was now a fairly cold breakfast.

Later, Charlie was sat at his desk and going through a report he had received from the financial investigation unit when Chief inspector Penney walked into the office. "Morning guv, had a good weekend,"

"Not really" came the reply, "Even the bloody fishing couldn't calm me down regarding Hamilton, we're going to have to go at him from the bottom up."

"Well we might have something", replied Charlie, "looking at these reports on Courtney and his business interests, it seems he's very clever at not paying tax, he has front companies in Switzerland, Cuba, Dominican Republic, The Philippines and a dozen others. It seems that they all lose money as it's moved from one to another. However one company in the Dominican Republic has funds transferred in from an account they have not been able to attach to any of his other companies."

"The Dominican Republic" repeated Penney, "Isn't that where Avatar is registered?"

"International Avatar Imports" replied Charlie, "the parent company, still that's hell of a coincidence, the finance guys are using their contacts to do a tax audit on Avatar both here and in the Dominican Republic."

"Let's hope they give us something quickly," said Penney "it's frustrating that we know who at least one of the killers is, we're pretty sure we know who ordered Osborne's death and is probably the main drug boss in London and we still don't have anything concrete to work on."

"I've had one idea" said Charlie, "I was talking to Doctor Stuart this morning and she's been in contact with Johnson regarding the makeup of the drug that killed Mercedes. It seems they produce something similar at his laboratory, so perhaps she could take a trip up to see him to look at his findings and I could tag along as her driver and assistant."

Penney thought for a moment before saying, "It might be worth a look around but unless we can talk directly to his security chief, I don't see we'll gain much besides, did he see you when he identified the body?"

"No I was interviewing the housekeeper Ms Trent."

"That maybe" replied Penney, "but I don't think it's worth the risk at the moment, although it might be worth talking to the doctor and having a look at his companies." "AJ Associates," said Charlie. "That's him is it? No doubt he runs the same tax dodges as Courtney, see what companies he controls." While talking, Penney was rifling through papers on his desk, suddenly one caught his eye and he started reading. It was about the person filing the stolen van report. It was a Lloyd Collins manager of Avatar Imports and it turned out that although it was registered at a convenience address, they had a distribution depot in North London. "Bugger!" exclaimed Penney, "someone must have dropped this in over the weekend, drop that for now Charlie, we need to go on a little trip."

Picking up their normal unmarked car from the pool, Charlie and the Inspector were soon heading out into the London traffic heading through Victoria Street, Grosvenor, and eventually Park Lane before winding their way over the A40 and joining the A41, the North circular and eventually the M1 leaving to join the A505 Dunstable road. According to the navigation system it was thirty-seven miles and would take one hour seventeen minutes. It was closer to two hours before they were advised they had arrived at their destination. They were in an industrial estate and the building they wanted was a modern glass and metal unit built next to a brick built factory, which appeared to be from the fifties and not currently in use. There was no mistaking that they were in the right place, as a large blue and white sign over the entrance proclaimed 'Avatar Imports'. The two men parked the car and walked into reception "I would like to see Mr Collins" said Penney. "I'm afraid he's busy at the moment," the receptionist replied. "So are we", said Penney flashing his warrant card, "please advise him I would like to see him now." The girl got on the phone and a couple of minutes later a man appeared from the door to her right. "Sorry gentlemen," he said, "please come through to my office." They followed him in, Penney noting that the office was very basic, a desk, a couple of chairs, some filing cabinets a calendar and a couple of pictures of trucks on the wall. It had the appearance of one of the waiting rooms usually associated with 'quick fit' tyre establishments. By comparison, Collins appeared the typical spiv with his black suit, white shirt and tie and several gold rings on his fingers.

They all sat down and then Collins asked, "So what can I do for you?"

"It's about the van you reported stolen" said Penney. "I didn't expect that to be investigated by a Detective Chief inspector," said Collins. "I expected a beat bobby." "Normally you would," continued Penney, "but the circumstances in which it was found and the method in which it was reported stolen means I need to ask you a few questions."

"You have it then," said Collins, "that's good news."

"Maybe" Penney replied "but we have reason to believe it was in the place we found it, at least two days prior to you reporting it stolen, can you explain that?" Collins shifted uneasily in his chair, before replying. "Yes, my car was in for a service and that van was only used for odd local deliveries so I took it home and then my wife and I went to France for a few days, it was our wedding anniversary so I treated her to a couple of days in Paris. When we got back I found the van had gone so reported it stolen, it could have been missing for three or four days at the most."

"You can confirm that can you?" asked Charlie. "If I need to," came the reply, "what's the point of these questions?" Inspector Penney lent forward stared straight at Collins and said. "Are you sure you don't know?" Again Collins looked uncomfortable. "You see Mr Collins, the van was found in an industrial unit rented by a known drug dealer, your van contained traces of cocaine, some of which appeared to have been there for some time and it was reported stolen the day after the drug dealer was murdered, now wouldn't you think that would make us a little curious?" Charlie noted a little sweat appear on Collins's brow and how he nervously ran his finger around the inside of his collar. "I assure you Inspector, I know nothing of a murder or of cocaine, in fact I'm shocked that you would think I did," he spluttered. "I don't think I accused you of knowing anything about it," said Penney. "I was just informing you of the facts and of why we're curious, by the way what is it you import here?"

"Shit, really" Collins replied adding, "you know the tatty gifts you get at seaside resorts or different attractions, come through and I'll show you."

Collins appeared relieved that they agreed, as it shifted the focus from the questions. Getting up, the three men went through a door at the rear of the office and into a large open warehouse space. There were several racks of boxes, marked with the names of various suppliers. There was less than either Charlie or the inspector had expected, a fact the inspector mentioned. Collins was quick to reply that the stuff never made money sat on shelves and was turned around as soon as possible after delivery, the next of which was expected in a couple of days. He opened one box and showed it to be full of toy guardsmen, which were destined for London gift shops, in another was little plates with 'Brighton' printed below pictures of the pier. Charlie accidentally kicked an empty box and on picking it up, he noted the lining. There were a few more empty boxes which he quietly noted were of the same construction. "What do you know about International Avatar Imports?" asked Penney. "It's our head office" replied Collins, "although I doubt if it's much more than a few people working out of a small office."

"Why's that? Asked Charlie. Collins shrugged and replied, "It's in the Dominican Republic and just a way of avoiding tax as far as I can see. Pity we can't register overseas and avoid tax but that's only for the ones with money, not foot soldiers like us eh! Inspector." Penney didn't reply but changed the subject. "Where do you live, or should I say where was the van parked, when it was stolen?" Collins was taken by surprise with the sudden return to questions. "Holland Park", he blurted Charlie and the Inspector both looked at one another. "Do you know an Andrew Rogers or Roger Andrews, sometimes known as Ginger?" Collins hesitated appearing to think, then shaking his head, replied. "No, that's no one I've heard of." It was clear to both of the others that he knew very well who Ginger was. "Well thank you for your time Mr Collins I will let you know when the van can be collected but it might be a few days yet and depending on the results of some tests, we may need to speak to you again." With that both Charlie and the inspector went back to their car.

"He's a lying smarmy bastard Charlie", said Penney. "I've got a good mind to get a search and forensics team in there just for the hell of it."

"I think you might come up trumps and all," replied Charlie, "several of the empty boxes were lined with panels of foil sandwiched foam the two layers of foil probably prevent X-rays but is more likely to be there to protect the contents from sniffer dogs." The inspector raised an eyebrow and looking at Charlie said. "My, my, we may make a detective of you yet Charlie. Make a note, when we get back, I want to know all there is about our Mr Collins, where he lives, is he married and if so what's the date of his wedding anniversary, what his financial state is regarding income and savings, I have a feeling Mr Collins has a lot to hide and with a bit of pressure he might just crack."

"Clear you didn't take to him much guv," replied Charlie, "think you're right though he's very nervous and it could be he had stuff there he didn't want us to see." Had they driven around to the back of the unused factory next to Avatar, they would have seen a large roller door that Mac and Karl had driven through the night before, and Collins was already in there ensuring the last of the deliveries were moved out as soon as possible.

With traffic build up from an earlier accident, it took over two hours and was late in the afternoon before Charlie and the Inspector got back to their office. After a few phone calls to different departments, Charlie was happy the Inspector's questions would mostly be answered by the next morning. A couple of messages had been left on the Inspectors phone, which he started to deal with. One was from Albert Johnson demanding to know when his daughter's body would be released. "I think we may be able to get you up to Scotland after all Charlie, that's if you don't mind accompanying a body. Said Penney, "we'll work on that tomorrow." Little did he know that tomorrow would become a day from hell.

CHAPTER TWENTY

Having acquired a hire car, Sticky drove back to his home; his stomach was churning as he turned into the estate. He had found that driving up to the empty house had got harder every time, leading to his bouts of heavy drinking before he could face going home. Eventually Sally's parents had suggested that for his own good he should move, rightly stating that he would never get away from the memories the house carried. They had found him a two bed roomed flat and along with his own parents had moved his stuff while he had been away. They had dealt with all sally's and Peter's clothes as well as Peter's toys. At Sticky's insistence, they had boxed and left personal items for him to decide what he would take with him. So it was with a sick feeling that he put the key in the door and entered.

Although the carpets and curtains remained in place, the living come dining room was completely empty as was the kitchen. The place had been spotlessly cleaned and he could see through the patio doors that the rear garden was also tidy and the grass neatly mowed. Upstairs he found the bathroom and bedrooms were also cleaned to the same standard, although in the middle of the main bedroom was a lidded cardboard box. He picked it up and decided to take it down to the kitchen where he could go through it on the worktop.

THE THISTLEDOWN CONNECTION

Placing it down, and with his heart racing, he removed the lid. The top of the box contained all of Sally's jewellery, including her watches, perfume and makeup items. He decided to keep everything except the makeup, which he removed from the box. He took the top off the perfume and sniffed at it. To his surprise it was different to the smell he conjured up in his bed at night, so he put the top back on and placed it to one side. Reaching into the box he pulled out some photo albums, and as he did so something fell to the floor. Placing the albums to one side, he bent down and picked the fallen item up to find he was holding a small eight-inch long teddy bear. It had a thin pink body with yellow ears, yellow hands and yellow feet, across its chest it had 'Get Well' printed in black. Peter had taken it everywhere. The pent up emotion he had been suppressing suddenly hit him like a wave, flopping his back against the wall he slid down into a sitting position, holding the teddy to his face and allowing the tears to stream from his eyes.

"Michael" a woman's voice suddenly cut into his thoughts. "Are you ok?" Sticky looked up to see it was his neighbour and Sally's best friend Jean stood in the kitchen doorway. He wiped his eyes and nodded then showed her the Teddy. "I gave him that," she said, adding "when he had his tonsils out."

"I remember," replied Sticky "after that he wouldn't go to bed without it, I wanted him to be buried with it, but we couldn't find it, I thought it was lost in the accident." "Where was it?" asked Jean "In that box" Sticky replied. Jean looked puzzled. "I helped your dad pack that and I don't remember seeing it." Sticky looked at the teddy then replied. "In that case I think someone wanted me to have it." Jean stepped forward and holding his hand helped him to his feet. Placing everything back in the box, Sticky replaced the lid and took the box out to the car. He then locked the house thanked Jean for being such a good friend to Sally and himself and then without looking back got in the car and drove off.

His new home was a top floor flat in a newly built four-story block and was positioned next to the river on the opposite side of the city to his old house. The lower floor of the block contained all the garages and allocated parking spaces. After parking the car and taking the box from the boot, he took the lift up to the flat. On entering, he was met with the smell of 'newness' only associated with fresh paint and carpets. He was thankful that the families had set everything up for him. The kitchen was equipped and stocked. The television and satellite system was installed and the lounge suite neatly placed. The main bedroom was en-suite and the bed was made and all his clothes hung in the wardrobes. The second bedroom had a double bed but little else other than a number of unpacked boxes. From the lounge there was a patio door that led to a small balcony where he could sit and watch the activity on the river. He made a mental note that he owed the family big time and vowed to treat them to a holiday because while he had been wrapped up in his own grief, he had given little thought to how much both sets of parents were hurting.

After making himself something to eat, Sticky settled into an armchair and started to watch the TV. To his surprise an item on the news showed him and Pony lowering Samantha Houghton on to the cruise ship. They went on to show her at the hospital, where she was apparently making a good recovery, although her face showed signs of several small cuts and there was obvious bruising by her left cheek and ear, Sticky was struck by her bright eyes and obvious attractive features. Her eyes dulled a bit and she was forced to hold back the tears as she spoke of the loss of her father. She stated that there was definitely, no arms or ammunition being carried on her father's yacht. As he would never allow it. She went on to describe the moment of the explosion, stating that she was sunbathing on the upper deck when the whole yacht seemed to lift out of the water catapulting her into the air and convincing her that the blast had come from under the hull. She then added that she would like to thank her rescuers and hoped to be able to do so personally in the near future. It then went back to the news reader who stated that a mystery surrounded those rescuers after someone had noted the helicopters registration did not appear on the civil aviation authority's website nor had the Johnson Marine ship been seen since the incident. A government spokesman was quoted as saying that Johnson Marine had applied to register four such aircraft and put the omission down to paperwork delays, something denied by a CAA employee, who stated that he felt that was not a plausible explanation. A spokesman stated that no-one from Johnson Marine was available for comment leading to several conspiracy theories The story annoyed Sticky, as along with a few other things that had worried him lately, this looked like another slip up by Hamilton and McGreggor. Something he intended having out face to face at their next meeting. Later that night, without the movement of the ship and the constant throb of the engines, and despite his anger at McGreggor, Sticky went off to sleep far quicker than he expected.

CHAPTER TWENTYONE

It was just before six in the morning when Charlie's phone rang, still half asleep he answered it to hear the Inspectors voice cut through the fogginess of his brain. "Get out of your pit and come and pick me up," he said with an urgency Charlie had not heard for some time, "we have a major problem unfolding" he added, "so don't hang about." Realising this must be serious, Charlie sprang out of bed, went to the bathroom and freshened himself up with a quick splash of water to his face and brush of his teeth. He didn't bothered to shave and was quickly dressed. He grabbed his keys warrant card and wallet, then ran down to the underground parking area and jumped in the car. As he drove out to join the main street, he switched on the radio and picked up the breaking news of the death of a cabinet minister. So that's the panic, he thought, but by the time he swung into the inspectors street, reports of other deaths were coming in. The inspector was waiting on the pavement and had grabbed the door and was getting into the car almost before Charlie had come to a stop. "Head for the embankment" he barked as he fiddled to fasten his seat belt. "Parliament end, it seems a cabinet minister has been found dead in a flat there."

"I heard on the way here, two bodies apparently", replied Charlie, "but since then there have been reports of several more who were at the same party."

"Shit", replied the Inspector "I'd not heard that, been stood around waiting for you."

It was still early and although the traffic was comparatively light, Charlie still had to use the lights and sirens on several occasions. Remarkably it was still only twenty to seven when they pulled up amongst the patrol cars, ambulances and press photographers already at the scene. Showing their warrant cards to the constable guarding the door, they entered and were directed up to a second floor flat. It was clear a party had been held there quite recently; a table contained the remains of a buffet style meal including several empty bottles, and partially drunk glasses of wine. One of the bodies was slumped against a settee, while the other was lying face down on the floor in front of an upturned coffee table, remnants of a white powder were evident on the face of the table, and there was also a small quantity on the wooden floor, along with a small plastic packet. "Certainly looks as if they were sharing a little coke" said Charlie. "Yes, but don't go sniffing it, looking at the speed at which these two died I don't want you to join them."

"Ah, Charlie he does care," said Dr Stuart, as she entered the room, both men turned towards her, Charlie smiled and noted that she managed to look elegant even at this time of the morning. While the Inspector blushed slightly then said.

"Of course I care there's too much paperwork to fill in if he croaks it." The Dr laughed then turning to Charlie said. "Got up in a rush this morning then." Charlie rubbed his chin and replied "Yeah no time to shave."

"It's not that," said the doctor "I was thinking more of the odd shoes you have on." Charlie looked down and realised he was wearing two black shoes but with completely different styles.

The Inspector just shook his head and then asked Dr Stuart if she noted anything in particular about the bodies. "Their faces" she replied "almost exactly like the look on young Mercedes their deaths must have been sudden and rapid."

"My God" exclaimed Charlie, "you're right but looking at the position of the bodies, I would say they were able to move away from the table after snorting, so it wasn't quite that instant."

"Fair point" cut in the Inspector, "if it had been instant, the second guy was unlikely to have taken his go." Doctor Stuart stood back and then said "That would make sense as when the stuff is snorted up the nose it would take a little while to be absorbed through the membrane, but when it was, it was fatal pretty quickly. I don't think I can do much else here I will need the bodies back at the lab. I'll take some samples then let you have results as soon as I can, my guess is the results will be similar to the Johnson case and we still don't know exactly what that was." Whilst she was talking, the Inspector had taken a phone call and was a little pale when he finally hung up. "I think we're going to be having a busy day, there have already been over thirty deaths reported around London including Mr Justice Isles who has just been found in the Judges quarters around the corner from here." A forensic, scenes of crime team, had just arrived so the inspector requested a report as soon as possible and leaving them to it, he and Charlie left.

Parliament Square housed the Middlesex Crown Court complex and nearby quarters were provided for the circuit judges, as they were required to sit on various cases. It took just ten minutes for the two men to drive around and then enter the Judges' quarters. The judge's body was lying on its back on the floor, the now familiar look of horror on his face. A dressing table, to the side of the room, contained the evidence of drug use. The remnants of one used line was next to a second unused line of cocaine, lying near that was a credit card presumably used for squaring up the lines. "Someone else was here Charlie, he's on his back, and he didn't fall that way, someone has rolled him over."

"Mrs C Grouse" replied Charlie; Penney looked quizzical, "It's the name on this credit card," added Charlie. "Mrs" said the Inspector, "that might explain why she didn't hang about, try to get the card details, without touching it, then get a trace and get her brought in, she might be the best lead we've got." Then leaving a constable to guard the site and wait for the scenes of crime unit, they decided to get back to the office and coordinate the reports from there. On the way back, they were informed that the death toll had reached the seventies and the Inspector had been summoned to the Chief Constables office.

As soon as they arrived at Scotland Yard, the Inspector went straight to the Chiefs office, while Charlie stopped and asked one of the junior detectives to find an address for the credit card holder and then have Mrs Grouse brought in for interview. On returning to his office, he retrieved the electric razor, toothbrush and toothpaste, kept in his drawer for such occasions, then he went to one of the rest rooms, shaved, cleaned his teeth, had another wash and combed his hair. There was nothing he could do about his shoes but at least he felt more comfortable, just a little hungry and thirsty. On arriving back at the office, a quick phone call put that right and a few minutes later a coffee and a couple of sandwiches were brought in. In the meantime he had searched through the files on his desk and found the paper he was looking for. He then phoned Dave and asked him to bring in anything else he had from Rogers's computer file. By the time Dave arrived he had pulled a list of names of that days victims from the main database. "I've managed to track about fifteen more names," said Dave but it's proving difficult." Charlie handed him a list. "Any of these look familiar?" he asked. Dave studied it then replied, "At least twenty of them, one is that judge and I think one of the others is a politician, where did this list come from?"

"That" replied Charlie, "Is the list of the people found dead from contaminated drugs this morning."

"Holy shit" exclaimed Dave, "then whoever took over Rogers's clients is bumping them off wholesale."

"Seems like it" replied Charlie "but is it deliberate or are they being used unwittingly in some mass murder."

When Penney arrived at the Chief Constables office, several Chief Inspectors from other divisions were already there as was Superintendent Reynolds. "Ah Paul, take a seat" said the Chief then continued, "You don't need me to tell you the position we're in is unprecedented. Everyone is screaming for answers and quite frankly we don't have any. I've just been told that the death toll has exceeded a hundred and is still rising, reports are also coming in from nearly every force in the South East of similar deaths, but not yet on the scale we're seeing in London. Whoever is behind this has just become the largest mass murderer in British history. So tell me that you have something." One by one each Chief Inspector reported on the situation in their respective areas. All the deaths were linked to either cocaine or heroin. All showed signs of almost instant death and all reported looks of frozen horror on the victim's faces. The majority were relatively unknown, but several were public figures one of the latest being a female BRIT award singer. "I have to address a press conference shortly and then I have to go on to meet the Cobra committee, what do I tell them?" Superintendent Reynolds replied, "The truth: there's a contaminated batch of cocaine and heroin on the streets that could have been distributed anywhere, advise people to destroy any illegal drugs in their possession."

"What about distribution?" asked the Chief. "It clearly started in London," replied Reynolds "but if normal patterns are followed, all the major cities will start reporting mass deaths in the next forty eight to seventy two hours."

"Do we know for sure it's just those two drugs?" asked Penney, "how do we know it won't turn up in other so called recreational drugs?"

There was a knock and the Chief Constables PA entered. "Sorry to disturb you," she said, "but this has just come up from Inspector Penny's office." She handed the Chief a note and he read it and then looking at Penny, he said, "Sorry Paul but this has to come out now." Turning to the others he said. "During the investigation into the death of Mercedes Johnson, Paul's team recovered some encrypted computer files. These contained a list of clients held by an Andrew Rogers which included the names of public figures as well as politicians and at least one High Court Judge. As this was very sensitive and, as you can imagine, would have provided the press with a field day, I asked Paul to sit on it until we could pinpoint the supplier. Now it would seem that most of the names on that list are also on today's list of victims." There was a stunned silence in the room as all eyes turned to Penney. "Have you got any further with your investigation Paul?" asked the Chief. Penney replied. "Well we're pretty sure the drugs are being supplied through a company called Avatar Imports and Rogers appeared to be sending money through their 'Head Office' in the Dominican Republic, which in turn sent money to a numbered account. That is well protected, but we're pretty sure we know who's controlling it, but so far I don't have any tangible evidence"

"So you have a name," enquired the Chief. "With respect gentlemen", said Penny as he wrote 'Sir James Courtney' on a piece of paper and handed it to the Chief. The Chief's eyes widened "You sure Paul?"

"One hundred percent," came the reply. "What do you need?"

"I want Hamilton off my back and I want to speak to Johnson."

"You got it" replied the Chief. "If this name is correct then it's no wonder we're being blocked." Just then a message popped up on the Chief's computer. "Oh shit" he exclaimed, "any of you heard of a rapper called Papa Mere." Several nodded; one Inspector said he was appearing at the O2 that evening. "I don't think he is," replied the Chief. "He and three of his band have just been found dead in his hotel room and they were smoking cannabis. This is getting out of hand. Paul get the details then you'd better get over there."

Penney rushed back into his office, taking Charlie by surprise. "We've got the go ahead for interviewing Johnson, I take it Dave spotted the tie up with the two lists of names."

"No" replied Charlie, "I did, then I asked him to bring in the names of any others he'd identified and found a few more."

"Oh well done, did we ever get those reports on AJ Associates?"

"Yes," replied Charlie "he has fingers in numerous companies everything including shipping, shipyards, oil refineries, drug manufacture and chemical research centres but nothing that ties him in with Courtney though."

"Ok then get Dave to find out everything he can about Johnson himself, I want everything even what toothpaste he uses, but tell him to be as discrete as possible as I'm sure Hamilton will be watching. Come to think of it find out all you can about him as well. For now we have to go and see John Greenhall he has a dead rapper and his band on his hands and they were smoking weed."

The two men left and drove over to the hotel. Stepping from the car, Penney waved away some of the press that approached him and quickly mounted the steps. John Greenhall met them in the foyer. "Making a habit of this John," said Penney.

"I'm trying not to" came the reply, "I've already had that from some of the press guys but I gather we are not the only ones today."

"Over a hundred and thirty so far, I gather," said Charlie "My worry is that some murder will be slipped in amongst this lot and we'll miss it."

"Never" replied Penney "Dr Stuart and her team would spot it if we didn't." The men had arrived at the hotel room; all four victims were either slumped in chairs or on the bed. All had the now familiar look on their faces and the remnants of reefers were either still in their hands or on the floor. "Ok John" Penney said "It's obviously drug related there's nothing we can do here. I'd like a list of other guests and can you check your CCTV to see if anyone else visited them. They're American but they must have bought the cannabis here. We'll get a team in as soon as we can but we're a bit stretched today."

"I bet you are," replied Greenhall. "I'll keep it locked and make sure no-one touches anything."

"The speed with which they all appear to have died I'd be afraid to touch anything" cut in Charlie.

"Who found them?" asked Penney. "Their tour manager, he has one of the adjoining rooms."

"I'd like to speak to him if he's about" replied Penney. Greenhall left and a short time later arrived with a balding overweight man dressed in an expensive looking suit, which appeared even more slept in than Penney's. He was red faced and sweating heavily. "This is Chief Inspector Penney" said Greenhall. "And you are?" asked Penney. "I'm Pinky Reed", the man spluttered, adding "I think this is all my fault, I bought the cannabis for them."

"I see," said Penney "and where did you buy it?"

"In a little wine bar just off Piccadilly Circus" Pinky replied before breaking down and uncontrollably sobbing. "Look" said Penney. "I'm sure you have a lot of people to speak to and arrangements to make and frankly we're too busy to arrest you for supply but do you remember the name of the wine bar and roughly when you bought it."

"It was called 'Your Vine' Pinky sobbed "around eleven last night."

"Thank you" said Penney "Do you think you're up to formally identifying the bodies for us?" Pinky nodded. Greenhall reopened the door and Charlie took Pinky in. He immediately started crying again. Then pointing to one of the bodies he sobbed "That's Papa, Mere", then one by one he pointed out Phil Martin, Rick Martin and Chris Horton. "Thank you", said Penney "we'll get the bodies out of here and arrange for their release as soon as possible. In the meantime if you can think of anything else or have any questions I'm sure Mr Greenhall here will help." Pinky thanked them and went back to his room. "Pinky," said Penney "this day just gets worse. Charlie get the local boys to look in on the wine bar and see if they have any CCTV footage from about ten pm until midnight. If they have, tell them to get it to over to Reynolds's team, they may be able to identify someone."

Henry Dawes had searched the hotels CCTV coverage and reported that other than the four deceased, no one had entered or left the room prior to their bodies being found. Penney thanked him and then he and Charlie left. As they stepped out of the hotel, they were immediately tackled by members of the waiting press. In answer to a question, Penney confirmed that a body had been found and identified as the rapper known as Papa Mere and the three other deceased were identified as members of his band. He added that the deaths appeared to be linked to the smoking of cannabis but until forensic enquiries were completed he could not categorically confirm that to be the case. Then ignoring other questions he and Charlie got into their car and headed back to the office.

CHAPTER TWENTY-TWO

Sticky woke at around seven thirty feeling refreshed. Having not planned anything for the day, he made a couple of pieces of toast and a coffee then turned on the TV news to see if there'd been any further developments regarding the previous night's reports. This morning though the news was dominated by the reports of the deaths of a Government Cabinet Minister and his male partner. There was speculation that their deaths were linked to the use of cocaine. During the report there was a news flash reporting the death of a leading High Court Judge, who had also been at a function attended by the Cabinet Minister the night before. Over the next half hour, reported deaths rapidly mounted; they included a well-known TV star, a radio presenter two famous soap stars and numerous members of the public. By nine thirty the number of reported deaths in London had reached over seventy and reports of deaths had started to come in from places such as Brighton, Oxford and Cambridge. Sticky was fascinated watching the whole thing unfold, it was like a mass epidemic and with no obvious cause being attributed to the deaths, and it was also worrying and causing a certain amount of panic amongst the public. The Prime Minister was hastily thrust in front of the cameras and announced that he was devastated at the loss of his minister and offered condolences to the families of all the deceased. He then announced that he had called a meeting of the Governments Cobra committee and that there would be a further statement as soon as more facts were known, he asked for calm and stated that although he was not prepared to be more specific at this time he could reassure the public the deaths were not caused by a virus or other infectious disease.

Sticky spent the rest of the morning moving items around and unpacking boxes of books and arranging them, as he wanted. He kept the TV on in the background, and at one o'clock, it was reported that the Chief Constable, of the Metropolitan police, had called a press conference. On it, he announced that the death toll had reached one hundred and thirty eight, and that all the deaths were related to the use of contaminated drugs, mostly cocaine and heroin. However he had received a report that an American rap star, who was due to appear in the O2 arena that evening, was found dead in his hotel room along with three of his band. It was believed all the men had been smoking cannabis. Therefore he advised anyone holding illegal drugs to destroy them and seek medical help, as at this time it appeared a large quantity of various drugs had been deliberately contaminated and launched onto the market. There was no way of knowing what was contaminated and what wasn't.

The news report then went over to the hotel where the rap star was found and several reporters started questioning the hotel's security manager. He confirmed the deaths and was doing his best to persuade them that he was in no position to make a statement and that their questions would be better addressed to the police. "Mr Greenhall," one of the reporters called, "Wasn't it here that Mercedes Johnson was found dead due to a drug overdose just a few weeks ago?"

"Yes" came the reply, "but I assure you they're unconnected."

"Still" said the reporter, "not good for the hotels image is it?"

"No", Greenhall replied "but this time there are a dozen other hotels reporting deaths, we act whenever we can or when we expect there may be a problem, but in reality there is little we can do to control what guests get up to in their rooms." With that he turned and walked away. Sticky had been watching intently, 'John Greenhall', he muttered to himself, 'well bugger me I wondered what happened to you.' He had met Greenhall on his first posting and although John had out ranked him at the time, the two of them got on well from the start. While deployed in Iraq after the second conflict, they occasionally came under fire from some of the dissident groups or got caught in the conflict between the Sunni or Shia factions. It was while patrolling a market in a Sunni controlled area, that a car bomb exploded taking off most of Greenhall's lower leg. It was Sticky who had flown the helicopter taking him and some other wounded back to the military hospital. He heard that he was then flown back to the UK, but had not seen or heard of him since another thing that caught his attention was the name Mercedes Johnson. That name Johnson seemed to be popping up a little too often for his liking. The other fact that had not gone unnoticed was the deaths were listed as being linked to cannabis, heroin and cocaine. All the drugs recovered by the different UN groups. It could just be a coincidence but his gut feeling told him otherwise.

With no logical reason other than an unsettled feeling and the possibility of renewing an old friendship, Sticky set off across the city hoping he would catch John Greenhall still on duty. It was raining as his taxi pulled up outside the hotel, which had reduced the number of reporters hanging around. The taxi driver spoke about the news of the deaths and added that the number of incidents being reported had now fallen. After paying the fare, Sticky hurried up the steps of the hotel, to be met by Danny Herbert who asked him if he had a reservation, explaining that following the earlier incident they were restricting access to the hotel. Sticky replied that he fully understood and that he had in fact come to see John Greenhall and asked that John be informed he was here. Danny radioed through and after an initial confusion over his name, which was rapidly resolved when 'Michael' was replaced by Sticky, Greenhall told Danny to show him to his office.

John met them at the office door grabbing Stickys hand and embracing him in a man hug. "God it's good to see you Sticky", he said adding "you've picked a bloody bad day to turn up though, I'm having a few problems at the moment."

"I know that's why I'm here" Sticky replied. "Can we talk somewhere?" Greenhall nodded to Danny who immediately took the hint and left. John ushered Sticky into his office and closed the door. "What's on your mind Mike?" Sticky sat down and looked straight at John, knowing that if there was one person he could confide in it was him "I've got a gut feeling that there's a conspiracy going on and I don't know how far up it goes. Pony and I have been involved in deniable operations as part of MI6 and several international groups designated UN1 to UN12." Over the next fifteen minutes he went on to tell Greenhall about the death of his wife and son and the operations in the Med as well as those in Afghanistan and America and how everything seemed to link back to Johnson. When he finished speaking it felt as though a big weight had been lifted. Greenhall had sat listening in silence, and then he said. "Jesus, Sticky I'm sorry to hear about your family, but are you telling me that chopper landing the girl on the ship was you and Pony."

"Yeah after blowing the ship out from under her."

"And blowing her father to bits" added Greenhall. "No he survived," said Sticky "well until our rescue boat got to him and broke his neck."

"That wouldn't be the first time that sort of thing has happened" Replied John, "But it does seem a bit of a coincidence that the deaths today are all linked to the same drugs that you know were recovered."

"Not just recovered" replied Sticky "but I know that at least two of them were loaded on ships belonging to Johnson and I would bet the American cocaine was also shipped on one of his boats. Then there's McGreggor, Campbell, McFadden and Hamilton all Scots as is Johnson."

"There's one more to add to that," replied John "our old friend Mac McCrae now heads up Johnson's security team. Look Mike, I see your problem, who do you go to?"

"Exactly" Sticky replied, "These guys will have contacts everywhere, and I don't have the facilities to prove anything. I wouldn't be able to get within a mile of Johnson. Even if I spoke out I think I would quickly become the victim of a nasty accident"

"Yes I'm sure you would, Penney already believes that Mac has bumped off the dealer that gave Johnson's daughter the drugs"

"Penney?" queried Sticky "Yes Chief Inspector Penney, he's the one in charge of the Mercedes Johnson case. You know what Mike that's your man he's got a brilliant mind and is incorruptible, which is why he's still only a Chief Inspector. Had he been one to turn a blind eye he would be deputy Chief Constable by now, he was here earlier. I can try and set up a meeting."

"OK" replied Sticky but either here or somewhere away from official premises."

CHAPTER TWENTY-THREE

Back at the yard, Charlie and the Inspector entered interview room four. Sat at the centrally placed table was a woman in her early fifties; she wore a business style black suit of skirt and jacket over a white blouse and whilst she couldn't be described as fat, neither could she be described as thin. Her hair was worn in a short style and immaculately brushed, the makeup she wore was little but expertly applied to emphasize her features and dark brown eyes. She didn't stand when the two men entered but sat with her hands clasped on the table nervously twisting her wedding ring. "Mrs Grouse" said Penney, "thank you for coming in"

"I didn't think I was given a choice" came the reply. Penney ignored that and continued, "The sergeant here will read you your rights and we'll tape the interview" Charlie switched on the tape and said "Recording of interview with Mrs Christine Grouse at 14.30 hours", after noting those present and completing the standard legal requirements. The Inspector enquired, "You're Clerk of the Court employed at Middlesex Crown Court is that correct."

"Yes."

"So how long have you and Mr Justice Isles been having an affair?"

"I resent that implication" Mrs Grouse angrily replied. "That may be" said Penney, "but perhaps you wouldn't mind answering the question and telling us what happened last night."

"I was at home last night watching TV" she replied, sitting back in the chair with a smug look on her face. Penney pulled a sealed bag from a folder and dropped it on the table the credit card could be clearly seen through the plastic. Penney banged the table making the woman jump. "That shit might work with your husband" he shouted but we have several hundred bodies out there and the total is rising, now unless you want me to charge you with supplying contaminated drugs, murder by administration of drugs and leaving the scene of a crime, then I suggest you drop the attitude and start talking."

"We've not had an affair" she replied. "David, Mr Isles, has been making advances to me for some time and until last night I never responded. He invited me to a party with several MP's and business people; I was curious and stupidly agreed to go. There was plenty of Champagne and wine, as I don't normally drink I got tipsy quite early." She paused wiping a tear from her eye. Carry on said Penney. "David noticed and said he thought I needed a black coffee, he asked me to walk him around to his quarters and said he would make me one."

"Sounds like he had more than coffee on his mind" cut in Charlie. "I'm sure he did" she replied "but I assure you I didn't. When we got to his quarters he tried to kiss me." Again she paused and wiped a tear and then continued.

"Suddenly he said let's make this more interesting, Sir James has just given me a little present. Then he asked if I had a card, I didn't know why but I gave him that one." Charlie cut in, "For the purpose of the tape, Mrs Grouse indicated the credit card recovered from Mr Justice Isle's apartment." Adding "carry on please."

"I was shocked when he took out the packet and tipped the powder on to the table. He then used the card to divide it into lines. I've never touched drugs and told him I wasn't going to start now. He laughed and said it's easy you'll enjoy it, then he bent down. I couldn't see exactly what he did but he suddenly stiffened, took one step back and crashed face first on to the floor. I bent down and turned him over." Then she started to cry. "His face, I can't get it out of my mind. I just panicked and ran." Penney said; "He said Sir James had given him a present, are you sure of that."

"Positive"

"Do you know who he meant by Sir James."

"Sir James Courtney I suppose", she replied, "he was at the party" Charlie and the Inspector exchanged glances a smile spreading across Penney's face. "Thank you" said Penney, adding, "Interview terminated at 14.45. We'll get the tape transposed into a statement for you to sign, then you'll be bailed pending the Crown Prosecution Service decision on prosecution." Getting a custody officer to take over, the two men headed back to their office. "A direct link to Courtney" said Charlie. "Yes" Penney replied "but not enough. Any lawyer could argue that he was talking about any number of presents."

"But if he was there then he could be linked to the other two deaths," said Charlie. "I bet his distribution network is connected to all the deaths, but it puts up the question, did he know the drug was contaminated?"

"I don't think he did," Penney replied, "he's a clever operator I don't think he would knowingly kill several guests at a party he attended. Also these deaths are going to badly hit the drug scene as prices will plummet until this settles, at best it could cost him millions, and at worst it could start a turf war amongst the suppliers. It's a, lose, lose situation for him." Charlie thought for a moment then replied. "Perhaps we should be looking at who's going to be a winner."

Back at the office, Charlie checked the latest reports. The reported deaths had slowed, but in London and the Home Counties, the total had now gone over four hundred. Doctors and hospitals were being inundated with addicts seeking help with withdrawal symptoms. Divisions were also reporting large falls in the number of street crimes, burglary and theft reports. "If this carries on, then the winners will be insurance companies and alternative drug firms," said Charlie. The phone rang and Penney spoke on it for a few minutes, then after putting it down, he said. "That was Reynolds, they have good information that batches of the contaminated drug have been sent to Liverpool, Manchester, Glasgow and Edinburgh, so we can expect a lot more deaths tonight. Apparently they also raided Avatar, he's sending up a report. Several people were arrested at the warehouse."

"I hope one of them was Collins," said Charlie.

Dave knocked and entered the office. "Sorry to interrupt guv" he said, "but I have the report on Johnson you asked for."

"Thanks" said Penney "anything of particular interest."

"Well in his early thirties he had established a reputation as a research chemist, then he started taking over other companies, particularly in shipping, shipyards and chemical research. The odd thing is that all the companies suffered some kind of disaster shortly before he took them over which badly affected the share price and suddenly Johnson came to the rescue. The more I read though, the more it struck me that he could have created the disasters in the first place. It's all in the report." With that he handed the report to Penney and left. Penney swung back in his chair and placed his feet on the desk then started reading. After a while he said. "Apparently he met Mercedes mother, a Julia McGreggor at university. They married and had Mercedes but when she was eight Julia was killed in a car crash. It was after that that he started expanding his business. All the research units he took over he closed and moved to his estate in Scotland where he now has the largest research and drug-manufacturing centre in Europe. By all accounts it's a fortress with access either by sea with his own dock or by a single road entrance, although it does have an airstrip and helipad."

"Perhaps I was right then, if he is manufacturing methadone or other counter addictive drugs, he could stand to make a fortune if these deaths continue" said Charlie. "It would have to be on a larger scale or even worldwide to be of any long time significance" replied Penney. "That's what bothers me," said Charlie, "what if this is just a trial run?"

"Then whatever the motive, it has either been a total success or a disastrous failure. I have a feeling that when the party scene kicks in tonight, the death toll is going to significantly increase" remarked Penney.

"What puzzles me is if Johnson is behind this, then why was the first victim we know off his own daughter?" asked Charlie. "Don't forget, we know she was not the intended victim but was in the wrong place with the wrong person at the wrong time. As far as we know Osborne was the target and was given the drug by Rogers on the orders of Courtney. But it went disastrously wrong. Now we know its Courtney's network that has been targeted, it could be payback to destroy Courtney. Whatever the motive we have to bring it to an end and hope to God your trial run theory is wrong."

"So do I, "replied Charlie. "Why don't we bring in Courtney and at least let him know we know he is involved. It might pressure him into a mistake, especially if we let slip that we know Johnson is the source." The Inspectors phone rang "Oh hi John" he said, "What's up?" After listening for a while he said "Are you sure of this?" After being told the affirmative he turned to Charlie and asked. "Can we have a meet at your place, you need to change shoes." Taken by surprise but knowing the request would not have come without good reason. Charlie agreed and after giving John the address and agreeing to meet in an hour. Penney put the phone down.

CHAPTER TWENTY-FOUR

Albert Johnson switched off the TV and turned to Mac who was sat opposite his desk. "Well" he said, "I didn't expect it to get on the streets that quickly, it seems Sir James Courtney now has at least four hundred less customers. I'm surprised by some of the names though."

"I'm not," replied Mac "I'm just surprised there are not more personalities amongst them." Johnson allowed himself a brief smile, then continued. "My sources tell me that the police raided Avatar this morning and have Courtney's number one in custody. It seems they suspect Sir James of being the money and brains behind the scenes, but they have been unable to crack the financial trail leading directly to him. Thanks to our little transaction the other night, I have all the information they need. I think it's time to give the police a little help."

"Won't that put the money he paid us at risk?" asked Mac. "Yes and No" came the reply, "we will lose the money but that was going to fund Hamilton anyway. The way this has been set up it will look as though the whole incident was organised by MI6." "So how do we explain our ships and the fact Hamilton arranged for the drugs to be landed here, you can guarantee McGreggor and Hamilton will implicate you should they go down?"

"Well" Johnson smiled. "I have prepared a statement should I be asked, how does this sound. At the request of my brother in law in a matter he described as being of National Security, I loaned him the use of four of my ships, I even helped convert one for covert use. I am mortified to learn what part they played in these tragic deaths." "Very convincing," replied Mac. "But that still leaves the drugs and the contamination."

"Jim Connelly, is dealing with that as we speak. As you know I own the old SMM Chemical works down the coast. All the equipment and quantities of chemical have been moved there, along with the only two chemists that worked on it. Muller and Johansen. Once everything is set up, Jim will ensure that neither of them will be in a position to talk, although I would have preferred to kill Muller myself." Mac raised an eyebrow, taken by surprise by the venom in that remark. "That's what you've got us for" he said, adding "you obviously want Sir James out of the way too, wouldn't it have been easier for us to have taken care of that as well?"

"No" snapped Johnson, there was an evil look in his eye that Mac had rarely seen before. He leant forward on his desk and looking directly at Mac he said. "Let me put you fully in the picture my friend, had you killed Courtney, the papers would have called it an evil deed and praised his achievements for Queen and Country. Our friend Muller developed a drug registered as JCM1403 which attacked the nervous system causing muscle retraction; we had several uses in mind. However, animal tests were a disaster so I cancelled the program. Muller was convinced he could make it work and behind my back he passed it on to an old university friend. Somehow from there and thanks to Courtney's arrogance it was used to kill Mercedes." He paused for a while reliving the moment in the hotel room. Then he continued. "So I don't want to kill Courtney. I want to destroy him. He will be exposed as a drug mastermind and the biggest mass murderer in British history. The fool even provided the cocaine that killed the Judge and Government Minister. As for Muller, Jim has instructions to ensure Muller tries his own drug first hand."

"Anything I need to do in the meantime?" asked Mac. "Yes there is, I have invited the pathologist that worked on Mercedes, a Dr Stuart, to visit us here tomorrow. I intend to give her the answers she's looking for and I want to ensure the police start looking for Muller. She will fly up to Glasgow in the morning, make arrangements for the chopper to bring her on up. You'd better make sure the labs can bear inspection. The changes to the Minerva have been completed in Glasgow, so tomorrow McGreggor will bring his team back together and motor up the coast, Hamilton will be with him. I've suggested they use their chopper and come on ahead. On the way I'll ask them to check out the old SMM Works. That'll put them nicely at the scene. When they leave here though, ensure the chopper doesn't make it back to their ship. It will be much neater if neither of them are around to answer questions."

Down at the old SMM chemical works, Muller stood back and surveyed the room. He was a thin beaky nosed man who wore heavy rimmed glasses. For several hours they had been cleaning the labs and ensuring everything was in place. Johansen, Connelly and himself had brought in all the chemicals and other equipment from the van and set it up. When Johnson closed SMM six months earlier everything had been mothballed so all the major equipment was still in place and in full working order. "What do you think Jan?" he said to Johansen. "Looks good to me" came the reply, "we can easily produce more batches here. It will be nice to work away from everyone and the constant surveillance."

"Yes" replied Muller "Then when things settle Johnson said I will be able to get on with my tests as despite everything Jan I know this drug can work."

"I wouldn't trust Johnson" Jan replied "Be very careful my friend." Jim called Johansen out saying he needed some help. Johansen left and as soon as they were out of Muller's sight, Jim grabbed him from behind, placing his hand over his mouth to stifle any shouts and at the same time jabbing a needle into his arm. Johansen's eyes widened with surprise then his body went limp and Jim allowed him to fall to the floor. Turning he walked back to the lab, "Where's Jan?" asked Muller. "At the van but I think he's sleeping on the job" Jim replied before placing his arm on Muller's shoulder and saying "listen carefully my friend, you think Johnson has moved you here to safely carry on your experiments, but no, he has moved you here to put all the blame for the recent

THE THISTLEDOWN CONNECTION

deaths clearly onto your shoulders and to remove any evidence he was involved."

"That cannot be true" Muller spluttered, "He promised me full support."

"Yes but he told me to ensure it looked as if you killed Johansen then committed suicide."

"What have you done to Jan?" Muller screamed. "Just this came the reply." Muller saw the syringe in Jim's hand and tried to turn and run. Jim was too fast and too strong for him and quickly subdued him and plunged the syringe into his arm saying, "Remember my words Stefan." With a look of total shock Muller was able to blurt out "Why?" before slumping to the floor. "I guess the boss wanted you to stop talking", said Jim "Frankly you've got on my tits for the last few hours." After a while, Jim drove out of the SMM complex, secured the gates and headed back to report that both men had been silenced.

CHAPTER TWENTY-FIVE

When they pulled up outside of Charlie's apartment, Sticky and Greenhall were already waiting. While Charlie went to park the car in the underground facility, Penney took the two men through to a lift and then up to the apartment. After a few moments Charlie joined them and they entered into his living room. This contained a three-piece white leather suite, a wall mounted Television, a glass topped coffee table and an oak sideboard. For a bachelor pad it was extremely tidy, reflecting Charlie's normal fastidious appearance. They all took a seat, but declined the offer of a drink. Greenhall introduced Sticky as Captain Wood of the army air corps. Adding that he was the pilot who flew him out after he was caught in the explosion. Penney nodded and asked where that fitted in with the current situation. Sticky recounted how he had flown Apache gunships in Afghanistan and how after the death of his wife and son he was seconded to special ops.

"You don't know this but he has been on TV a lot lately" cut in John, "The incident in the Med" said Sticky. "I was flying the helicopter that landed Ms Houghton on the cruise ship, it was us that blew up Houghton's yacht in the first place." Charlie looked stunned. "Our government sanctioned that?" he asked. Sticky nodded, "Al-Qaeda's main money man was on board, and Houghton had directly processed several arms deals with the Taliban."

"None of this helps regarding today's death toll "Penney snapped. "I'm coming to that", replied Sticky. "Before the Houghton incident, we took out a terrorist said to be heading for Britain to organise a Kenyan style shopping centre massacre. We sank him and his boat off North Africa, but not before recovering four hundred and fifty kilograms of cannabis resin and transferring it to a Johnson Marine boat."

"Now I'm interested," said Penney "you're certain it was one of Johnson's boats?" "Positive," came the reply. "McGreggor told us it was to be used for research and conversion to drugs to aid Multiple Sclerosis."

"McGreggor?" queried Charlie. "Yes Lieutenant Colonel McGreggor, he's head of our unit."

"He's also Johnson's brother in law" said Penney. "Damn," exclaimed Sticky, "I knew things weren't right. McGreggor also told us another unit had recovered two hundred and fifty kilos of heroin in Afghanistan and shipped it via Iran, while a third group had recovered four hundred kilos of cocaine in Mexico. When I heard the news this morning, it all seemed too much of a coincidence."

"Why not come direct to us?" asked Charlie. "I'm not sure how well I'm being monitored, but I was certain Hamilton would know as soon as I went direct." "Hamilton", said Penney "this gets better, where does he fit in?"

"As far as I know, there are twelve deniable ops groups and Hamilton controls the whole thing."

"In that case you were right to be cautious Captain, Hamilton has been blocking my investigation and placed an injunction denying us access to Johnson. He's also prevented us from access to the files on Johnson's head of security."

"Mac McCrae" said Sticky, "I can tell you he's clever and a quick thinker, he's also pretty fearless under fire. There's more than one soldier that owes him their lives including John, it would be a shame if he's sold out."

"It looks to us that he has, we can implicate him in at least two murders." The unmistakeable 'Bing bong' of a text message being received cut into the conversation. Sticky reached for his phone and read it. "I've been summoned back to the ship early, she's due to sail at seven thirty in the morning so I will need to make a move." Penney thanked him then asked if there was anyone else in his unit that was likely to feel like him. "Two possibly three" he replied but added "that there were a couple of Scots that would need watching." As he and John were leaving he asked if there was a mobile number he could contact them on. Charlie gave him his. Sticky entered it into his phone as Charles noting the first three numbers then reversing the next four and doing the same with the last four. "I have a pay as you go phone at home, I think there's twenty quid credit on it, and I will use that one to contact you if I have anything" he said.

John then drove Sticky home where he collected the little he needed, although he had to search the still unpacked boxes to find the phone. John waited and then drove him to Euston station. After saying their goodbyes, Sticky just had time to buy an evening paper before catching the seven thirty pm train. If all went well this was due in at Glasgow five minutes past midnight. Which would give him time to get to the docks and hopefully get some sleep before they sailed.

As soon as they got back to the yard, Inspector Penney was called to the Chief Constable's office for another briefing. Charlie was making his way to his office when he met Dr Stuart. "I've been looking for you," she said. "Johnson has asked me up to Scotland tomorrow. I'm flying up to Glasgow from London City airport, from there, he has arranged to fly me on to his lab. Apparently he has identified the source of the drug and wants to brief me on the details."

"We're pretty sure he's the source of the drug" replied Charlie. "The Chief has given us permission to speak to him, can you advise him you will be travelling with an assistant, I will come with you."

"Carrying my school books eh Charlie?" Charlie blushed. "More like watching your back and getting a look around without having to go through the Scottish authorities" came the reply. "Ok consider yourself my assistant but the flight is at eight thirty in the morning don't be late. Oh and wear sensible shoes."

Penney was the third to arrive in the Chief's office, but was quickly followed by the others, the last of whom was Reynolds. "Gentlemen" the chief started. "Nationally, the death toll is now over seven hundred. We have called in help from the forces as well as undertakers from all over the South East. There are TV and radio reports asking people to report any deaths via a hot line number we have set up, undertakers will be dispatched to collect the bodies as soon as practical. It's pointless sending in SOC teams, even if we had them, all the victims seem to be habitual drug users. We have also advised people not to touch any unused drugs or drug equipment with their bare hands, but to use gloves and package everything in sealed bags, for collection or to be dropped at no questions asked centres the government and councils are currently getting set up. We are keen to see they are not disposed of in any other manner."

"Not that that will stop some throwing it in the nearest bin" cut in one of the Inspectors. Turning to Reynolds the Chief asked. "What scale of deaths could we be looking at?" Reynolds replied, "As far as we know we are looking at three drugs, coke, heroin and cannabis. Samples we've collected appear to show the coke is probably Columbian, the heroin more than likely originated in Afghanistan and the cannabis."

"Is Moroccan black" cut in Penney. Reynolds looked surprised, "that fits in with information I received this afternoon." Penney added. Reynolds continued, "Following information we received from Paul, we raided Avatar

Imports and found large quantities of cheap gifts, some of which were packed in boxes designed to beat sniffer dogs, some of the broken items showed traces of cocaine. Then one of our guys found a door-linking Avatar to the disused warehouse next door, well it seems it was not as disused as we thought. We found equipment for cutting and packaging numerous drugs, as well as a van that contained packages ready for dispatch. We arrested the manager a guy called Collins. Under the threat of mass murder charges, he confessed to managing that part of the operation. He informed us that a batch of drugs were delivered by a new supplier two nights ago. He described the driver as a Scot of heavy build and having a military bearing. The other guy had blonde hair, was about six four and spoke with a slight foreign accent."

"That fits the description of the guys who killed Osborne and Rogers," said Penney "and as far as the Scot goes, we're sure he's Albert Johnson's head of security, an ex SAS officer called Mac McCrae."

"It seems to me" said the Chief, "that we know the name of the main supplier and money man, we know where and who contaminated the drugs and who delivered them to Avatar. Yet we're sitting with our hands up our backsides unable to pull any of them, but at least we've taken out the supplier stopping anymore getting on the streets."

"That doesn't help," replied Reynolds. "We didn't recover a lot from the warehouse and we don't know how much went onto the streets."

235

"I can help you there" chipped in Penney, "according to my informant there was four hundred and fifty kilograms of Moroccan, two hundred and fifty kilos of heroin and four hundred kilograms of cocaine."

"Jesus" exclaimed Reynolds. "It's said that the UK is currently becoming the coke capital of Europe, and in fact Scotland does have the highest use in Europe. Estimates say one in forty Scots are now using it. With the latest figures suggesting there are three hundred suppliers, three thousand middlemen and up to seventy thousand dealers. The stuff we recovered was cut with Levamisole, a worming agent for horses and cattle. It's known to rot the skin. In some other samples, it was clear the dealers had cut it again with Benzocaine a dental anaesthetic. In some cases its cut so much that the purity can be as low as five percent. Where the good stuff goes for one hundred and twenty pounds a gram, the cut stuff can go for as low as thirty-five pounds a gram. Each gram can produce ten lines, so four hundred kilograms would be four hundred thousand grams, producing up to four million lines and once cut that could be four times that. So, in answer to your question Chief. We could be looking at deaths in the millions and that's just the cocaine."

The Chief cut through the ensuing silence. "Let's stay realistic for a moment, most users will buy a gram or two, the first line they used would kill them so rather than four million we're back to less than four hundred thousand add in the cut factor and the publicity, then using Superintendent

Reynold's figures we may be looking at one million. But we have not seen anything like that yet, we are only just closing in on one thousand."

"Yes," replied Reynolds, "but Collins told us that batches have been sent to Liverpool, Manchester, Glasgow and Edinburgh. So we are likely to see another explosion of deaths in those cities tonight."

"Then we go on the offensive", said the Chief. "Our information seems to show the poisoned drugs were delivered sometime on Monday, as we started to see the first deaths Monday night and this morning. We make TV and radio appeals on every available channel telling dealers and users to ditch anything they've acquired since Sunday and everything that emanated from London. Then we pull every known dealer off the streets, in every force and every county. We'll need to use all available police and community officers and every custody suite we've got. I'll let slip to the press what we're doing and ensure there are television crews at some of the raids. If we can create enough panic for a few to ditch their stash, then that will be a few lives saved." Looking at Penney he continued, "I'm confident that the perpetrators will all be in custody in the next forty eight hours, but getting all the contaminated drugs off the streets will not be that easy." He then dismissed everyone to get on with their tasks, but asked Paul to stay behind.

Penney waited and when the room was clear, the Chief explained that Dr Stuart had been invited up to see Johnson and had asked if Charlie could go as her assistant. "I'm happy for him to go if you are," he said. "Gets us in without going through the Scottish system and alerting Johnson."

"Fine by me" replied Penney. The Chief looked straight at Penney and asked where the other information regarding the quantity of drugs had come from. Penney explained the meeting with Sticky and how Hamilton and McGreggor had fitted in. The Chief then handed Penney a printed sheet. "I got this through this afternoon, gives some bank details and money transfer actions that link Courtney directly to a major drug deal. Going by the dates and the delivery address being the Avatar warehouse, I'm sure it's the contaminated batch. Get Dave to confirm the details while I get you an arrest warrant for Courtney along with a search warrant for his home and offices."

CHAPTER TWENTY-SIX

There were very few empty seats available as Sticky made his way through the carriages, however he had purchased a first class ticket and as he entered this, section it was noticeably quieter with only six or so passengers spread throughout the compartment. He found himself a forward facing seat with a table and sat next to the window, placing his bag on the seat beside to him. Exactly on time, there was a jerk as the train started to move and the engine took up the slack in the carriages. It slowly built up speed to around thirty miles an hour, then remained at that level as it negotiated the myriad of points and lines leading from the station. Once clear, it built up speed again as it worked its way past the back of various London streets. From the window, Sticky noted that the further they went, the rows of older terraced houses, commercial buildings and warehouses, gave way to more modern properties and occasional green spaces. Even so it was an hour before fields and open spaces became a more regular sight.

Declining a meal offered by a steward, he opted instead for a coffee and muffin then he reached into his bag and took out the paper. Not surprisingly, the headline read

'OVER A THOUSAND DEAD IN CONTAMINATED DRUG HORROR'

It went on to say that although initially deaths occurred in London this had spread to other counties and there had even been reports of at least fifteen in France. The Governments Cobra committee had met and all medical facilities were on alert, temporary morgues had been set up and undertakers and coffins had been shipped in. London's Chief Constable had made a statement that the police were certain the illegal drugs had arrived in London only three days before, therefore he advised anyone that had obtained drugs in the last seventy two hours to destroy them immediately or place them in the special collection areas throughout the city. He confirmed that the drugs affected were cocaine, heroin and cannabis resin known as Moroccan Black. Information obtained after a raid on a London distributor, confirmed that some of the drugs had been sent to Manchester, Glasgow and Edinburgh therefore he advised anyone in those cities to avoid new purchases. He also believed that up to thirty percent of the contaminated batches had been ordered on the 'Dark Net' and were currently en-route via mail. So any new drugs obtained via the AIE website should be destroyed. If people took this action he believed the number of deaths could be contained. In the meantime the police nationally had taken a proactive stance and were currently in the process of detaining every known dealer throughout the country.

The steward interrupted his reading and delivered his coffee and muffin, Sticky thanked him and pushed the paper aside while he took a drink. At that moment, the train came to a stop and he noticed it was raining quite heavily. He idly watched as people alighted hurriedly pulling on jackets, pulling up hoods or trying to open umbrellas. Other passengers were rushing to get on and doing just the opposite. He allowed himself a smile as one woman's attempts to lower her umbrella resulted in her companion's hat being sent rolling along the platform. After a few moments, they were on the move again so he turned to removing the wrapper from the muffin when a familiar voice said "Mind if I sit here?" He looked up to see Carter who, not waiting for an answer, had thrown his bag onto the seat opposite and then sat down. Picking up the paper he said. "Bit of a shocking incident this, I wonder where the drugs originated from?"

"I was wondering that too," replied Sticky "I wouldn't be surprised if someone in the Government put them on the streets deliberately."

"Well it certainly seems to be reducing the number of addicts," replied Carter "but do you really think they could be capable of that?"

"After the few weeks I've just had I think they could be capable of anything" replied Sticky. Seeing someone opposite looking at them, Carter held out his hand "I'm

James by the way, where're you headed?" Sticky took his hand "Peter, I'm going to Glasgow."

"Me too" Carter replied, "be good to have some company" The other passenger then seemed to lose interest. Carter spotted the steward and ordered a coffee and a couple of sandwiches for himself and a second coffee for Sticky.

Leaning forward on the table and lowering his voice to a whisper, Carter then said, "What do you really think Sticky, it can't be a coincidence that the drugs affected are the same as those McGreggor told us about and the ones we recovered."

"Exactly" whispered Sticky "and I found out today that Johnson was married to McGreggor's sister."

"Talk about keeping it in the family," said Carter. "Campbell let slip that McGreggor is somehow related to Hamilton. We know that Johnson owns the docks and presumably the ships we've been using as well as the biggest chemical works in Europe. But family or not, why would someone in Hamilton's position get involved with this?"

"Do you remember reading about the death of the socialite, Mercedes Johnson?" replied Sticky,

"Yeah",

"Well she was Johnson's daughter and McGreggor's niece, could this be revenge on the drug industry?" Carter sat back and thought for a moment, finally saying. "I think it must go deeper than that. Hamilton is a shit but he's well up in MI6, I can't see him knowingly throwing everything away on something that could put him behind bars for life. I reckon we've all been stitched up here including McGreggor and Hamilton." "Maybe" replied Sticky "but I don't trust either of the bastards." The coffee's and sandwiches arrived and while they consumed them, Sticky related his contact with the police, John Greenhall and the information that Mac McRae was known to be connected to two murders and was acting as Johnson's head of security. Even though they were both in the SAS, Carter had heard of but never met Mac. Speaking in low tones had attracted the attention of the other passenger again, so they both sat back and started discussing the rain and the papers headlines as well as politics in general.

At exactly five past midnight, the train pulled into Glasgow Central station. The men got up, collected their bags and made a show of saying goodbye. They each left the carriage by separate doors. Sticky made his way through the station exiting into Gordon Street, where several cabs were waiting for fares. He noted Carter getting into the first in line. He hailed the next one and on entering asked for the BAE buildings on South Street. "Which end?" asked the driver, adding "It's a pretty long building"

"The dock entrance I think" replied Sticky "but to be sure follow the cab in front" The driver looked in the mirror and raised an eyebrow. "You know how long I've waited for someone to jump in and shout follow that cab, then you do it so politely, ruins the effect." Sticky laughed then settled back as the driver turned left into Hope Street before taking a right into Argyle Street. A large, almost plain green clad building on his left contrasted to the eight-storey glass window building to his right. The street was an eclectic mix of old and modern buildings ending with a large tower block before they passed under a flyover and continued on towards Clydeside where a domed flying saucer like building was well lit against the night sky. The cabbie continued on following the taillights of Carters cab, which was about twenty yards ahead. Eventually they entered South Street and shortly after, Sticky caught his first sight of the BAE buildings, which appeared to run for half a mile or so on his left. "See what you mean," said Sticky "bloody miles of them" Eventually Carters cab pulled up outside a glass entrance that had a large red and white sign declaring 'BAE SYSTEMS'. His own cab pulled up behind, Sticky paid and thanked the driver adding a, well received, five pound tip.

Both cabs drove away leaving the two men stood on the pavement. Lights were on illuminating the foyer, however there was no sign of any human activity. A light blinking on around twenty yards to the right of the main door caught their attention. At this point the building protruded out and the light had come on in a doorway. From this a uniformed man appeared and beckoned them over. As they approached him, he asked "Are you for the Minerva?" His Glasgow accent was so thick that Sticky wasn't sure what he had said but it was of little consequence as Carter replied "Yes." They followed the man in and after going through several corridors, they emerged back out of the building alongside a dock. The Minerva was tied up alongside and as they made their way towards the gangplank, Carter said. "She looks different somehow."

"I was thinking that," replied Sticky "could just be the colour, it looks green in this light." An unknown crewman welcomed them aboard and pointed out that Tea or coffee was available if they required it. Sticky declined saying he preferred to get his head down if he had to be up before seven. He asked if Pony was on board and was told that Mr Moor had arrived about an hour earlier. Thanking him and saying goodnight to Carter, he went directly to his cabin, threw his bag on the floor, quickly set the alarm, undressed and within thirty minutes was fast asleep.

CHAPTER TWENTY-SEVEN

Armed with the warrants, Chief Inspector Penney called a team together in a briefing room to outline where and what he wanted searched. Charlie had been relieved and had gone home to prepare for his flight up to Scotland in the morning. Penney would take Dave with him along with a team of four officers to question Courtney and search his home. Another Inspector would take a team of six to search his offices. "I don't expect to find drugs or paper lists of contacts and dealers" said Penney "Everything is probably electronic therefore don't overlook any electronic device, computers, memory sticks, discs even E readers bag and remove them all give, the IT crowd something to do other than play patience. Somewhere amongst that lot should be a key to all his dealings, but that doesn't mean you overlook any files or safes, be the most thorough you have ever been. I don't need to remind you what's at stake here." Turning to the other Inspector he said. "Keep me informed of anything significant." After that was acknowledged, he said. "Ok then let's get on with it."

The two convoys of cars headed out of Scotland Yard, one heading for Courtney's offices on the embankment, while the other containing Inspector Penney headed for Courtney's Chelsea Mansion. As they swung in through the open gates, the driver was forced to slam on the brakes and swerve to avoid a Bentley convertible, which was heading out. Both cars avoided the collision but the police car was left blocking the gates. As Penney stepped from the car, an irate Sir James Courtney shouted at him from the convertible. "Get that out of the way, this is private property and I have a plane to catch."

"Not tonight you don't Sir James" replied Penney, "I have a warrant here for your arrest and a further warrant to search your home, so please step from the car and come with me."

"Dammed if I will", came the reply, "that's bullshit, no one would sign a warrant for my arrest." Penney took the paper from his jacket. "Afraid they would and did, they say when the shit hits the fan you find out who your real friends are; at the moment sir I think you'll have a job to find any." Courtney looked furious and revved his car as if to ram Penney and the police car in his path. Then he switched off the engine and stepped from the car. "I don't know what you're expecting to find err"

"Chief Inspector Penney" Penney volunteered. "Then as I said Inspector I don't know what you expect to find, a cannabis plantation or drug fuelled orgy maybe." Then he turned and walked towards the house. Penney and two police officers followed him as Dave and the other officer manoeuvred the cars.

After entering a library or study which contained several well stocked book cases as well as a desk and computer,

Courtney turned to Penney and asked "So where do you want to start?"

"I'll start by formally arresting you on suspicion of supplying and dealing in Class 'A' drugs and in the supply of contaminated drugs leading to multiple deaths. You do not have to say anything. But it may harm your defence if you do not mention when questioned something which you later rely on in court. Anything you do say may be given in evidence." Courtney just shrugged then in a menacing tone, he said, "I hope you have some proof to back that up Inspector or heads are going to roll."

"I think it's your own head you should be worried about," replied Penney. "We have a witness statement that confirms you gave cocaine to Mr Justice Isles deceased and no doubt also provided the drugs that killed the minister and the other man at the party you attended."

"Pure speculation," Inspector "none of that would add up its circumstantial."

"Maybe" said Penney "but add that to the fact the drugs were delivered and distributed by your company Avatar and the fact we can prove you paid for them and I think it becomes a little more substantial."

"That's bullshit," replied Courtney, dismissively waving his arms. "You can't possibly connect me to any drug payments or this Avatar." Dave had entered the room and told the other officers to bag and remove the computer. Penney pointed to Dave and said. "For some time, Detective Constable Jones here has been tracking payment details we obtained from encrypted files on Rogers's laptop. He was very precise with his payments taken and the payments he made. These went through Avatar and Avatar's registered office in the Dominican Republic, which by the way, the local police informed me, is little more than a tin shed. From there the money disappeared into several front companies all of which traded through the same numbered account, the same account from which Rogers's salary was paid. Now we were sure you owned that account but just could not find the link." Courtney smiled "As I said you have nothing."

"Not until today" continued Penney, "then someone kindly provided us with the link, including delivery details, amount paid and the track on the account it was paid to. It seems the person that provided you with those drugs wanted to ensure he destroyed you completely."

Courtney's face was white with rage, "Who?" he demanded, "Who would want to destroy me?"

"Albert Johnson" replied Penney. "Johnson" spluttered Courtney, "the industrial chemist, Why? Why? I don't even know him."

"Your pride and arrogance, that's why." replied Penney. "That and the fact you killed his daughter Mercedes."

"I never killed that girl" Courtney blurted, desperation now replacing the previously smug attitude. "Not directly" agreed Penney, "but when you ordered Rogers to kill Osborne, the DJ who had upset your precious ego, you effectively ordered her death." Courtney leant against the wall, "I can't believe this, I can't believe this" he repeated "well I'm not going to prison for that." One of the officers who had been checking the bookcase found a safe and pointed it out to Penney. "Can you open that for us please?" he asked, Courtney hesitated then said, "I suppose if I don't you will get someone else who will." He then walked over stood in front of the safe and dialled in the combination, then before anyone could react, he quickly opened the door and reached inside. Just as quickly he withdrew his arm and swung around holding a semi-automatic pistol in his hand. "As I said Inspector, I'm not going to prison."

"That's not going to help," said Penney "Put it down." Courtney raised his arm and Penney lunged forward trying to knock the gun from his hand. Courtney was too quick and brought the butt of the pistol down onto Penney's head knocking him sideways where he crashed heavily into the desk breaking his collarbone in the process. DC Jones and the other officer went to rush forward. "Stay where you are." Courtney barked, "Apologise to the Inspector for me won't you," he added as he placed the pistol against his forehead and pulled the trigger.

As blood poured from the head wound of the unconscious Inspector. DC Jones could see there was nothing more he could do for Courtney so he used tissues to try and stem the flow of blood, while the other officer rang for an ambulance and additional backup. Within thirty minutes Penney was

THE THISTLEDOWN CONNECTION

on his way to hospital while a scenes of crime team dealt with Courtney's remains and Jones and the others continued to gather what little evidence they could. Several packets of Cocaine were found in the safe as well as documents that would eventually expose the whole of Courtney's drug dealing empire, leading to the downfall of many high-ranking politicians from all the main parties.

The ringing of the bedside phone brought Charlie awake, his immediate thought was that he'd overslept but the bedside clock read ten past five. He lifted the receiver to hear Dave's voice on the other end. "Sorry if I woke you Charlie," he said "But I thought I'd better speak to you before you heard it elsewhere."

"Why what's happened?" he replied. "We went to arrest Courtney and he pulled a gun, Penney tried to stop him but he clubbed him with the butt and then shot himself."

"Is Paul ok?" queried Charlie, unusually using the Inspector's first name. "Yes, he has four stitches in his head and concussion as well as a broken collar bone and cracked rib from where he fell against the desk, moods not to good either because they want to keep him in."

"I bet it's not," replied Charlie, "I'd better call off the Scotland trip and come in."

"No that's another reason I'm calling, Penney said make damn sure you go he wants this sorted."

"Ok, give him my regards I'll get back to you when we arrive, by the way have there been any overnight developments."

"About another hundred dead in London and reports of several deaths in Edinburgh and Glasgow. Overall though it looks like our campaign is working." Charlie thanked him, put the phone down and went for a shower. By the time he had shaved, put some items together and had a coffee; it was time to head for the City airport.

Rather than take his car, Charlie got a taxi, and arrived at the airport over an hour before the departure time. Walking into the small terminal, he looked around and not seeing Dr Stuart anywhere, he decided to check if she had already booked in, just as he started for the check in desk, a familiar voice said "Ready to carry my bags then Charlie." He spun around to see the Doctor smiling at him; she was wearing a black two-piece trouser suit and white blouse with her long blonde hair bought forward over her shoulder and reaching almost to her chest. She wore very little make up, but what she had on emphasised her features and striking blue eyes. "Well" she said, holding up her overnight bag. "Oh yes, sorry" replied Charlie realising he had been staring "I'm not used to such good looking company Doc." "Such a smoothie" came the reply "and I've told you before its Lucy away from the office." Charlie took the bag and booked them both in. Right on time at seven thirty, the plane took

252

off, climbing steeply away from the buildings of London before turning to start its fifty-minute flight to Glasgow.

On arrival, they were met at the bottom of the aircraft steps by a dispatcher who led them to a car that then drove across the airfield to a stand where a private jet was waiting. "I thought we were going on by helicopter," said Lucy. "Mr Johnson thought this would be a little more comfortable for you" came the reply, "it's also a little quicker." Within a few minutes they were settled in and offered a coffee while the pilot went through his checks and waited for take-off clearance. Twenty minutes later they taxied out and took off heading for Johnson's estate. The flight took slightly longer than Charlie had expected, with the jet flying out towards the coast before banking right over a large Island. "That's Arran," said Lucy "and ahead of us is Kintyre."

"You know Scotland then" replied Charlie. "I used to sail around here with my dad." She replied before going quiet, Charlie noting her eyes misting as she relived some memories. They flew on over Kintyre and headed across the sea. "So what's the island ahead?" asked Charlie. Lucy composed herself and looking out the window, replied "It's probably Jurra, we once sailed up the sound of Jurra to a little place called Craobh Haven only a little place but it had a lovely marina and I remember a little shop called the Giving Tree, always thought that was a great name. Just then the plane banked right again passing the Isle of Jurra on its left, finally another turn found them flying over a heavily wooded area and a small inlet where Charlie could see a motor yacht moored against a wooden jetty. Seconds later the aircraft touched down on Johnson's private runway. As they stepped from the aircraft, an open topped Jeep pulled up. The driver was wearing a blue uniform and was carrying a holstered pistol; he helped Lucy into the vehicle then jumped into the driver's seat letting Charlie to clamber into the back.

It was a short drive to the main house, but the driver continued past the main entrance before turning left down a small hill to where the chemical factory was located. A man was waiting on the front steps; he was wearing a smart suit, which looked a little odd on his large frame. Charlie's heart raced, as he instantly knew this was Johnson's head of security and the man who either killed or had a hand in killing both Osborne and Rogers. As if to confirm it, the man stepped forward and said, "Welcome to Thistledown, I'm Mac McCrae, head of security, Mr Johnson is waiting for you in the main office." Lucy shook his hand saying, "I'm Dr Stuart, and Charlie here is my assistant." Charlie nodded and reached for their bags avoiding having to shake hands. They were led through to a reception area, where they were checked in and given visitor passes, then McCrae led them down to Johnson's office. He knocked and without waiting for a reply opened the door and showed them in. "Ah Dr Stuart I presume" said Johnson without getting up from his desk, "rather an interesting business this, don't you think?" he added. "I wouldn't say interesting," replied Lucy. "Over one and a half thousand deaths and God knows how many more to come, I would say disastrous."

"Only for the people involved in the drugs scene and most of them are not a great loss", said Johnson then, smiling, he added "look at the benefits, I'm told the crime rate has fallen by sixty percent in two days, shows how much the two are linked." "That might be so replied Lucy but first I can't discriminate on worthiness a death is a death and I'm keen to find a way of stopping it."

"It seems Mr Johnson isn't too worried about that" cut in Charlie.

Johnson sat back in his chair and stared straight at Charlie, with a look that made him feel fairly uncomfortable. "I lost my daughter to a contaminated drug sir, so no I don't have much sympathy for drug users or those that profit from their sale. However I do have a great interest in chemicals, their manufacture and their makeup, so when one comes along that is virtually undetectable and can kill within seconds, then I'm very interested."

"So have you made any headway in identifying it?" asked Lucy. "Yes I'm afraid I have" came the reply. "I say afraid as it appears this chemical originated from here." Charlie went to speak, but Johnson held up his hand and said, "Let me explain, as a by-product of samples of nerve agent recovered from Iraq, one of our scientists called Muller isolated a drug we registered as JCM1403 or (NRC) nerve retraction compound. It attacked the nervous system causing muscle retraction. In diseases such as hypokinetic rigid syndrome (HRS) more commonly known as Parkinson's disease, many patients have little control over the motor senses resulting in rapid muscle movement. Sometimes quite destructive surgery takes place to alleviate the symptoms, it was thought that NRC could be refined to produce a similar reaction in the nerves and reduce the shake without the need for surgery."

"How far did you get with that?" asked Lucy. "Nowhere" came the reply, "it was all wishful thinking, and animal tests showed you couldn't direct it to specific muscles or nerves. In most cases it went straight to the heart which immediately contracted and stopped. As you have seen in the last few days it also affected the face muscles leaving human victims with a look of horror on their faces. If you're looking for an antidote doctor I'm afraid it acts too quickly for one to be of use, and so far we have found no way of neutralising it. The only solution I can offer you is to destroy any stocks."

"So how did it get from here out into the drug scene?" asked Charlie. "My guess is via Muller and his assistant Johansen, I pulled the plug on the project and all supplies were put into quarantine. Muller was convinced he could perfect it and, unknown to me, had smuggled some of the drug to an ex-university friend and was giving him instructions on performing various experiments. It seems his friend was in debt to drug dealers and to clear the debt was asked to provide something to deal with some pathetic DJ who had upset the wrong people. He thought it would be fun to try out the latest version of Muller's drug. Unfortunately Mercedes decided that was the night to experiment and agreed to share the drug with the DJ." Johnson's face clouded over as he added. "I knew what had killed her as soon as I saw Mercedes in that hotel room."

"Where's Muller now?" asked Charlie. "Both him and Johansen were gone by the time I got back."

"What about the drug?" asked Lucy. "As far as we can tell, all that was produced here is still here, but we don't know how much his friend produced. I heard the Police raided his place this morning and recovered some items as well as the man's body." And I bet I know who killed him thought Charlie, glancing at McCrae. "Let's hope they've got it all then" he said, adding. "Can we look around?" "Certainly came the reply, it will be my pleasure." Johnson asked McCrae to ensure lunch would be available in the main house in about forty-five minutes, and then they were shown to changing rooms where they changed into white boiler suits, head coverings, gloves and special shoes. They then went through the airlock and through to the main factory. Charlie was amazed at the size of the place although each section seemed to have no more than one or two people in attendance. Millions of tablets were flying through the different processes ending either in bottles or foil strips and boxes before being packaged in containers. And disappearing through rubber faced doors to the dispatch department. "Virtually completely automatic" said Johnson

"We only use people to sort the odd glitch and to restock the cardboard, paper and bottle machines."

"Impressive" said Lucy "but where does all the research take place?"

"Follow me" came the reply. They were taken to the lower part of the complex and entered a corridor, which had a large glass panelled wall between them and the workers the other side. In turn several sections appeared to be completely sealed units with their own airlock systems of entry.

They stood silently watching for a few minutes then Johnson said "Interestingly we are working on a drug that prevents the death of dopamine producing cells that should be a lot more effective against HRS."

"Individual labs all inside one lab," commented Lucy."

"Indeed," came the reply "several of those sections contain some nasty viruses and diseased cells, so as you see they are sealed and each has three different airlocks to get in, and a different three to leave. Personnel are showered, chemically cleaned and then showered again, so far we have had no leaks or nasty accidents."

"Except for Muller" replied Charlie. "Except for Muller indeed" snarled Johnson. "Over in the far corner we actually have a good supply of cocaine, heroin and cannabis, and no we don't supply it to dealers, although it could be profitable. All of it is used in the production of other drugs, while currently the cannabis is being used to try and develop a drug for MS sufferers that is producing promising results."

"So Muller would have not only had access to the drug but the same three drugs that are causing all the deaths at the moment" said Charlie. Johnson raised an eyebrow, "You talk more like a policeman than a scientist my friend, but you're right, yes he would and as I informed the police this morning, our latest batch of drugs, scheduled for delivery last week, have failed to arrive. But enough of this, let's get out of these damn suits and go for some lunch, I have one of the best cooks in Scotland." They got changed then took a waiting jeep back up to the main house. Little was said but Charlie had a feeling that Johnson knew exactly what he was, in which case so did McCrae.

CHAPTER TWENTY-EIGHT

Sticky woke with a start; it took a few seconds to adjust, then he felt the throb of the engines and the sharp rise and fall of the ship as it ploughed through the waves. He realised that it must have been the result of hitting one of these that had brought him awake. In fact the ship had motored down the Clyde and it was a wave hitting the ship beam on as it rounded Garroch Head that had not only awoken him. But had also awoken all of his companions. He looked at the clock and realised it was five to six, so he decided to get up shower, shave and see if he could find some coffee. Thirty minutes or so later, he walked into the dining area to find Carter already there trying to pour coffee against the roll of the ship. "It woke you up as well then," said Sticky. "Woke me up, it threw me out of the bloody bed", replied Carter, "got a right bruise on my backside." Sticky laughed then grabbed for a table to steady himself as the ship again plunged down from the top of a wave. "Hope this isn't going to go on all day" said Pony as he entered the room "I get badly seasick at times." Sticky shook his hand, "Glad to see you mate" he said, "but just don't go throwing up over me, I'm more worried they'll want us to fly off this thing in these conditions."

"I'm not worried about flying off," replied Pony. "It's landing back on that would put the shits up me."

Over the next half an hour all the group arrived and the movement of the ship appeared to steady down. There was a lot of general conversation and Sticky learnt that Pony had spent most of his time at the flat of the young woman he had befriended on the flight home. In fact, if you believed his account it appeared as though they never left the bedroom. Carter had just pinned down McFadden and Campbell and was trying to elicit why they had seemingly disappeared in Gibraltar. The exchange was just getting a little heated when McGreggor entered the room, closely followed by Hamilton. "That'll do Carter," he barked, "any questions can wait, I will explain all later, The Captain tells me it will be a lot calmer from here on in, then once we leave the Sound of Bute, we'll be in the more sheltered waters between Tarbet and Portavadie. We are heading up Loch Fynne to Brenfield near Lochgilphead. By then I want you ready for action, but in the meantime try and get some breakfast we'll meet in the briefing room at eight thirty." With that he moved over to the corner of the room and entered what appeared to be a quite animated conversation with Hamilton. As if on cue shutters were raised on the newly fitted catering area and everyone went over to see what was on offer. Pony decided it would be best to ignore the cooked breakfast and go for cereals, while Sticky settled for toast and bacon.

Carter came and joined them, "Ready for action" he said. "What bloody action are we going to find on the west coast of Scotland?"

"I've got a feeling it will have something to do with Johnson, his place is up this way somewhere" replied Sticky, "What did Campbell and Mcfadden have to say for themselves?"

"Bugger all of any consequence, they just kept repeating that they were doing as they were told, in fact if McGreggor had not walked in I would have smacked Campbell in the mouth."

"Am I missing something here?" enquired Pony. "If you had not been so loved up in Gibraltar, you might have noticed that Campbell and Mc Fadden weren't on the flight back with us" replied Sticky, "so we just wondered what they might have been up to." Pony thought for a moment and then said: "I have noticed that they seem to be well in with McGreggor and there was always one of them with each team that went out, except us." "Really!" replied Carter and Sticky in unison "well we never noticed."

"Ok, Ok stop taking the piss, what else should I know?" Carter motioned for Wright to join them, then in lowered tones they went through the conversation they had had on the train the night before and their suspicions regarding Johnson, the drugs and the relationship between Johnson and McGreggor. By the time they finished it was time to make their way to the briefing room and an expected showdown with McGreggor.

Unlike many other areas of the ship, the briefing room was unchanged, each man entered and as the last one took his seat Hamilton and McGreggor walked in. Switching on the table top screen to reveal a map of the UK, Hamilton said; "Time to be completely honest with you gentlemen."

"Again" mumbled Carter. Hamilton smiled. "I don't blame you for thinking that Mr Carter, you are all intelligent men indeed some of you have surpassed what we expected of you and are far ahead in your assessment of the current situation than we could have anticipated. That's why I'm going to give you the full picture with nothing held back. Lives and careers depend on it, although I think it's a little late for my own. Firstly let's get the problem of Mr Campbell and McFadden out of the way. Unlike the rest of you, both men have worked for MI6 for several years and are experts at working undercover and behind enemy lines." All eyes turned to the two men who just sat passively looking towards Hamilton. "When we put you together, their job was to asses you in operational and non-operational situations. Their reports show me that we have an exceptional team. The fact that some of you quickly realised there was some link between Mr McGreggor and Mr Johnson did give us a few headaches. Then recently, while you all had a break, I'm afraid they didn't and were sent to meet up with other agents and obtain the information you will shortly receive."

McGreggor stood up and switched on a wall screen showing a picture of a man. "Albert Johnson," he said, "owner of AJ Associates, chemical research and production plants, dockyards, shipping and this ship you're sitting on."

"And your brother-in-law" said Sticky. "That he is" McGreggor replied without faltering "he married my sister and fathered my niece Mercedes. In turn, I'm married to Mr Hamilton's sister, which probably explains why I got seconded to MI6. I suggested to Albert that we use his ships and worldwide facilities for our undercover operations. He was excited at the prospect and provided us with unprecedented help. In return we provided him with the occasional batch of captured drugs, which he genuinely used for the production of other legal lifesaving substances." He paused and with no-one making any comments, he continued. "After the untimely death of my sister, he changed. He expanded rapidly, taking over many other companies, all of which seemed to have had some sort of event or disaster that squashed their share price or brought them close to bankruptcy. It was obvious that Albert was engineering it, so we put someone into his security team."

"Mac McCrae," said Sticky. "No I'm afraid not" came the reply. "Mac has gone rogue we think that he and his accomplice Karl Steiner created a lot of the 'disasters' and have been involved in at least three recent killings."

"Shit!" exclaimed Sticky banging his fist on the table.

McGreggor looked at him disapprovingly saying; "I share your frustration Captain Wood, but please don't break the table I will be needing it."

"So where is this taking us?" enquired Carter. "Patience, please Mr Carter, I will get to that shortly. Like many people who get power, for Albert it was never enough. Those that wouldn't sell out to him he destroyed and I started to worry about his mental health. Then the death of my niece Mercedes seemed to have pushed him over the edge, especially when he found out the drug that killed her was developed in his labs. Our informant tells us that it was developed by two scientists, called Muller and Johansen." A picture of the two men appeared on the wall screen, then McGreggor continued. "When Albert stopped further research, Muller passed it outside and this inadvertently resulted in the death of his daughter Mercedes."

"I can see how that would blow your mind" said Wright, "Did he kill Muller?"

"No, in return for the promise of having his own research facility, Albert got Muller to contaminate a batch of drugs then sent them out on the streets in revenge."

"Christ!" spluttered Pony, "all those deaths in the last couple of days was down to him."

"Yes and there were over two hundred more last night." A murmur went around the table as McGreggor continued. "Muller and Johansen along with the remaining drugs and all evidence linking Albert to the contamination were moved to an old chemical works on Kintyre. Where they were told they could continue their research. In fact as soon as they were located there, Albert ordered their deaths."

There was silence in the room then Hamilton spoke again. "There is little we can do about the drugs currently on the streets, although the governments' action regarding amnesty drops, as well as targeting dealers and known sources, seems to be having an effect. Over the next week we should see the deaths drop off to zero. On the plus side, if there is one? Johnson's actions have resulted in a drop in crime, more addicts seeking help and he has managed to set up Sir James Courtney, removing one of the biggest drug import rings, estimated to be responsible for thirty percent of all drugs coming into the UK. Rather than face arrest, Sir James shot himself last night."

"Wow!" said Phillips "I always believed that drug dealing went high up the ladder, but look at some of the ones reported dead in the last few days, then add in Sir James and it makes you wonder about the whole stinking system."

"Quite" said Hamilton, "call me a cynic but if you consider illegal drugs are estimated to be worth sixty billion pounds to the economy you have to ask just how much governments really want to reduce their use."

McGreggor then cut in. "This is all very well gentlemen but you now have all the background and know as much as we do. However, like it or not, the deniable ops groups have inadvertently provided the drugs that are now responsible for the mass killings the country's witnessing. We can claim that we had no way of knowing Albert would take this action, but we are using his ships and equipment, and Mr Hamilton and I are related to him. Can you imagine the repercussions from that information? The likely result would be the shutdown of all the UN deniable ops groups putting many of our agents and the security of the country in danger. As well as causing massive embarrassment to the British government. Mr Hamilton and I are prepared to fall on our swords, but have a plan that will hopefully shift responsibility and keep our program intact."

He then pressed a button on the remote control he was holding, and zoomed in on the picture of the UK to show their current position, which was someway south of Brenfield. He then zoomed in further, showing a fenced building located in the trees on the northern part of Kintyre. "In these woods just off the B8024 south of Achaolish is a chemical works recently closed down by Johnson, our informant tells us this is where Muller and Johansen are. It's now ten minutes past nine and at exactly ten o'clock I want Wood, Moore, Wright and Carter on the chopper. All the details are in the briefing packs Campbell is distributing. You are to recover Muller and Johansen from the facility and fly them back to the ship. At 0-eleven-hundred, we will call the police and inform them that the contaminated drugs and equipment can be found there. So you need to get in and out sharpish."

"I thought you said they were dead" said Pony. "I said Johnson had ordered them to be killed, but dead or alive, get them out. Mr Hamilton and I will drop off at Brenfield and with Clarke and Phillips as our protection officers, we will drive around to Thistledown, which is Johnson's facility in the woods north of Achnamara." Again the picture zoomed in showing the fenced area, small dock, main house, runways and chemical works. We expect to arrive by car at around thirteen hundred. We'll inform them we'll be leaving by helicopter, which will give you a reason to fly in. All the rest of you are to travel on the chopper. Wear your blue combat uniforms and be fully armed."

"Is it just me or am I missing something here?" asked Carter. "So far you have not mentioned the target or the objective. Why are we going fully armed, just to meet your brother-in-law?"

"A good point, firstly, I'm hoping you will find Muller and Johansen alive, their testimony will implicate Albert in the current mass murders. It would make life simple if he took the same route as Courtney but that is unlikely. Then there are these two," the wall screen showed pictures of McCrae and Steiner. "Both are wanted in connection with at least three murders and I don't think either of them are likely to come quietly. Johnson also has his own security team although this is limited to three men on the main gate and a further three at the dock. Added to that he has two two-man mobile units. One man on the main house entrance, and on the top floor there's a control centre which oversees the whole complex with a system of sophisticated cameras and sensors."

"Only about four to one then", said Pony, "no problem."

"Actually" replied Hamilton. "Only one at the most would leave the gate areas and before the chopper lands, our inside man will take over the control room making them blind. Johnson, McCrae and Steiner will be the main problem, as they won't hesitate to shoot to kill. Don't give them the chance. For that matter, if any of the security team pulls out his gun, take him out."

"I'm sure they will," replied McGreggor, before running over the whole plan regarding the securing of Thistledown, finishing up by saying. "Once everything is secure we'll hand over to the local police and withdraw."

"Just like that, if only" muttered Pony. McGreggor ignored him but added. "You need to keep in mind, that if this goes right, MI6 will be credited with closing down the threat to life from contaminated drugs, if it goes wrong we'll be blamed for it and the whole of the UNO project will be lost." Hamilton looked around the table. "It's been a pleasure working with you gentlemen, but I'm afraid our links to Johnson means Lt Colonel McGreggor and I will both be…." He paused and looked at McGreggor before continuing "Um 'retiring 'but let's just get this one thing put right before we go."

Thirty minutes later, Sticky and Pony climbed into the helicopter, they were pleased to see that the machine was in the same configuration as it had been the last time they flew, making running through the pre-flight checks a lot simpler. The fully armed pair of Carter and Wright climbed in the back, with Carter loudly complaining of his hatred of choppers. There was a flash of daylight and a jolt as the roof panel opened and the helipad started to rise up. On request, the Captain turned the ship into the wind, then with the all clear given, the engines were started. Once the rotors were up to speed, Sticky gave the thumbs up, and with a loud hiss, the clamps were removed. Judging it perfectly, for when the ship crested a wave, he lifted off swinging the machine to port and towards the A83 that ran along the coast of Kintyre and the hills beyond. Within a couple of minutes, they crossed the road and climbed above the trees. Maintaining low level, they skimmed above the patchwork of forests before intersecting the B8024 close to the shore of the opposite coast. They had seen very few buildings en-route, but as Sticky banked left, Wright spotted a track running up to the clearly fenced chemical factory contained within a thickly wooded area ensuring it was virtually undetectable form the road. They hovered overhead, before Pony pointed out the large empty car park and seconds later they touched down.

Before the rotors had stopped, Carter and Wright leapt out and were running towards the building. Large notices proclaimed 'DANGER CONTAMINATION' and 'STRICTLY NO ADMITTANCE'. "Seems like they don't want us in" said Carter. "When did we take any notice of that" came the reply as Wright kicked open a door a lot easier than expected. Cautiously they made their way through the corridors, checking several completely empty rooms as they went. As they moved into the next passage, Carter tapped Wright on the shoulder and placed his finger to his lips to indicate silence as he nodded towards a door where a shaft of light could be seen emanating from beneath. With Wright down on one knee and with his gun pointed straight at the door, Carter stood to one side caught hold of the handle and flung the door open. Muller and Johansen were lying face down side by side in front of one of the benches, "Looks like we're too late this time" said Wright as he shouldered his gun and stood up. As they entered Johansen moved and groaned. "Maybe not." said Carter as he bent down and checked both bodies. "They're unconscious but both are breathing let's get them out of here." Wright radioed Sticky and confirmed they had found the targets and were on their way out. A minute later they both appeared each carrying one of the men over their shoulders with comparative ease. Muller and Johansen were dumped unceremoniously on to the floor of the chopper and seconds later they took off and were heading back to the ship. "In and out with twenty five minutes to spare", said Carter looking at his watch. Pony radioed the ship confirming the condition of their passengers, while in turn the Captain passed the message on to Hamilton.

At the same time that Carter and Wright had been entering the chemical works, Hamilton, McGreggor, Clarke and Phillips had stepped ashore and had climbed into a waiting car. All four were dressed in smart suits with shoulder holsters containing their Glock 19 nine-millimetre pistols with spare magazines attached to their belts. They had barely covered three miles when the message came through regarding the scientists. "Alive but unconscious," said Hamilton. "That's good", replied McGreggor. "They have the antidote on board so will soon have them talking, my main concern was them choking on their own vomit while unconscious. Albert will be in for a shock, when he gets that bit of news." With the car speeding on towards what seemed to be their swansong, they sat back and mulled through their thoughts and the various scenarios that could play out during the rest of the day.

With the smallest of bounces, Sticky landed back on the ship, the clamps immediately locked and as the rotors shut down a medical team appeared with two stretchers and quickly unloaded and carried the two unconscious men to the sick bay. The helipad remained in place, as they were due to fly again within the hour. Crewmen appeared and started refuelling and performing system checks, so the remaining four men climbed out and made their way down to their cabins. They agreed to meet in fifteen minutes for refreshments and to go over the attack plans once more before lift-off.

CHAPTER TWENTYNINE

On arriving at the main house, Dr Stuart and Charlie followed Johnson up the front steps and through the large double oak doors. The wide entrance hall had panelled walls on which hung an eclectic collection of paintings, including portraits, hunting scenes and landscapes. All appeared to be originals and although Charlie had no knowledge of artists he guessed they were of considerable value. Lucy admired the wide carpeted staircase, which was positioned centrally to the hall sweeping up with branches to the left and right leading to the upper floor. A uniformed security guard was sat at a desk in the hall and promptly stood as Johnson entered. "The dining room is ready for you sir", he said "shall I inform the chef you're ready."

"Yes" came the reply, "tell them to start service in ten minutes." Turning to Lucy he said. "This way doctor, I'm sure you're hungry by now." With that he led them through a large panelled door and into the superbly furnished dining room. "What a fabulous room" gasped Lucy as she looked around at walls hung with tapestries and felt the thick burgundy coloured carpet beneath her feet. In the centre of the room was a long table with twelve seats and settings. While at the far end there was an oak sideboard containing several crystal decanters placed on silver trays. Above this was a coat of arms with a large sword at either side.

"Those are huge swords." remarked Charlie "They must have had some muscles to swing those around."
"Indeed" replied Johnson, "those and the coat of arms belonged to the previous owners whose family had lived here for four hundred years. The swords are the Scottish claymore and are thought to have been used in the battle of Killiecrankie in sixteen eighty-nine. They're typical of the type being around fifty-five inches in length and weighing almost six pounds, you'll notice the hilt is around a foot long so it could be held with two hands, in fact outside of Scotland it's more commonly known as the two handed sword. I consider myself fairly fit but I don't think I would like to fight with that for long."
"Me neither" agreed Charlie. With that a young woman entered the room from a side door, she was carrying a tray containing three lidded soup bowls. "Ah here we go, please take a seat." Johnson sat at the head of the table while Lucy took one of the side seats to his right, and rather than sit on the opposite side, Charlie took the seat next to her. The bowls contained a traditional chicken broth flavoured with a selection of vegetables. Little was said as the three devoured the warm liquid. Putting down her spoon, Lucy remarked that, that had been extremely good. "I hope you are still hungry," replied Johnson, "we have venison, boiled potatoes and vegetables to follow, I like to have my main

meal now and just something light in the evenings, is that ok with you?"

"Fine" Lucy replied, "Neither of us had time for breakfast this morning." The meal was followed by coffee, both having declined something stronger. Johnson did pour himself a whisky and then sat back in his chair.

"What time is your flight back?" he asked "Five thirty" replied Charlie. "Plenty of time yet then, I'll ensure my pilot can get you back to Glasgow in time."

"Thank you" said Lucy. "And thank you for your honesty as well as your hospitality, we now know what caused the deaths of your daughter and it seems the thousand or so drug users. There is little more we can do to prevent further deaths other than hope all the contaminated drugs get taken off the streets and destroyed." Johnson smiled. "Must be hurting a few of the dealers, I heard this morning that Sir James Courtney committed suicide when he was found to be one of the country's main suppliers. It creates a bit of a dilemma doesn't it"?

"In what way?" asked Charlie, "Well as we said before, while these dangerous drugs are off the streets, more addicts are seeking help, the crime rate falls, as they stop stealing to fund their habits, and the suppliers suffer major loses which will result in infighting and price drops. That in turn will affect the wholesale drug prices, which we know funds arms and terrorism. Once drug use becomes relatively safe again you're back into high crime and drug gang warfare. The dilemma is, which is the better of the two evils?"

"Of course on the other side the fall in prices could lead to more young people being dragged into the drug scene, we've already seen recent price drops having that effect." replied Lucy.

The policeman in Charlie cut in. "It could have the reverse effect, suppliers and dealers will quickly realise the contaminated drugs came from Courtney's network and with the resulting shortage prices could go up leading to increased crime and drug warfare between suppliers as they fight to become the new top dog, so I don't see a dilemma, more a disaster." Johnson glared at Charlie. It was clear the response was not what he expected, so Charlie continued. "The one thing I don't get is why Muller should want to contaminate the drugs, I can see you might want to avenge your daughter, but what motive would he have and how would he get the drugs out of here past all your security?" Charlie noted the flash of anger in Johnson's eyes as he leant forward, stared at Charlie and said, "Perhaps you weren't listening Detective Sergeant, I told you Muller and Johansen had left when I got back, and the latest batch of drugs I was expecting had gone missing." With Lucy looking shocked that Johnson knew who Charlie was, Charlie replied, "I assure you I was listening very carefully, I'm sure Muller's drug killed your daughter and knowing that would be a good reason for him to do a runner before you returned, but where is he now?"

"Dead as far as I care," snapped Johnson.

"Sorry to disappoint you Albert but I'm afraid he isn't." said a voice Charlie and Lucy spun around to see McGreggor walk into the room closely followed by Hamilton. Johnson looked unfazed as he turned to Charlie and Doctor Stuart and said. "Meet my illustrious brothers–in–law, Lieutenant Colonel McGreggor and his boss Sir Henry Hamilton. What brings you two here? I'm afraid you've just missed lunch."

"As I said Albert, a couple of hours ago my men recovered both Muller and Johansen down at the old SMM chemical works and the local police are currently recovering their equipment."

"They're both dead so what?" Said Johnson. "I'm afraid they're very much alive, true they were unconscious but after receiving an antidote they're now singing away like little birds." Unseen to all in the room, Johnson pressed a button located under the table. McCrae had just finished his lunch and was talking to the young waitress, when the alarm buzzer went off on his radio. "Dining room" the controllers' voice stated.

As McCrae headed for the side door, Connelly stood behind the controller on the top floor. "I'll take over" he said, "have a break," with that he brought the butt of his pistol sharply down on the controller's neck. The man's unconscious body slumped forward, forcing Connelly to drag him from the chair and out of the control room. He left him on the landing floor and returned to the room locking the door behind him. Then he took the controller's seat and quickly scanned the monitors. In the hallway Clarke and Phillips were talking to the security guard and joking about their respective bosses when Clarke's phone bleeped indicating a text message. He pulled it from his pocket read it, then nodded to Phillips. Who, in expectation of the message, had moved closer to the guard and asked for a pen. The man opened a drawer and reached in, spotting the movement too late as Phillips brought his elbow down on the guards neck smashing his head into the table with a sickening crack that saw his body go limp and fall to the floor. After a quick check, Clarke pronounced; "He'll live." Then with the guard secured, Phillips went to the main entrance to prevent any possible reinforcements gaining entry, while Clarke took up a position where he could cover the stairs and doors leading off the hallway.

At that moment, Sticky was flying in behind the trees to the south of the estate. Pony put away the phone he had used to message Clarke, and then pointed out a spot amongst the trees ahead. With the machine brought to a hover just above the branches, the winches were immediately activated to lower the ropes on either side. Within seconds, Wright, Carter McFadden and Campbell had abseiled to the ground, the switch was thrown to retract the ropes, and as soon as they were clear, the helicopter climbed back above the trees and sped forwards. As they cleared the trees, they could see a runway running from right to left and parallel to the front of the house. A small jet was parked over to their right, while immediately in front of them a square area was marked with a large 'H'. Sticky brought the craft in and landed directly on top of it. "Hamilton said aim to arrive around thirteen thirty." said Pony "you're a minute early." They shut down the engines, then, as they climbed from the chopper, Pony nodded towards a small fuel tanker that was heading towards them. The tanker pulled up alongside and Steiner climbed out of the cab. "Will you be needing any fuel Captain", he asked. "No more than five hundred kilo's" replied Sticky. "We should be flying four people out of here so I want to keep it light." "Leave it to me" came the reply. Pony nodded then whispered, "Well here goes, let's hope Clarke and Philips have disabled the guards. They walked casually towards the house and had just reached the steps to the main door when, unnoticed to them, the fuel truck sped away towards the far side of the house.

To the two man mobile patrol, the helicopter had seemed to come in low and then appear above the trees before heading directly for the landing pad, the drop had been so quick it had not been detected. As they watched the engines shut down, one of their radio's crackled. "Romeo one, McGreggor's helicopter has just come in low and has either disturbed one of the fence sensors or the wildlife, go check it out please."

"Bloody sensors," said one of the men always bleeping away, probably another bloody deer." Meanwhile the other patrol call signed Romeo two had been told to check out sector six on the north side of the estate, which happened to be as far from the main house as possible. Within minutes, Romeo one's driver had passed through the woods and was speeding around the perimeter track when his companion spotted a tree branch lying against the fence. "Looks like our problem," he said, "that bloody chopper was probably so low it snapped it off." He stopped the vehicle and got out. As if from nowhere four figures appeared pointing machine pistols directly at them. "Face down please hands out in front of you." The men never hesitated and were quickly relieved of their radios and pistols. Then with their hands and feet tied they were placed back amongst the trees. "We'll send someone for you later." said Carter, "We just need to borrow your jeep for a while." The four quickly mounted the vehicle and headed in the direction of the house, coming out of the trees in time to see the fuel tanker driving off. They continued across the runway then swung onto the road running in front of the main house, barely stopping for Carter and Wright to leap out and run up the main steps. Campbell and McFadden then sped off with instructions to secure the chemical works.

In the dining room the recent revelations were beginning to sink in. "I take it Connelly has been working for you then." said Johnson "I needed someone to keep an eye on you." replied McGreggor "but I never expected you to go this far." McCrae switched on his radio to speak directly to Steiner.

"Connelly has the control room take him out," he barked. "Give it up," said Hamilton. "The police are probably taking control of your main gate as we speak and my men are in control of the chemical works and are well towards taking control of this house." With that Pony and Sticky entered the room. "Captain Wood" declared McCrae, "and Pony of course, long time no see, surprised that you two have gone all James Bond."

"Not as surprised as I was to hear you had gone bad Christ man, you were one of the best marines I knew."

"Maybe" came the reply. "But the day after I flew with you holding Captain Greenhall's leg together, my brother got blown to pieces by an IED have you looked at what they're paying you to take that? Well I decided that if I'm going to get killed I might as well be well paid for it."

"As much as I regret breaking up this touching reunion" said Hamilton, "The fact is McCrae and Steiner are wanted for at least two murders as well as aiding and abetting the distribution of contaminated drugs. While you Albert, are implicated in multiple deaths due to the drugs you ordered contaminated."

"So you intend to arrest me then do you?" mocked Johnson. "That could be embarrassing for the government" came the reply "it would be a lot neater if you took Courtney's way out."

"Go to hell" barked Johnson.

Steiner skidded the fuel truck to a halt next to a rear entrance of the house, at the same time the other patrol jeep appeared and screeched to a stop next to him, alerted by the call to Steiner they had raced back to the house. Leaping from the cab, Steiner shouted, "Get to the dining room," then he ran into the house and sprinted up the rear staircase. On reaching the landing he found the controller just regaining consciousness and trying to sit up. Steiner shook him, "Peters, Peters, who's in there?" he shouted. With the fog lifting from his brain, Peters replied "Just Connolly." Finding the door locked, Steiner called out, "Connolly open up." There was no reply so he stood back and kicked the door as hard as he could; the result was a sharp pain through his leg but no movement. He then drew his gun and fired four shots into the lock before again aiming a kick near the door handle. This time, to the sound of shattering wood, the door swung open. He rapidly scanned the room and noted that both it and the controller's desk appeared empty. On the monitors he could see the scene being played out in the dining room below and more alarmingly several police vehicles at the main gate. As he walked towards the desk, the door behind him started to swing shut, he turned to see Connolly stood behind a filing cabinet, his hands resting on top pointing a pistol directly at him. "Drop the gun," Connolly demanded, but with a built up anger at himself for making such an amateur mistake Steiner started to raise his own gun, immediately there was a quick 'pop' 'pop'. Steiner saw a flash then his face took on a surprised expression as he looked down at his gun and realised his arms were not responding, he looked back to Connolly then his legs buckled and he slumped to his knees before falling forward face first unto the carpet. Peters staggered in still rubbing his neck, he looked at Steiner then Connolly. "Shit you've killed him," he said "No more than he would have done to me, now you'd better sit down."

The sound of the gunfire from above, coupled with the two security men bursting into the room, led to a scene of mayhem in the dining room. The first of the security guards had his gun in his hand and in panic, fired a wild shot in the direction of McGreggor. Instantly Sticky felt as though his legs had been kicked away from beneath him and he fell forward cracking his head on the table and slumping to the floor. Seeing Sticky go down, Pony had drawn his weapon and fired two quick shots, the guard, who had fired the shot, was flung backwards dropping his gun and falling against the wall leaving a blood trail on the surface as he sunk to the floor. In unison Hamilton and McGreggor ducked below the table, while Charlie flung a startled Doctor Stuart from her chair both crashing heavily to the floor, where he placed his body over hers in an effort to protect her. The second guard dropped his gun and dived to the floor placing his hands over his head weeping in shock. At the same time, a calmer McCrae pulled his gun and fired at Pony the impact of the shot knocking him off his feet. Carter had been in the hall and at the sound of the first gunshot rushed to the dining room door, flinging it open in time to see Pony hitting the floor. Instinctively, Carter fired a burst from his machine pistol and McCrae crashed back into the sideboard scattering the glasses and decanters.

The few seconds of gunfire and panic was followed by a silence broken only by the quiet sobbing of the second guard. McGreggor and Hamilton climbed to their feet and Carter was pleased to see Pony sit up holding his chest and examining the mark on his bulletproof vest. Charlie stood up and helped Lucy to her feet. Looking concerned, he muttered. "Hope I didn't hurt you." She just gave him a long stare and then asked if anyone needed her help. "Captain Wood does," said Carter adding, "I think the other two are beyond it." Hamilton looked around, "Where's Albert?" he asked. "He must have made a dash for it in all the commotion" replied McGreggor. Carter walked over towards McCrae and glancing out of the window, saw Johnson climbing into the parked helicopter. "He's making a break in your chopper", called Carter before shouting into his radio for Phillips and Wright to try to stop him." McCrae raised his head and smiled. "Don't bother," he whispered between laboured breaths. "He's forgotten his own orders." Carter looked puzzled then watched the helicopter rise from the pad, it turned towards the sea and as it went forward there was an explosion, amongst the flash of flame and smoke, pieces of helicopter and burning debris could be seen falling to the ground. "I take it that was meant for us" said Hamilton McCrae just smiled then looked at Carter "Nice shooting marine" he said before finally taking his last breath.

Sticky sat up holding his head where a large blue lump was forming. Dr Stuart came over and took a quick look. "That might smart for a couple of days" she said "you never know, it might even knock some sense into you. Where else are you hurt?"

"I think I've been shot in the leg" replied Sticky, next to the map pocket in his flying suit was a small hole with a clear indication of blood that was now spreading rapidly down his leg. Placing her fingers in the hole, Lucy tore his trousers revealing a surface wound running across the muscle, there was another hole that went through the back of the map pocket and exited the other side confirming the bullet had passed straight through. Some small coloured grains fell from the hole prompting her to reach into the pocket. "Well" she said, "You'll live, it's just a surface wound but I'm afraid there's no hope for your friend here." With that she held up a small teddy with a bullet hole through the area where it had previously said 'get well.' Once a dressing had been applied to the wound, Sticky got to his feet. "Can you walk?" enquired Carter. "Yes I'll be fine", came the reply. "That's good" chipped in Pony "cause it looks like we will be walking home, and just when I was beginning to like that chopper." Remarkably Lucy found that the guard was still alive, the two bullets having both gone through his right shoulder breaking his collarbone and scapula but missing any vital organs or blood vessels. For McCrae and Steiner though there was no such reprieve.

CHAPTER THIRTY

In the control room, Connolly apologised for hitting the shocked Peters, who had watched the incidents in the dining room and the helicopter exploding above the runway displayed on the bank of monitors. Then on Connolly's instructions, he had the scrambled off duty, guards to deal with the various fires caused by the helicopter. In the meantime, all of McGreggor's men were quickly ferried down to the docks to board Johnson's private yacht. On the way Phillips and Wright took one of the jeeps and released the two guards they had left in the woods and after a quick look down the barrel of Carters gun, and a desire not to be around for any police investigation, the yachts captain set sail with instructions to meet up with the Minerva. During the incident, Connolly had cut all the power to the main gate, now with the members of UN12 out of the way, he restored control and finally allowed the police vehicles and ambulances to proceed in convoy.

A very irate Scottish Police Inspector came striding through the door abruptly stopping and taking in the scene in front of him. He was followed by a team of paramedics who quickly went to work on the wounded guard. "What the hell has happened here?" The Inspector demanded "and why were we held at the gate?"

"We got you in as soon as possible but we had to take over the control room first" replied Hamilton. "Have you been briefed regarding Muller and Johansen?"

"Yes."

"Then you will know that Albert Johnson, McCrae here and Karl Steiner were behind the recent drug deaths. The other couple here are Dr Stuart and her assistant who came up to enlist Johnson's help in identifying the contaminant."

"Little did I know he had produced it" cut in Lucy, before adding, "Do you think we could go; this has been a terrible shock and we need to catch a flight back to London."

"I don't see why not," replied Hamilton "I'll get Connolly to track down the jets pilot and get you under way."

"Hold on" said the Inspector "I need to take statements and I'll decide when people can leave."

"Not on this occasion" replied Hamilton "I think you'll find I outrank you and if you need statements, they can make them in London. However what happened here is a matter of National security, so you will be provided with any statements you require."

"I don't suppose any of them will reflect the truth." Fumed the Inspector before turning on his heels and storming out.

Forty-five minutes later an air ambulance took off carrying a stretcher containing the wounded guard and the hall security officer, who had regained consciousness but was found to have a broken cheekbone. The remains of Steiner and McCrae had been loaded into body bags ready for transportation, while a police team continued with the grizzlier task of doing the same with the remains of Albert Johnson. Connolly had called up the jets pilot and with only some remnants of debris at the far end of the runway. A police vehicle drove Lucy and Charlie out to the aircraft which they quickly boarded, fastened their seatbelts and prepared for take-off. The Jet rapidly sped down the runway and lifted off banking to the left and out over the sea. Charlie looked at the Doctor and noticed she was uncontrollably trembling. He unfastened his belt then moved over and held her hand. "You Ok?" he asked. "I think shock is setting in" she replied. "I'm used to the aftermath but I've never been in the middle of it before, and if you ever jump on me again it had better be a little more loving than the last time" she smiled. Charlie smiled back saying. "I promise to do my best." They both spent the rest of the trip in relative silence, while running the day's events through their minds. At Glasgow, Charlie spoke briefly to the pilots and thanked them before he and Lucy caught the connecting flight to London City where they both fell asleep before the plane had even left the ground.

Back in Scotland, Hamilton briefed the Police Inspector, who by now had given up any hope of a formal investigation, being left in no doubt that 'D' notices and other government intervention would make this impossible, so he settled for concentrating on the cleaning up of the site and taking control of the remaining staff. To that end, the chemical works was closed down and evacuated and all the technicians, security personnel and household staff were ordered to assemble in the main hall and bar of the on-site community centre. All those that had been in the chemical works or accommodation area, were far enough away from the main house not to have heard anything, although the reception staff had been well aware that the heavily armed Campbell and Mcfadden had entered and ordered them to carry on as normal but not allow anyone to leave. Luckily no one had either entered or wanted to leave in the relatively short time the two men were there.

With everyone, including the security and household staff, gathered in the community centres bar, all sorts of stories and rumours were beginning to spread, before Hamilton strode in and loudly called "Could I have your attention please?" The bar fell silent, Hamilton continued, "You must all be aware of the recent deaths associated with illegal drug use. What you may not be aware of is that those drugs originated from this plant." A gasp and murmur spread throughout the gathered technicians, "That cannot be right" one of them called. "I'm afraid it is" came the reply. "Let me continue, a batch of drugs which came here for treatment were condemned, Muller and Johansen foolishly mixed them with another condemned drug with the intention that they be incinerated. However Mr McCrae and Mr Steiner decided to make some money by selling it on to dealers. When Muller tried to stop them both he and Johansen were kidnapped and left for dead." Another gasp spread through the audience, "Are they OK?" someone asked. "They will live but you're unlikely to see them back here again. This afternoon, Mr McCrae and Mr Steiner were both killed in a shoot-out while resisting arrest. I'm afraid to tell you that my brother-in-law and your boss was also killed by Steiner." A couple of the female technicians and the housekeeper began to weep and were comforted by others someone shouted; "What happens now"

Hamilton looked around the assembled crowd, "Is Mr Harris here?" A man dressed in a white coat over a dark suit held his hand up. "Could you come forward please?" The man who appeared to be in his mid-fifties and about six foot tall walked up to Hamilton. He had dark hair and sharp features and carried himself with an air of confidence. Hamilton shook his hand and continued, "As of now Mr Harris will take over the full responsibility for running the chemical works and report directly to me. Mr Connolly will take over as head of security and household and also report to me. I will be based at the main house and will remain for some time while all of Albert's, that's Mr Johnson, different interests are stabilised. In the meantime unless you're instructed otherwise by Mr Harris, take the rest of the day off and go back to your normal tasks tomorrow. Mr Harris I will see you in Albert's office at ten tomorrow morning."

With that he turned and strode out. McGreggor had watched the whole performance. "So that's going to be the official story then, my God you're a good liar." Hamilton smiled and replied; "I've obviously worked with politicians to long. My future at MI6 was over anyway so I will resign. 'So that I can look after the family interests' that should keep everyone off our backs and maintain Albert's good name."

EPILOGUE

On arrival in London, Charlie phoned the yard but was told that Inspector Penney had not been released from hospital and that he should go home and complete his report the following morning. He walked Lucy through the terminal and flagged down a taxi. As it pulled up, she turned and kissed him on the cheek and said "Goodnight", then she got in and he stood and watched it drive away. He then got another for himself and headed directly back to his flat. Once inside he dumped his bags and had a shower. Feeling fresher and in a pyjamas trousers and dressing gown, he made himself a coffee and sandwich then opened his laptop and began typing up his report. Before he finished he turned on the TV to catch the late night news the main headline concerned the death of Albert Johnson and had a breakdown of his rise to fame, and the companies he had built up and controlled, before going on to recall the tragedies in his life with the loss of his wife and the more recent death of his daughter.

The story then followed the line given to the technicians and Thistledown staff by Hamilton. It reported that while helping the Metropolitan police regarding the spate of drug deaths, Johnson realised the killer drug had originated from his chemical plant. They had been stolen by the heads of security, Mac McCrae and Karl Steiner, and their actions had led to the accidental death of Johnson's daughter, Mercedes. When Johnson challenged them, Steiner killed him but other guards stepped in, one of them shooting Steiner while another killed McCrae. However in the shoot-out one of the guards was shot twice and is now in a critical but stable condition. It went on to state that a helicopter belonging to Johnson's brother-in-law, Sir Henry Hamilton, was also destroyed. The reporter continued by saying the Metropolitan Police have confirmed that both McCrae and Steiner were wanted in connection with the death of the DJ Ralph Osborne in Paris and the death of a drug dealer named Andrew Rogers in London. It was believed they had used these two deaths in order to infiltrate Sir James Courtney's drug distribution organisation resulting in the killer drug being circulated on the streets. The story concluded by saying that Sir Henry Hamilton had resigned his government post with immediate effect and would be staying in Scotland to oversee Johnson's affairs. Charlie turned the television off then read the report he had typed up. Well he thought I was there and what they have just said and what I've written are two very different bloody stories. However, he decided that his version was going to be submitted, but with no doubt it would be buried somewhere and the 'official' version would continue to run.

On board Johnson's private yacht, the men had also watched the late news and while the crew bought the story and were sad at the loss of their boss, the men of UN12 just knowingly smiled to themselves. Carter brought Sticky a drink and said, "Got to give it to Hamilton he doesn't half come up with some bullshit fast, but I wonder how he'll keep Muller and Johansen quiet as well as the two poor buggers we left tied up in the woods."

"I heard that Wright and Phillips released them but I'm sure Hamilton will have something nasty he can use to keep them quiet" replied Sticky who was sitting with his now bandaged leg resting on a chair. "How is it?" asked Carter nodding to his leg. "Fine just stings a bit but no serious damage." In the early hours of the morning, they came alongside the Minerva and all of McGreggor's men transferred across. The yacht was ordered to return to Thistledown, which was now under Hamilton's control. The men all grabbed a few hours' sleep and when they assembled for breakfast McGreggor joined them having been flown down in a police helicopter and then ferried out in one of the on board RIB's. Checking everyone was present he said "Well done yesterday gentlemen the end result was not exactly as planned, but as it happens it gives it a much neater finish."

"I'm sorry about your brother-in-law" said Phillips. "Yes, well we were close once but seeing as he intended most of us to be blown to bits in the helicopter it somewhat dampens my sorrow." Turning to Sticky he asked. "Are you ok to fly

Mr Wood?" Yes fine" Sticky replied. "Ok then we'll drop you and Pony off in Glasgow where you will have instructions for collecting a new chopper. The rest of us will continue down the coast, then when you re-join us you will be pleased to hear we have a little job off the West Coast of Africa, enjoy your breakfast."

Charlie got up early and arrived at the Yard in time to grab some breakfast before he started work. As he was collecting a coffee Dr Stuart walked in. "Mind if I join you?" she asked. "Not at all, I was hoping I may see you, did you see last night's news?"

"Yes, slightly different to what I remember."

"Exactly," said Charlie, "but I have put my report in exactly as I saw it; no doubt it will be sat on."

"No doubt at all", came a familiar voice. They both turned to see Chief Inspector Penney standing behind them, with lint pad covering the wound on his head and his right arm in a sling. "What are you doing in?" Charlie asked. "Oh just thought I'd catch up and I wanted to be the first to tell you my news." They both looked at him expectantly. "I'm getting too old for this fighting with criminals, so I've taken up a new post, there will be twelve homicide squads set up all run by Detective Inspectors who will all report directly to me. You Charlie will be in SW1 area run by a new Inspector." Charlie's face dropped, "shit" he muttered "have I got to train another Inspector?" Penney laughed, "No a new Detective Sergeant, you're the new Inspector. I've recommended young Dave if that's ok with you."

"You serious." asked a delighted Charlie, "wow but I'll have a hell of a lot to live up to following you guv."

"Well naturally" said Penney, "but I'm sure you'll get there." Lucy held up her coffee "Congratulations Inspector…," she paused. "Hang on, I've only ever heard you called Charlie what's your last name? Charlie looked at Penney, "He banned anybody from using it, its Farthing Charlie Farthing." Lucy looked at them both and then erupted in laughter. "Penney Farthing, no wonder you banned it. Still Dr Farthing has a nice ring to it." This time Penney erupted in laughter.

ABOUT AUTHOR

Christened William Michael but known all his life as Mike. He is the youngest of four children and was born in Halsetown in the borough of St. Ives Cornwall in 1946. 'Mike' studied and worked in engineering, and married his wife Jenny in 1969. After the birth of their twin daughters during the strike hit periods of the early seventies, he left engineering and joined the civil service. Following a series of privatisations in 1995, he again moved on and became the publications manager with one of Europe's largest regional airlines. Where for sixteen years, he wrote, edited, maintained and controlled various operational and technical manuals. His first Novel 'The Man Within' was published in 2009. Now retired, he and his wife live in Devon and have three grandchildren.